SAFE AND SOUND

ALSO BY J. D. RHOADES

Good Day in Hell
The Devil's Right Hand

SAFE AND SOUND

J. D. Rhoades

ST. MARTIN'S MINOTAUR

NEW YORK

SAFE AND SOUND. Copyright © 2007 by J. D. Rhoades. All rights reserved. Printed in the United States of America. No part of this book may be used or reproduced in any manner whatsoever without written permission except in the case of brief quotations embodied in critical articles or reviews. For information, address St. Martin's Press, 175 Fifth Avenue, New York, N.Y. 10010.

www.minotaurbooks.com

Library of Congress Cataloging-in-Publication Data

Rhoades, J. D., 1962–
    Safe and sound / by J. D. Rhoades. — 1st ed.
        p. cm.
  ISBN-13: 978-0-312-35489-3
  ISBN-10: 0-312-35489-4
  1. Keller, Jack (Fictitious character)—Fiction.   2. Bounty hunters—Fiction.   3. North Carolina—Fiction.   4. Kidnapping victims—Fiction.   I. Title.

PS3618.H623S24 2007
813'.6—dc22

2007005173

First Edition: July 2007

10   9   8   7   6   5   4   3   2   1

To the memory of Brent Hackney, 1948–2005. Reporter, press secretary, and editor. Brent was the first person who read my writing and gave me a weekly column in the Southern Pines, North Carolina, *Pilot*. He was also one of the first to suggest I write a novel.

Still, to quote Mark Twain, he was a good man, and he meant well. Let it go.

ACKNOWLEDGMENTS

In the past couple of years since my first novel, *The Devil's Right Hand*, came out, I've been fortunate to meet and hang out with the wonderful and supportive people who make up the crime fiction community. A list of all the folks who've offered encouragement would take up several pages, but here's a partial one: Duane Swierczynski; Ken Bruen; Jason Starr; Allan Guthrie; John and Ruth Jordan of *Crimespree Magazine*; David Thompson and McKenna Jordan of Murder by the Book in Houston; Janine Wilson at Seattle Mystery Bookshop; Toni and Steve Kelner for crash space, pep talks, and the tour of Boston; Laura Lippman for sound advice and excellent company on a long journey; J. A. Konrath for his generosity in sharing the things he's learned about the business end of writing; Tasha Alexander and Kristy Kiernan (aka The Honorable Companions); Nathan Singer; Bob Morris; Pat Mullan; Stephen Blackmoore; Lori G. Armstrong; Victor Gischler; Sean Doolittle; Chris Everheart, Kim Mizar-Stem; Stacey Cochran; and, of course, David Terrenoire. See you on the road, my friends.

As far as the research goes, thanks to Chris Wilson of Cape Town for pointers on Afrikaner slang and idioms; and to former Staff Sgt. Mark "Markey D" Ivey, currently of Darmstadt, Germany, for laughs. Yo, respect...

Thanks also to my long-suffering webmistress at jdrhoades
.com, Beth Tindall.

As always, thanks to Scott Miller and the crew at Trident Me-
dia Group for their excellent representation; and Ben Sevier and
Marc Resnick of St. Martin's Minotaur for their enthusiasm
and support and for letting me pretty much do whatever the hell
I want.

Play with murder enough, it gets you one of two ways. It makes you sick, or you get to like it.
—Dashiell Hammett, *Red Harvest*

SAFE AND SOUND

one

"You're lucky one way, you know," the man said. The accent was clipped, the vowels oddly pronounced, so that the words came out *You're luggy one wuh, you nuh*. People tended to mistake the accent for Australian. But he was an Afrikaner, a descendant of the Dutch pioneers who had struck out into the South African wilderness in the 1800s to escape British rule. He was originally from the harsh, arid plateau known as the Karoo, although he hadn't been there in a long time. His name was DeGroot, and he was worried.

"Some people actually enjoy this type of thing," the man went on. The naked man tied to the heavy wooden chair in the middle of the room said nothing. He tried to stare straight ahead, but his eyes kept darting to the table where DeGroot had laid out his tools. The room was empty except for the table, the chair, and the plastic sheeting covering the floor. The man in the chair could hear the harsh crinkling sounds of the Afrikaner's boots on the plastic as he walked around.

"I don't enjoy it," DeGroot said. "But you do what you have to."

The man in the chair hated the way he was sweating. He hated how he desperately wanted to know what it was that DeGroot was doing behind him. There was the snap of a switch and a high pitched whine. A sharp, electric smell filled the air. He felt the Afrikaner step up behind him, felt the man's breath on his ear.

"I scheme your training's like mine," DeGroot said. "Everyone's got his limits. Everyone talks eventually." He stepped around to face his captive. He was holding a pair of wires in his hands. The wires ended in a pair of large alligator clips. The other ends were somewhere behind him.

"You tell yourself you'll be different. You'll be the one who holds out." The man smiled, almost sadly. "It's who we are. We're the best." He was opening and closing the clips absentmindedly as he spoke. The man in the chair stared with horrified fascination at the jaws opening, closing, opening, closing . . .

"But in the end, we're human," the Afrikaner said. "Flesh and blood. We're all the same underneath. We hurt, we bleed, we scream, and"—he looked directly at his prisoner—"we talk. It takes longer for some than others, but we do. So save yourself some pain, eh? Tell me. Where've you been? And who've you been talking to? And most important, where's your key?"

"I haven't told anyone," the man in the chair said. "I swear it."

The Afrikaner shook his head. "I wish I could believe you, *boet*. We've been through a lot together already. But I can't take chances." *I kint take inny chanzes.* He stood up and approached the man in the chair, the electrodes clenched open in his hands. "Don't feel bad about screaming," he said. "It's not like anyone can hear you, way out here."

. . .

There are few places hotter than a tarpaper roof in the late summer in North Carolina. The small group of men working around the tar kettle were stripped to the waist, the skin of their backs and chests cured to the color of old leather by the twin blasts of the sun from above and the waves of heat shimmering up from the sticky black goo they spread around the chimney that stuck up from the gabled roof. They were mostly silent, moving with an economy of motion. It was too hot to move fast, and they didn't know one another well enough for small talk to come easily. Mostly they kept their heads down, concentrating on the job of spreading the tar evenly. They looked up, however, as the ladder that leaned against the side of the building shook and rattled. Someone was coming up. They looked at each other curiously. The whole crew was already at the top; they were expecting no one else. All work and motion stopped as they turned to see who was invading their space.

As they watched, a head came into view, followed by a pair of broad shoulders. The man who clambered off the top of the ladder was tall and lanky, with shoulder-length blond hair pulled back in a ponytail. He straightened up and looked at the men standing silently by the edge of the roof. His gaze took them in, one by one. Finally, he stopped, his eyes fixed on a wiry dark-haired man who had moved to the middle of the group as if trying to lose himself in the tiny crowd.

"Afternoon, Edward," the blond man said in a soft drawl. "We missed you in court the other day."

The other men looked at Edward, then moved slightly aside. He was the newest member of the group, and no one felt inclined to try their luck against the dangerous-looking interloper. They were especially disinclined to stick up for him since he had previously introduced himself as Gary.

Edward looked from one of his coworkers to the other and

saw no help there. He looked back at the blond man and squared his shoulders.

"I ain't goin' back," he said.

"Yeah," the blond man said. "Actually, you are." He advanced on the smaller man calmly, moving as easily as if he were on level ground. He reached into his back pocket and pulled out a set of handcuffs. Edward looked desperately one way, then another, then over the edge of the roof. He turned back to the blond man.

"Fuck you," he said, and ran off the edge.

It wasn't meant as a suicidal move; in lunchtime small talk, the other men had regaled Edward/Gary with the story of how one of them had lost his footing, slid off the edge of a roof, and landed on his feet without any ill effect other than a sore ankle for a few days. Edward didn't have that kind of luck; he never had. He screamed as he landed, his ankle breaking with a sickening crack. He rolled over onto his back, howling like a wounded animal, pulling his knee up to his chest in a futile and belated attempt at protecting the shattered joint. He looked up to see a short Latino man standing over him. The man was in his midforties with deep brown eyes and a thin mustache that drooped on either side of his mouth. He was holding a shotgun pointed at Edward.

"Hold still," the man said in a soft Spanish accent. "We will get you a doctor."

Edward screamed again, the tears of pain and frustration rolling down his face. Dimly, through the haze of his own agony, he heard the metallic rattling of someone coming down the ladder. He looked up to see the blond man standing over him. The blond man turned to the Latino and held out his hand silently. The Latino man sighed and handed over the shotgun. He reached into his back pocket and pulled out his wallet. He riffled through the contents for a moment, then pulled out a bill and handed it to the blond man.

"You were right," he said. He shook his head.

"I usually am, Oscar," the blond man said, not unkindly.

"What?" Edward snarled. "Right about what?"

The Latino man shrugged. "I did not think anyone would be stupid enough to try to escape by running off a roof. Mr. Keller here bet me five dollars I was wrong."

"Fuck you," Edward said again.

Keller pulled out a cell phone. "Look, you want me to call an ambulance before we run you in or what?"

The man with the rifle tracked the progress of the red Jeep Grand Cherokee as it wound its way up the mountain. Even at this altitude, it was beginning to heat up, but he paid no attention to the sweat that ran down his face. The huge rifle was heavy and awkward, but the rifleman moved easily with it. He kept the crosshairs of the telescopic scope locked on the tinted windshield, his finger resting lightly on the trigger. As the Jeep reached the bend in the road, the man's finger tensed ever so slightly. The Jeep stopped. The headlights flashed once, twice. The rifleman relaxed the pressure. If the Jeep had not stopped and signaled, he would have put a .50-caliber bullet into the driver's side window, then another into the engine block. Each of the rounds was the length of a man's hand and traveled at three thousand feet per second. The rifle was originally designed to disable vehicles at extended ranges; against flesh and bone it wreaked terrible damage. The rifleman had seen the weapon cut a man in half at fourteen hundred yards.

As the Jeep approached the cabin below him, the rifleman saw a flash of movement at the edge of his field of vision. He swung the rifle to bear, his finger taking up the slack on the trigger again. The crosshairs centered on the back of a blond head. He tracked the figure of the small child running across the tiny yard in front of the cabin. She was about five years old, dressed in a light-blue flowered dress. The rifleman held the sight on the girl for a long second. He blew out the breath he had been holding and let off the trigger. He kept his eye to the sight and focused again on the red Jeep. It pulled to a stop in a cloud of dust. A man got out. The rifleman swung the scope to bear on the passenger side. No one got out. The driver was alone. The rifleman took his eye away from the scope. Only then did he wipe the sweat from his brow.

"Shit," he said under his breath. A slight breeze blew up and he closed his eyes, savoring the coolness on his flesh. He opened them again and looked out over the vista before him.

He was standing in a rusting steel hut at the top of an abandoned fire watchtower. The tower itself was situated atop the highest of the local mountains. His vantage commanded a view of hundreds of square miles of forest that covered this part of the Blue Ridge. The ever-present haze that gave the mountains their name was light today. It obscured his view only slightly. The tower and the cabin at its base were far enough from the main road that even the muted whisper of traffic that most people tune out at the edge of hearing was gone. The silence of the ancient hills seemed to be a noise in itself, an emptiness that roared at him from the valleys below. In that enormous sound that was not a sound, the Jeep door's opening and closing seemed muffled, as did the voices that followed. One was high and childish, the other one deeper. It was a voice the rifleman knew as well as his own. But it was only one voice and he had hoped to be hearing two. He sat down on the wooden floor of the tower and leaned against the steel side. The massive rifle lay across his lap.

The tower vibrated slightly as the man below mounted the steps that spiraled up from the bottom of the tower. The vibration grew stronger as the second man drew nearer, until his head poked up through the hole in the middle of the floor.

"Anything?" the rifleman said.

The second man shook his head. He climbed the rest of the way into the observation deck. He walked over to the side and looked out.

The second man was tall and broad-shouldered, in contrast to the rifleman's wiry compactness. The second man was light-haired and fair-skinned, where the rifleman was dark-haired and Mediterranean-looking. Yet there was an indefinable similarity between them that occasionally led people to ask if they were related or even if they were brothers. In some senses, they were.

"We're going to have to call DeGroot," the rifleman said.

"He's not going to like this," the second man replied.

The rifleman lifted up slightly and fumbled in his pocket for a coin. He pulled one out. "Call it," he said as he flicked the coin into the air with his thumb.

The second man smiled slightly. "Tails."

The rifleman caught the rapidly spinning coin out of the air with one hand and slapped it down on his other wrist. He took his hand away. "Heads."

The second man grimaced. "I'll make the call. You get to feed the kid. I got groceries."

The rifleman sighed. "Spaghettios again."

"It's all she eats." The second man smiled tightly. "And we've eaten worse."

The bells hanging on the doorknob jingled. Angela Hager looked up from the counter as Keller and Oscar entered the front door.

Keller gave her a thumbs-up as he placed a sheaf of paperwork on the counter. She picked it up. Her hands were covered by soft black leather gloves.

"Did he give you any trouble?" she asked him.

"Nah," Keller said. "But he didn't do himself any good."

"What does that mean?" she asked.

"He ran off a roof," Oscar Sanchez said. "Trying to get away."

She arched an eyebrow at them. "Why would he do that?"

"Because he's a dumb-ass," Keller said. "If he wasn't a dumb-ass, he wouldn't have run in the first place."

"If you can spare me," Oscar said, "I am going upstairs for a bit."

Angela looked concerned. "Is the leg acting up?"

Oscar shrugged. "It hurts a bit, yes. But it is better than it was."

"There's some ibuprofen in the medicine cabinet," she said. "Take some of that." Oscar only nodded. He went up the stairs to the small apartment that he shared with Angela. She winced slightly at the sound of his halting tread on the stairs. She turned to Keller. "So how's he doing?" she asked.

"Not bad," Keller said. "He still underestimates how crazy or stupid some of these jumpers can get." He fished in his shirt pocket and pulled out the five that Oscar had handed him earlier. "By the way," he said, "slip this back into his wallet sometime."

She took the bill, looking at it quizzically. "What's this for?" she asked.

"Oscar didn't think Edward would be stupid enough to try and run off a roof to get away. I bet five bucks that he would. But I was just doing it to make a point."

Angela tried to hand the bill back to him. "It won't work," she said. "He'll know. He knows exactly how much money he has. To the penny."

Keller shrugged. "He needs it more than I do," he said. "What with trying to get his immigration problems straightened out. He's got a good lawyer, and good lawyers cost money."

She grimaced. "You got that right," she said. She sat down in the chair behind the counter and massaged her temples as if her head hurt. "And he's gotten back to the idea of bringing his sons here from Colombia. And that's going to cost another fortune." She shook her head. "But you know how he is. He made a bet. He lost. If you try to give it back, he'll think you're patronizing him. And he'll be impossible to live with for days."

Keller came around the counter and sat down. "So how do you feel about having his kids here?" he said.

She gave a short, sharp laugh. "Boy, there's a can of worms."

"Sorry," Keller said. "If you don't want to . . ."

"No, no," she said. "That's not what I meant." She looked down at her hands. "You mind if I take these off?" she said. "I'm roasting."

"You know you don't have to ask me," Keller said softly.

She looked up and smiled. "Yeah," she said. "Well, I'm still working out exactly where we stand, now that . . ."

"Now that you're with someone else," he said. "Well, we're still friends," Keller said. "I hope."

"Yeah," she said. "We still are." She began pulling the gloves off as she spoke, exposing the web of burn scars that covered the backs of her hands. "Anyway. He's been talking about it off and on. He misses his boys and he worries about them. But a couple of weeks ago there was a news story on that Spanish-language station he listens to. A young boy got kidnapped in Bogotá."

"It's not like that's anything new in Colombia," Keller observed.

"Yeah, but this one really got to him. See, he'd always sort of assumed that it was just the kids of rich people who got snatched and held for ransom. But these kidnappers made a mistake.

9

They got the wrong target. Instead of the rich kid they thought they were getting they got the maid's son." She shuddered. "When they discovered their mistake, they slit the boy's throat."

Keller's face darkened. "So it hit him. Anyone's vulnerable."

She nodded. "It's making him crazy. So . . ." She fell silent.

"So you can't say anything about the way you feel," Keller said. "If you put up any resistance at all . . ."

She finished the sentence for him. "If I put up any resistance at all, I feel like a complete selfish bitch."

"Well, you're not," Keller said.

"Aren't I?" she said, her voice bitter. "They're his sons, Jack. He's got every right to want to see them grow up. To see them grow up safe. And I'm supposed to stand in the way of that because I'm worried that I won't be able to hack it? That I'll be a lousy stepmother to them? Or that I just won't be able to stand having teenage boys around my apartment?" There was another silence before she spoke again. "You know the last thing my husband said to me before he shot himself?" She paused, took a deep breath. "I was lying there on the rug, both legs broken, the house beginning to burn down around me. He dropped that fucking baseball bat he'd just beaten me bloody with and pulled out his gun. I thought he was going to shoot me. I was praying he'd shoot me so I wouldn't have to burn to death. Instead, he looked at me and said, 'None of this would have happened if you'd just agreed to have kids.'" She slammed her hand down on the counter. It made a sound like a gunshot in the silence. "Like I was going to bring a child into a house with that psychopath. I couldn't protect myself. How was I going to protect—" She stopped, drew a deep shuddering breath as she got herself under control.

Keller got out of his chair. He knelt by hers and took her scarred hand in his. "You need to tell him this, Angela," he said softly. "He needs to know how you feel. Because it'll come out. Somehow. No one knows that better than me."

She smiled down at him, ran her free hand through Keller's hair before putting it on top of his hand. "Ahhh, Keller," she said. "Why did I let you get away?" She let go and waved off the response. "Don't answer that. I know why." She smiled sadly. "And now it's too late. We've got other people in our lives." She glanced up at the clock on the wall. "And speaking of late," she said, "you'd better get a move on if you're going to make it to Fayetteville in time to see Marie."

He stood up slowly. "Yeah," he said. "But remember what I said."

"I will," she said. "I'll talk to him." She stood up. "Things easier between you two now?"

"A little," Keller said. He didn't elaborate.

"How's her new business going?" she said.

"Picking up," Keller replied. "She said she needed my help on something. I'll call if I'm going to be gone long."

"No worries," Angela said. "Most of our clients have been pretty well behaved lately. Maybe it's your reputation, since you've been on TV and all."

He made a face. "Great. Thanks to TV, I have a reputation as a total wacko."

She laughed. "Yeah, but damn few people want a total wacko like you coming after them. Hey, you use what you've got." She gave Keller a kiss on the cheek. "Say hey to Marie for me."

two

Keller pulled the Crown Victoria into one of the angled parking
spaces along Hay Street. The broad sidewalks near the Cumber-
land County Courthouse were lined with older buildings. The Hay
Street area had been populated with strip clubs and streetwalkers
catering to horny soldiers far from home for the first time until a
city cleanup program in the 1980s closed the venerable fleshpots
like Rick's Lounge and the Seven Dwarfs. But that didn't eradi-
cate vice in Fayetteville so much as relocate it. The strip joints
had moved out to Bragg Boulevard and turned into upscale "gen-
tleman's clubs." The hookers had moved indoors and into the Yellow Pages, where they euphemistically called themselves escorts.
Now Hay Street was more friendly to "legitimate" business, but
those businesses seemed slow to get the word. Some of the storefronts were deserted, but various civic organizations had brightened them up with brightly colored designs painted on the empty
windows. Other storefronts held small law offices, clothing stores
offering "urban wear," and a pair of hair and nail salons.

Keller got out of the car. He stopped in front of another store-front. The lettering on this front window read JONES INVESTIGA-TIONS. A bell attached to the door rang as Keller entered.

There was a pressed-wood reception desk with a phone and a computer in the front office. Keller had helped assemble the desk when Marie opened the office. It was empty; so far, there was no money to pay anyone to man it. He and Marie had also spent a weekend constructing the thin wall that separated the single office from the reception area. Behind the desk, the door was open. Keller could hear voices coming from inside.

Marie was seated behind another cheap desk. The wall behind her was sparsely decorated: her newly framed PI license, a couple of pictures of her in her police uniform, and a picture of her with her father that Keller remembered last seeing at her house. A picture of Marie's son, Ben, smiled at her from a frame on the desk.

The woman seated across from Marie stood up and extended a hand to Keller. She was tall and broad-shouldered. She looked to be in her early forties, but there was a single broad streak of pure white in her wavy dark brown hair. "Tamara Healy," she said. Her voice was a contralto roughened by tobacco and whiskey. "I'm with Black, Diamond, and Healy."

Keller took the hand. Her handshake was firm, like a man's: straight up and down, one pump, two pumps, release. She sat back down. Keller took the other chair. "You're a lawyer," he said.

She gave a short laugh. "I thought Miss Jones was the detective," she said.

Keller began to feel a vague sense of unease. He looked at Marie and cocked an eyebrow.

"Ms. Healy . . ." Marie began.

"Tammy," the woman broke in.

Marie forced a smile. "Tammy has a client who's involved in a custody dispute."

Keller tried not to grimace. He knew Marie hated domestic cases. He didn't blame her. They usually involved surveillance of husbands or wives suspected of fooling around. The suspicions proved true with depressing regularity.

"I'll wait in the lobby," Keller said.

"Pull the door shut as you leave, will you?" Marie said. Keller did so. He took a seat at the empty reception desk. He looked around for something to read. There was nothing. Then Keller realized that he could hear the conversation on the other side of the cheap paneling almost as clearly as if he were in the same room.

"Problem is," Healy was saying, "Dad's run off with the kid."

Keller grimaced. He didn't really want to hear this. He got up and went to the window. No good. He could still hear the voices.

"Did you call the police?" Marie was saying.

"No," Healy said. "Dad made his move before there was a custody order. With no court order, either parent has a right to the kid. No court order, no crime."

"So get a court order."

"We got one. But we can't get it served. We're not really sure where Dad is, either."

"I can run a skip trace on him," Marie said.

"Well, that's where it gets a little complicated," Healy said. "This guy isn't your standard anything, Ms. Jones. He's in the military, for one thing."

"I can contact his unit . . . or is he AWOL?"

"No," Healy said, "he's not AWOL. At least as far as we know. But the Army won't tell us anything. They act like he doesn't exist."

That got Keller's attention. His pacing had brought him back to the office door. He knocked, then entered. Marie looked up at him.

"We should have sprung for the thicker paneling," Keller said. "I can hear every word you're saying in here."

Healy gave a sharp laugh. "Well, you might as well sit in, then." A flash of annoyance crossed Marie's face and Keller took the other client chair.

"So you know this guy's military," Keller said, "but no one will tell you anything about him. That can only mean one thing. He's Special Ops, isn't he?"

Healy nodded. "Delta."

"Well, that's it, then," Keller said. "You won't find him. It's like pulling teeth to even get the Army to acknowledge there is such a thing as Delta, let alone tell you where any of their people are."

"That's where I was hoping Ms. Jones could help," Healy said. "And maybe you could as well. Scott McCaskill tells me you're pretty good at finding people."

Keller shook his head. "I bring in bail jumpers," he said, "not commandos."

"You've been in the military," Healy said. "You speak the language. You know your way around."

Keller snorted. "Scott obviously hasn't told you everything," he said. "I didn't exactly leave the Army on the best of terms."

"So you don't want to help?" Healy said.

Keller looked at Marie. She refused to meet his eyes. The words he was about to say died in his throat. He had promised to be there for her. He had promised not to let his own demons drive them apart. He turned to Healy.

"Okay," he said. "I'll see what I can do."

"Good." Healy stood up and handed a file across the desk to Marie. "I'll tell the client to call you," she said. She held out her hand. Keller stood up and took it. "Nice meeting you, Mr. Keller," she said. She closed the door as she walked out.

Keller turned to Marie. "I can try calling—"

"Jack," she interrupted, "what the hell are you doing?" Her voice was low and furious.

15

"Whoa," Keller said. He held up his hands in a warding gesture. "If you don't want my help, just say so."

"Why are you doing this?" she demanded. "You don't think I can handle it on my own?"

"I know you can," Keller said. "It was Healy who brought it up. And she played me pretty well to get me to agree."

"She's a lawyer," Marie said absently. "It's what they do." She rubbed her hands over her face and sighed. "Okay," she said. "I'm sorry. I'm just a little . . . I don't know, I'm trying to figure out where we are right now."

"You're not the only one," Keller said.

She laughed.

"So you're taking this one?" Keller said.

Marie spread her hands. "What am I supposed to do?" she said. "I'm trying to get a business off the ground, Jack," she said. "I've got a kid of my own to feed and an ex who's three months behind on his child support. I can't turn down work."

"Okay," he said, "I'll lend a hand."

She stood up, slowly, grimacing slightly. She had been shot in the abdomen by the last person she had tried to apprehend, and the wound still pained her. She limped slightly as she came around the desk. "Thanks, Jack," she murmured as she came into his arms. She nestled the top of her head beneath his chin. "I don't have any more appointments today," she said softly, "and Ben's at day care till five. No one's at the house."

"And that means?" Keller said.

She poked him hard in the ribs and laughed. "You know damn well what it means, Jack Keller."

"I'll drive," he said.

She laughed and gave him a squeeze. Then her face turned serious again. "Did you think it was going to be this hard?" she said.

"What?"

"Being together. You and me."

He tucked her head back under his chin and stroked her light brown hair. "I didn't think at all about it," he said. "It just kind of happened."

Her voice against his chest was muffled, but he could still hear the tension in it. "So is it worth it?"

He kissed the top of her head. "Yeah."

DeGroot was frustrated. He sat down in a wooden chair in front of his subject and took off his surgical mask and goggles. The subject was presumably HIV negative, but one never knew. He wiped a spatter of blood from the goggles with a towel.

He realized now that he had made a mistake. He had tried to rush things, instead of going by the book. He should have known better. Through a dozen wars, across Africa and Asia, he had perfected the craft of extracting information. Physical interrogation should start with small indignities: a cuff, a slap, denial of food or sleep. Then the pressure should be ratcheted up in small increments, between periods where the subject is left alone to consider the next level, his imagination becoming the interrogator's ally as he worries and wonders how bad it could get. The extreme methods should be saved for the last resort. But DeGroot had let the time pressure get to him. He wondered briefly if his earlier speech to the subject had been a bit of denial on his part, wondered if he was becoming one of those people who enjoyed inflicting pain.

"Maybe I'm gettin' *bossies* in my old age," he said out loud to the subject in the chair. The word was slang for *bosbevok*— "bush crazy." "Maybe it's time to retire, eh, *boet*?" The man didn't answer. His head still hung forward slackly so that DeGroot couldn't see his face. A drop of blood fell from his face to join the pool on the chair between his legs.

DeGroot picked up the galvanized steel bucket beside his own chair. It was empty. He sighed. Besides the dodgy electrical wiring, the running water in the safe house was a meager trickle of rust-stained water from the faucets. He would have to revive the subject with water from the ancient pump outside. As he stood up, his cell phone rang. He muttered under his breath and answered it. "Go" was all he said.

The voice on the other end was agitated. "We still haven't found Dave," he said.

The Afrikaner looked at the man in the chair. "Keep looking," he said. He turned away. "Do you have his key?"

The brief pause was all the answer he needed. DeGroot cursed under his breath. "No," the voice said. "We figured he had it with him."

"BOBBYYYYY!" the man in the chair bellowed. "MIIIIIIKE! HELP MEEEEEE!"

DeGroot looked up in shock. The subject was awake, struggling against his bonds and yelling at the top of his lungs.

DeGroot heard a confused "Dave? Was that Dave?" before he swore and snapped the phone shut. He advanced on the man in the chair, his arm poised for a backhand blow. He stopped short. Lundgren was smiling at him through his mouthful of broken teeth. His one remaining eye glittered with triumph. "Psych," he whispered. "Psyched you out, you fucker."

"Clever *boet*," the Afrikaner said. He knew the schoolboy taunt was designed to make him lose his temper. It worked. He drew his gun and shot Lundgren in the head.

three

Carly Fedder was not taking the disappearance of her daughter well. Her eyes were red from crying, and her hands shook as she lit a cigarette. It was the third one Marie had seen her light since she and Keller had arrived.

They were seated in the living room of her two-bedroom apartment. Carly Fedder lived in one of the cookie-cutter apartment complexes that were expanding outward into the rural areas surrounding the growing city of Fayetteville.

"The son of a bitch," she said. She took a deep, angry drag on the cigarette. She was slim, blond, and blue-eyed. She looked like a high school cheerleader who had managed to keep her figure, but fatigue had worn furrows in the corners of her mouth and eyes.

"Mrs. Fedder—," Marie began.

"It's Ms.," the woman interrupted. "We were never married." She took another drag.

Marie tried to ignore the anger that hung in the air like the smoke from the cigarette. "How do you know David Lundgren took your daughter?"

She looked at Marie as if the question was idiotic. "Because he told me he was going to take her. He said he wasn't going to wait for the courts."

"What did he mean by that?" Marie asked.

Carly didn't answer. Instead she looked at Keller and said, "What's he doing here?"

Keller stared back. He kept all expression from his face. He decided to let Marie answer.

"Mr. Keller is a friend of mine," Marie said. "He's helping me. He has some . . . military experience."

"Great," Carly snapped. "One of them." She turned to Marie as if Keller had ceased to exist. "What if I don't want him along?"

"Suits the shit out of me," Keller said as he stood up. "I only came along as a favor to Ms. Jones."

Carly's laugh was nasty. She addressed Marie again. "Oh, now I get it," she said. "I'll bet you've got him jumping through hoops right now, honey. But when you run out of tricks, he'll leave. They all do."

Keller gritted his teeth. "I'll be in the car." He was almost to the door before he heard a small voice behind him. "I'm sorry."

He stopped and turned. Carly was turned toward him, but her eyes were cast down to the floor. "I'm sorry," she said again. She looked up at him, her eyes brimming with tears. There was something contrived, almost theatrical, about it, as if she had studied the signs of contrition and was putting them on.

"I'm not the only one you need to apologize to," Keller said. He jerked his chin at Marie.

She turned to Marie. "I'm sorry," she said quickly, "I'm just really wound up about this." She smiled. "Tammy said you're a mother. You understand, don't you?"

Marie gave a different smile back, the smile of one being polite to someone she'd rather be strangling. "Sure," she said. "And the sooner we get to work, the sooner we get your daughter back. Have you got any pictures of her?"

Carly leaped up. "Of course," she said, too brightly. She walked over to the television, where a small forest of framed pictures covered the top. She picked one out and handed it, frame and all, to Marie. "That's her," she said. "That's Alyssa."

Marie studied it for a moment, then handed it to Keller. It was a standard portrait photograph, the kind available in department stores across the country. The girl in the photo appeared to be about five years old. Like her mother, she was blond and blue-eyed. Whatever the photographer had been waving off camera to make the little girl smile, it had obviously delighted her. Her face was scrunched up in the expression of pure, spontaneous joy that adults lose along the way and never seem to regain.

"Pretty," Keller said.

"She's my life," Carly said. Again, the words sounded as if they were being read off a script. But the tears that followed seemed real enough. "Find her. Please, please find her."

"We'll try, ma'am," Marie said. It was a voice Keller hadn't heard from her since she left the police force, a voice of competence and reassurance.

"Tell me about Alyssa's father," Marie went on.

"What about him?"

"Where you met, for one thing."

Carly took a tissue out of a nearly empty box on the coffee table and blew her nose. "I was waitressing at Bennigan's. He and some of his buddies came in one night. We got to talking. He was young, good-looking, built . . ." She shrugged. "We hit it off."

"How long were you together?" Marie asked.

Carly looked away. "We were never really together, not in any kind of boyfriend-girlfriend way. He was gone a lot. He'd give me a call when he was in town. I knew he was in the service, but he never would talk a lot about what he did, so I figured it was some kind of Special Forces deal."

"Why?" Keller said.

She looked confused. "What do you mean?"

"You make it sound like you weren't all that close. If you were just fuck buddies, why'd you think his not opening up meant he was Special Ops?"

She reddened slightly at the words. "It was just . . . something about the way he carried himself. I've dated a few guys in the service before, but he was different. Nothing fazed him, nothing rattled him. Like he was above it all."

"How did he react when you told him you were pregnant?" Marie asked.

"He wasn't happy about it," she said. "But I told him I wasn't going to have an abortion. He didn't get mad or blow up or anything, he just walked out." She took another tissue. "He called a few days later, said we'd be taken care of. He was going to arrange an allotment from his pay for support."

"Did he see much of Alyssa?"

Keller saw the muscles in her jaw clench. "He was gone when she was born. He called me a few days later. I asked him where the hell he'd been."

"What did he say?"

"He seemed surprised I had even asked the question. Like I said, we didn't usually talk about where he was or what he did. I told him that all that had changed now, that I had to know I could count on him. He said it couldn't work like that. I hung up on him."

Marie looked puzzled. "So he didn't visit with her?"

Fedder shook her head. "He didn't call anymore. The checks came, but . . . no Dave."

22

"But you said . . . ," Keller began.

"Oh, he called once, a few days before he took my daughter. He said he'd heard what I was up to, the way I was living, and he wasn't going to let his daughter grow up in that environment."

Keller and Marie exchanged glances. "What did he mean by that?" Marie said.

She looked defiant. "Look, I moved on with my life, okay? I'm thirty-five years old. I'm a grown-up. I can live any damn way I please."

"Was he unhappy about another relationship?"

"I don't know what the hell he was unhappy about," she snapped. "And just what did he mean, his daughter? If he's not going to be there for her . . ." She was getting wound up. Marie tried to calm her. "Ms. Fedder," she began.

"Look, are you going to help me find my daughter or are you and this tin soldier here going to cover up for him, like everybody else?"

Keller started to respond. Marie silenced him with a warning glance. "What do you mean, everybody else?" she said.

"I called the JAG office, the Provost Marshal, everybody I could think of. I got nowhere. It was like Dave had ceased to exist."

"What exactly did they tell you?" Keller asked.

"Nothing," she responded sullenly.

"So you asked them a question and you got silence back?" Keller said. "Come on. They said something."

She sighed. "They said that they could neither confirm nor deny the whereabouts of Sergeant David Lundgren," she said.

Keller nodded. "Sounds familiar."

She laughed bitterly. "I'll bet. Bet you've said it yourself."

"Ms. Fedder," Keller said as he stood up, "when I was in Saudi, my squad and I got separated from our unit. It was late at night, out on the desert. A passing helicopter mistook our Bradley for an enemy tank. The Army killed nine of my men, men I was responsible for. If I hadn't been outside to take a leak, I'd be dead, too. I still have nightmares about it." He walked toward the door. "The Army acted like it had never happened, and tried to get me to do the same." He paused with his hand on the door-knob. "You might want to consider that before making any judgments about me being some sort of tool for the Army."

She was unfazed. "And what about you, Mr. Keller?" she said. "You haven't judged me?"

He thought about it for a moment. "Okay," he said. "It's a fair point. Tell you what, I'll make a deal with you. You don't call me a whore and I won't call you one." He walked out.

Keller waited in the car for another five minutes, until Marie came out. She slid into the driver's seat. She didn't look at Keller or start the car. Finally, she said through clenched teeth, "You mind telling me what that was all about?"

Keller looked out the window. "Guess we didn't hit it off."

"You didn't hit it off because you acted like a total jackass. What the hell is the matter with you, Jack?"

"I don't trust her," Keller said. "She's not telling you the whole story."

Marie shook her head and started the car. "Well, she still wants me on the job, God knows why. I sort of danced around the question of your involvement. From now on, you let me deal with the client, okay? You seem to have lost your people skills." She began backing the car out of the parking space.

"Suits me," Keller said.

Marie slammed on the brakes. "So now you're pissed at me?" She took a moment, then a deep breath. "Okay," she said. "I get it. Look, Jack, you didn't want this job in the first place. Just forget the whole thing."

He looked at her. "I said I'd help, and I will," he said. "I'm not trying to back out."

"If you're going to be this big a pain in the ass, I don't need your help," Marie snapped. She finished backing out, then slammed the car into gear. Tires squealed as she sped out of the parking lot. They drove in silence for several minutes. Finally, Marie said, too casually, "You seeing Lucas again anytime soon?"

Keller's eyes narrowed. "Why, you think I need to see a shrink about this?"

"Well," Marie said, "something about this situation's put a bug up your ass. Lucas has helped you a lot. He's gone to bat for you. And since you won't talk to me . . ." Her voice trembled slightly on the last word.

Keller looked out the window. "I'll call him," he said after a few moments. "He's been bugging me about taking him to the beach anyway."

"When?" Marie said.

"This weekend. First I've got to make some calls to Fort Bragg. See if we can get somebody to tell us how to find Lundgren."

"Where are you going to start?"

"Probably the Provost Marshal. If there's legal papers to be served, it's their lookout. After that, I'll try the Inspector General. What about you?"

"I'm talking this afternoon with the operator of the day care where Alyssa was when Lundgren took her. You want me to drop you at my office?"

"Yeah, that'd be good." The tension between them had eased, but only slightly. Neither spoke until they had gotten back downtown and Marie pulled up outside the office. "Okay. Let me know what you find out," Marie said.

"Right," Keller said as he got out. "See you later."

"Later," she said. It wasn't until she had driven off that he realized she hadn't asked if he was coming over.

four

"EighteenthAirborneCorpsHeadquartersCompanyOfficeofthe
ProvostMarshallCorporalDetwilerspeakingcanIhelpyou?" the
female voice on the other end of the line compressed the pre-
scribed greeting down into an unrecognizable blur of words, just
like any other Army clerk Keller had ever met.

"Corporal," he said, "my name is Jackson Keller. I'm attempting to locate a Sergeant David Lundgren regarding his . . .
regarding a legal matter."

"What sort of legal matter, sir?"

"It involves his daughter."

"Support matters are handled by an allotment from the soldier's pay. If you give me his unit designation I can give you the
name and number of the officer to contact."

"It's not a support matter. It's about custody."

"That would be the office of the Judge Advocate General, sir.
It would be handled by the JAG office at his unit level. If you
give me his unit number, battalion first . . ."

Keller took a deep breath. He remembered well the first rule of military bureaucracy: Whatever the problem is, make it someone else's responsibility. "I don't think JAG represents him, Corporal. We believe Sergeant Lundgren kidnapped his daughter."

The clerk didn't miss a beat. "That would be Criminal Investigation Division, their number is 555-4976, hold on and I'll try to connect you." Keller tried to say something else, but before he could get a word out, there was a click, then silence. Keller waited. A few seconds later, another click and a dial tone. He had been disconnected.

Keller sighed. He doubted that CID would get involved. Just like civilian cops, military police loathed domestic situations. He was convinced that he was going to get nowhere here. Still, he wanted to be able to tell Marie he had tried everything. He dialed the CID number. He waited for the clerk to complete his greeting, then began again. "I'm trying to locate a Sergeant David Lundgren—"

"That case is being handled by Special Agent Wilcox. Please hold."

Keller was taken aback. *What case?* he thought to himself.

After a moment, a man's voice came on the line. "Major Wilcox, can I help you?"

"Major Wilcox," Keller said. "My name is Jackson Keller. I'm trying to locate—"

"Sergeant David Lundgren, right," Wilcox said. "May I ask what your relationship is with Sergeant Lundgren, Mr. Keller?"

"I've been employed by the lawyer representing the mother of his child. We need to try to find him."

"Support matters are handled by—"

"It's not child support, damn it!" Keller snapped. "He's taken his daughter. There's a court order for her return."

There was a pause. "You mean to tell me he might have a child with him?"

27

"You mean you aren't—." Realization struck Keller like a hammer between the eyes. "Holy shit," he said. "The Army really doesn't know where he is, do they?"

"Where did you say you were, Mr. Keller?" Wilcox said.

"I didn't," Keller said and snapped the cell phone shut. He tried to call Marie. He got the message saying she was either unavailable or had left the calling area. He fumbled for a moment for his wallet, then pulled out Tamara Healy's business card. He worked his way though a receptionist and a paralegal before being allowed to leave a message on her voice mail.

"It's Jack Keller," he said. "They're not stonewalling you. The Army doesn't know where Lundgren is. They've got CID looking for him. And that . . . I don't have to tell you, that's weird." He hung up.

Wilcox put down the phone. He took a moment to look again through the Lundgren case file. Finally he realized he was just stalling for time to avoid making the next call. He sighed. He hated having to report to anyone else. It was especially rankling when it was a civilian. Still, orders were orders. He picked up the phone and dialed. It was answered after one ring. "Gerritsen."

"This is Major Wilcox at Fort Bragg," he said. "I was just contacted by a Jackson Keller. He said he was looking for Lundgren."

"Did he say why?" Gerritsen asked. Wilcox could see Gerritsen in his mind's eye. The preppy-boy good looks, the dark glasses . . . He shook a pair of Rolaids out of the plastic bottle on his desk.

"He said he worked for an attorney. There's a custody case going on. Lundgren's apparently the father."

"Right," Gerritsen said.

"You knew about that," Wilcox said.

"We did, yes."

"And you didn't tell me."

"We didn't think it was important at the time," Gerritsen said.

"And what about now?" Wilcox asked. "Is it important now?"

"It may be," Gerritsen said.

"Thanks for sharing all this information with me," Wilcox said.

The irony was lost on Gerritsen. Most irony was. "Thank you for calling, Agent Wilcox." Gerritsen placed just enough stress on the word "agent" to let Wilcox know he was only humoring him by using the title. "We'll check this out and get back to you."

Wilcox hung up without responding. He popped the Rolaids into his mouth and went to shake another out of the bottle. It was empty. Time to buy more.

five

Marie felt like she had gone through the looking glass when the day-care director introduced herself as Miss Melanie. It was also on her office door. She was a short, plump brunette, with red cheeks and a perpetually sunny smile that never left her face even when talking about the taking of one of her charges. The perpetual singsong quality of her voice never changed, either. It was as if spending day after day with children had destroyed her ability to converse normally with adults.

They were sitting in Miss Melanie's office just off the main playroom of the Tiny Tots Daycare Center. The office was minuscule, barely a cubicle. Every wall was covered with chaotic children's drawings of unidentifiable subjects. It was just after lunch and the children lay on thin mats laid out in rows on the linoleum floor. Miss Melanie had left the door open to keep an eye on the playroom. "We're a little shorthanded today," she said with her sweetly grating voice.

"Miss . . . ah, ma'am," Marie said, "I know this may be a bad time for me to just drop in . . ."

"Oh, it's no trouble at all, hon," Miss Melanie said, leaning forward to pat Marie on the knee. "It's nap time, so we can set and have a nice talk."

"Did you know that Alyssa's mother and father were having domestic problems?"

"Oh, no, dear," Miss Melanie said. "Nothing like that."

"Her mother ever say anything to you about being afraid her father was going to take her?"

"No, no," Miss Melanie said. "If she'd said anything like that, we'd have wrote it down in the book up front. So the staff would know to keep a lookout. No, ma'am, she never told us."

"Can you tell me what happened the day Alyssa was taken?"

Miss Melanie never lost her smile. "Well, shug, I'd like to. But the folks from the insurance said we'd best not talk to nobody about it. You know how them lawyers are."

Marie was taken aback. "You mean someone threatened a lawsuit?"

"No. Not yet at least. But, you know. Lawyers."

"Yeah," Marie said. "Lawyers." She stood up. "Thanks again," she said.

"Anytime, shug," Miss Melanie beamed up at her. Marie made her way through the rows of children lined up on the floor. A few gazed up at her curiously. None of them were asleep.

As Marie stepped out the front door, she noticed a young black woman leaning against the side of the prefabricated metal building that housed the day-care center. She was smoking a cigarette. The woman eyed Marie suspiciously as she walked over.

"Hey," Marie said.

"Hey," was the reluctant reply.

"My name's Marie Jones," she said, extending her hand. "I'm a private investigator. Mind if I talk to you a moment?"

The woman ignored the extended hand. "It about Alyssa Fedder, I don't know nothing."

"You don't know anything, or you've been told you don't know anything?"

The woman gave Marie a look of amused contempt. "They any difference?"

"Not to me, I guess."

"Damn right," the young woman said. She took a short, abrupt pull on her cigarette. "Already one of us lost her job over this. An' that ole bitch in there ain't bothered to replace her."

"So they leave you shorthanded."

The woman blew the smoke out on an angry blast through her nostrils. "Shit. We always shorthanded."

Marie looked sympathetic. "Trying to cut down on costs, I guess."

"You got that right. Ole bitch. I ought turn this place in to the state, 'cept I need the job. Don't know why Violet ain't done it."

"So Violet's the one that got fired?"

The woman threw the cigarette down angrily. "Now you got me sayin' too much. Who you say you was again?"

"I work for Alyssa's mom. She's worried sick about her daughter."

"Huh," the woman said. "That'd be a change."

"What do you mean?"

She ground the cigarette into the dirt with the toe of her running shoe. "I tole you, I ain't got nothin' to say. An' my break is over."

"Okay," Marie said. She started to walk away. After a few steps, she heard the woman's voice. "Hey."

Marie turned around. The sullen look had left the woman's

face. When she spoke again, the defiant hardness had left her voice. "That little girl in any danger?"

Marie spread her hands, palms up. "I don't know," she said. "I have to find her first."

The woman looked around furtively. "Lady got fired name Violet Prickett. She know something about it, and the ole bitch ain't got nothin' to hold over her no more."

Marie nodded. "You got an address? A phone number?"

The girl nodded. "She move in with her son. He stay in Wilmington. We talk sometimes." She told Marie the number. Marie memorized it; she didn't want to be seen writing it down in case Miss Melanie was watching.

"Thanks, ah . . ."

"Janica," the woman said. "You find that little girl you tell her Miss Janica said hi. She'll know who you talkin' about." She shook her head sadly. "She a sweet little thing. I hope you find her."

Violet Prickett lived in one of the areas near the Cape Fear River where older houses had yet to be bought up by affluent white people and turned into "historic" homes. The house, while clean and recently painted, was losing the battle with gravity and dry rot. The front porch visibly sagged in places, one of the carved support posts slightly askew. The screen door behind which Prickett stood had been torn and patched and torn again.

Prickett was a slightly built woman who appeared to be in her early sixties. Marie was surprised at her age; most of the other women at the day-care center had appeared to be in their twenties. She stood ramrod straight behind the door, no expression on her face. Her skin was a light brown, only slightly creased with laugh and worry lines.

"Ms. Prickett?" Marie said. "I'm Marie Jones. We spoke on the phone?"

"It's Mrs.," Prickett said.

"I'm sorry?"

"You said Ms. It's Mrs.," Prickett said. Her diction was crisp and precise, like a schoolteacher's. "I was married twenty-nine years. I raised seven children. I'm not ashamed of it."

"No, ma'am," Marie said. "Mrs. Prickett, I really need to talk to you."

The woman made no move to open the door. "You work for that Fedder woman," she said. "Why should I talk to you?"

Marie decided to gamble. "Because I'm not sure my client is telling me everything I need to know. I'm doing my job, but I want to know who I'm doing it for."

Prickett didn't move. "And if you find out something that makes you think twice about giving that little girl back to that woman," she almost spat the last two words, "what then? You going to give the money back?"

"Well, actually," Marie said, "I haven't been paid yet."

Prickett remained silent for a long moment. Then she smiled sadly. "You really are new at this, aren't you, Miss Jones?" She opened the door. "Come on in."

Marie entered. The front room was dimly lit by the light through the big front windows. There was a worn couch by the door, covered by a crocheted afghan. A matching and equally ancient easy chair stood beside it, facing a console television.

"I was just getting ready for some tea," Prickett said. "You want some?"

"Yes, ma'am," Marie said. "One sugar, please." She sat down on the couch. There was a coffee table in front of it, with copies of *The Watchtower* and *Modern Maturity* arranged in neat rows.

There was the rumbling of feet on stairs somewhere out of

sight. A slim young black man came into the room. He stopped short when he saw Marie. "Who are you?" he demanded.

Marie stood up. "Marie Jones," she said, extending her hand. "I'm—"

The young man cut her off. "I know who you are," he snapped. "You're that investigator." Before Marie could respond, he turned and shouted toward the back of the house. "Mama?" he called. "Mama!"

"Don't you shout at me like that, Curtis," Prickett said as she came back in the room, carrying a tray with a teapot and two cups. "I haven't gone deaf yet."

Curtis was unabashed. "I thought we talked about this, Mama." He gestured toward Marie.

"This lady, son," she said, setting the tray down on a clear space on the table, "is a guest in our home. And she's shown better manners so far than you have. Now, don't you have to get to work?"

"You said you weren't going to—"

She cut him off decisively. "I changed my mind," she said. "Which is my right. Last I checked, I am a grown woman."

He stood firm. "Haven't white people caused us enough—"

"That's *enough*, Curtis." The tone was calm, but Curtis's mouth snapped shut as if he'd been slapped. His mother walked over to him and hugged him. The top of her head nestled comfortably under her son's chin. "Now go on to work. I'll be all right," she said. Curtis gave Marie a stormy look over the top of his mother's head, but he hugged back. "You be careful, Mama," he said in a low voice. She nodded. Curtis left, giving Marie one last hard look.

Prickett sat back down. "I apologize for my son," she said formally as she picked up the teapot.

"No apologies necessary, ma'am," Marie said. "He's trying to take care of you."

"You're very sweet." She poured a cup of tea for Marie and one for herself. "I suppose that should worry me, coming from a police officer."

Marie was startled. "Mrs. Prickett," she said hastily, "I'm not—"

"No, no," she said. "I know, you're one of those private detectives. But you haven't been for long. And you used to be a policewoman, didn't you?"

"Yes, ma'am," she said. "If you don't mind my asking, how could you tell?"

Prickett blew on her tea. "Just something about you. The way you speak." Her eyes crinkled at the corners with amusement. "The way you say 'ma'am' sometimes, like you don't really mean it."

Marie flushed. Prickett smiled. "Don't worry, Miss Jones, most times you do. Mean it, that is. I can tell you were raised right. Sugar's in the bowl right there." As Marie spooned the sugar into her tea, Prickett asked "So why aren't you a policewoman any more?"

Marie hesitated, the cup halfway to her lips. "Mrs. Prickett," she said. "I don't think that has anything to do with what I need to know."

Prickett was unperturbed. "Well, now," she said. "Seems to me I'm about to give you a lot of information that might come back to bite me if I give it to the wrong person. You said you wanted to know who it was you were doing this for. Well, so do I."

Marie took a sip of her tea. The hot liquid had to fight its way past the lump that had suddenly appeared in her throat. Finally, she said, "I got shot. Me and another officer. He died."

"Oh," Prickett said. "I'm sorry to hear that, dear. And they blame you for that?"

"They didn't need to," Marie said. "It was my fault."

"Seems to me I saw something on the TV about all this. You

and some bounty-hunter fellow went after those two that did all that killing."

Marie gritted her teeth. One of the things she had hated most about the whole experience was having the distorted details on every local newscast for weeks. "Yeah . . . I mean yes, ma'am."

Prickett nodded. "I remember now. That was quite a story." She took a sip of her tea. "Seems to me I remember that bounty hunter from the TV. Big, good-looking fellow. You two—"

"Mrs. Prickett," Marie said. "Can we talk about something else now?"

Prickett looked startled, then contrite. "I'm sorry, Miss Jones," she said. "I'm being a nosy old woman. Go ahead and ask your questions."

Marie took out a pad and pen. "How did Lundgren get possession of his daughter?"

Violet arched an eyebrow at her. "Possession? That little girl wasn't a possession, Miss Jones, however her mother may look at it. She was a child."

Marie took a deep breath. "Yes, ma'am, I'm sorry," she said. "How did Sergeant Lundgren get his daughter?"

"That's simple," Violet said. "He called and asked to pick her up."

"Didn't her mother object?"

Violet snorted. "I should say she did."

"That's not what Miss Melanie . . . um, your former boss . . . said."

"Hmph," Violet replied. "That woman would say anything to keep herself out of trouble. Well, the only reason no one is going to say anything about it now is none of us want to do anything to help that Fedder woman."

"Mrs. Prickett," Marie said, "let's cut to the chase. It's pretty clear to me that no one where you worked liked Carly Fedder.

Did you have any reason to believe that Alyssa's mother was abusing her?"

Violet sat a long time, staring into her teacup. Finally, she shook her head. "No," she said in a low voice. "At least not physically."

"How do you mean?"

Violet looked up. Marie saw tears in her eyes. "I've never seen a child so starved for affection," she said. "She'd get up on your lap at story time . . . and when it was over, she'd just hang on, like she was afraid she might drown if you let her go." She took a tissue out of the pocket of her dress and dabbed at her eyes.

"So you felt her mother was neglecting her."

Violet nodded. "Sometimes she'd wear the same dress to school two, three days in a row. I'd ask her why, and she'd just say it was her favorite. When I asked if Mommy didn't want to take it and wash it, she'd just shrug and say, 'Mommy doesn't care.' Violet's voice broke on the last word. "And the way she said it . . . so matter of fact . . . like caring was more than a little girl should expect . . ." She brought herself under control. "So, yes, it's fair to say none of us liked that woman."

"Did you ever call Social Services?"

Violet looked out the window. "God forgive us," she said. "We should have. We should have. But Miss Melanie let us know that anyone who did that would be out of a job. And we needed the jobs. Most of those girls working there had little ones of their own to look after. So we tried to give Alyssa all the love we could."

"Until her father came for her."

"When he called to ask after her . . . Well, Miss Melanie told him everything was fine, that there were no problems. I snuck into her office and got the number off her message pad. Me and a couple of the other girls called him after work. We told him he needed to come get his daughter." She sighed.

"How did you know that he wouldn't turn out to be worse?" Marie asked.

"We thought about that. I arranged a time to meet him. We talked for almost three hours." She shrugged. "Maybe that's not much. But he seemed sincere. He talked about what he'd seen, how it had changed the way he looked at things."

"What did he say he'd seen?"

"He couldn't be too specific. But he let me know he'd seen fighting." Her eyes went far away. "My husband, God rest him, was in Korea," she said. "He wouldn't talk about it much, either. But when he came back is when he settled down. I saw the change in him then. It's when I finally agreed to marry him." She collected herself and looked at Marie. "So I decided to trust Sergeant Lundgren."

"Did he say where he'd been?"

"No," Violet said. "But I figured he'd been over to that Afghanistan."

Marie nodded. "That makes sense. But how was he going to take care of a little girl? He's Special Forces. He could get sent off anytime."

Violet nodded. "I asked him about that. He just smiled, sort of mysterious. Said he had everything he needed now to take care of her."

"Now? He said now?"

Violet looked troubled. "Yes. Come to think of it, that was a strange way to put it. Wonder what he meant by that?"

Good question, Marie thought. "So," she said, "did he say anything about where he was going? Where he was taking her?"

Violet shook her head. "Just that she'd be safe. Among friends."

Marie stood up. "Mrs. Prickett," she said, "thank you for seeing me."

Violet stood up as well. "Thank you, Miss Jones," she said.

"I've been wanting to tell somebody the straight story on this. I know you'll do the right thing."

"Yes, ma'am," Marie said. *As soon as I figure out what the hell that is,* she thought.

Alyssa was bored. She had already seen all the stuff that was on TV, and most of her toys were back at her house. She still had FredtheFrog, and the baby doll she had named Abby. Miss Violet had made sure her dad got those. She wished her dad would come back. He had bought her a couple of games to play with, but then he'd left for a little while. The two guys Dad had introduced as her uncles were nice to her, but they didn't seem interested in board games.

She got up and walked to the kitchen. Uncle Mike and Uncle Bobby were sitting at the table talking. They seemed upset.

"Can I have some juice?" she asked.

They jumped like she had stepped up behind them and said "boo!" She giggled. Then she saw the look on Uncle Mike's face and she didn't feel like laughing any more. "Sure, honey," he said as he got up to go to the fridge.

"What's the matter?" she said.

"Nothing, sweetheart," Uncle Bobby said. "We're just having a grown-up talk, okay?"

Uncle Mike brought her some juice in her sippy cup. She took a swallow and stood there looking at them.

"When's my dad coming back?" she asked.

"A little while," Uncle Mike said. "A little while longer."

She sighed. When her mom said "a little while," it could mean anything from minutes to days. But she knew better than to ask again. She might get smacked. Her new uncles had never hit her, but you never knew. She went back into the living room and turned on the TV. She kept it on low, so she could hear the conversation in the other room. It was a trick she'd learned. If the TV was on, they didn't think you could hear them. She had to strain her ears to listen and even then she could only catch a few words. They were talking about something being blown. Maybe something had blown up. Or maybe it had fallen over in the wind. Grown-ups were weird.

That scared feeling came back in the pit of her stomach. She picked up FredtheFrog and squeezed it tight against her chest. She felt something hard beneath the worn green felt. She wondered if she should tell Uncle Mike or Uncle Bobby about the secret that FredtheFrog had swallowed. But Dad had told her to keep it to herself. She'd keep the secret till her Dad told her it was okay.

six

Angela looked up from behind the counter as the bells on the front door jingled. The first man who walked in was young, slender, with short, perfectly cut blond hair. He was dressed in a dark blue business suit that looked as if it had been tailored to fit him. His eyes were hidden behind a pair of Ray-Bans. The woman who accompanied him looked as if she had been stamped from the same mold, except that her hair was light brown, slightly longer. She might have been attractive except for a weak chin beneath a small, thin mouth that seemed permanently pursed in disapproval. She was also conservatively dressed, if less expensively, in a pantsuit of the same shade of dark blue.

The man took off his shades. He tucked them in an inside jacket pocket. His hand came out of the pocket with a slim brown wallet. "Ms. Hager?" he said. Without waiting for an answer, he flipped the wallet open, showing a flash of gold badge that swiftly disappeared as he tucked the wallet back in his pocket. "I'm Agent Gerritsen. Federal Bureau of Investigation. This is my partner, Agent Rankin." Rankin performed the same conjuror's trick, the badge flashing like summer lightning, then disappearing into a coat pocket.

"I'm Angela Hager," she said, standing up. "What can I do for you?"

"We're attempting to locate a Jackson Keller," Gerritsen said. "I understand that he's employed here."

"Mr. Keller is an employee of mine," Angela said guardedly. "May I ask what you want to see Mr. Keller for?" she asked.

"First off," Gerritsen said, "do you know where he is?"

"It's his day off," Angela said.

"That wasn't what we asked," Rankin said.

"No," Angela said. "I don't know where he is. As I said, it's his day off."

"He's not at his house," Gerritsen said. "We also had people check Miss Jones's office and her home in Fayetteville. He's not there, either."

"You seem to know an awful lot about him already," she said.

They ignored the observation. "Does he have a cell-phone number?" Rankin said.

"First, I think you need to tell me what this is about," Angela said.

The two FBI agents looked at each other. Finally, Rankin nodded. Gerritsen turned back to Angela. "Do you know why Mr. Keller is looking for a Sergeant David Lundgren?" he said. "Sergeant Lundgren isn't a client of yours, is he?"

"No," Angela said. "Mr. Keller is helping out Miss Jones. She's a friend of his. She's a private investigator."

"For the time being," Rankin said.

"What's that supposed to mean?" Angela said.

"Interfering in a federal investigation is a serious matter," Rankin said. "It could also have repercussions for your license as well."

"I think you should get out," Angela said.

Gerritsen took a card out of his coat pocket. "If Mr. Keller gets in touch with you," he said, "please ask him if he'd call me at this number." He held out the card. Angela didn't take it. Finally, Gerritsen sighed and put the card on the counter. He turned and walked out behind Rankin.

Angela sat down. She was shaking. She pulled the phone over toward her and dialed Keller's cell phone.

As Keller pulled his car onto the concrete slab driveway of Marie's house, he noticed a vehicle parked on the road, across the street and one house down. He flicked off his headlights and sat in the car for a moment. As his eyes accustomed themselves to the darkness, he identified the vehicle as a Ford Taurus. He could make out the outline of a pair of shadowy figures in the front seat. He got out of the car, his eyes on the other vehicle. He thought he could see the shadow behind the wheel turn and say something to the person in the passenger seat. He began walking toward the Taurus. The headlights of the vehicle came on and the engine started. Keller broke into a run. The Taurus pulled quickly away from the curb and sped past him. Keller tried to get a license number, but the bulb on the license plate light was out and he couldn't make out the number in the darkness. He thought he could see the bright yellow decal of a local rental company on the rear bumper. The Taurus reached the stop sign at the corner, failed to slow down, turned, and was gone. Keller stood in the middle of the road, watching.

In a few moments, he saw headlights approaching. Marie

drove up in her gray Honda. Keller stepped over of her way and over to the curb as she pulled partway into the driveway. "Hey," she called over to him as she rolled down the passenger-side window. "What were you doing standing in the middle of the street?"

"I'll tell you inside," he said. Marie shrugged, rolled up the window, and pulled the rest of the way into the drive. Keller opened the passenger side and reached into the rear seat, where Marie's son lolled in the car seat, fast asleep. Ben was big for his five years, with a shock of tousled curly brown hair. Keller undid the straps holding Ben in the car seat and lifted him out. Ben murmured grumpily and squirmed a bit, but settled down as his head came to rest on Keller's shoulder.

"Thanks," said Marie, hauling a small bright green backpack out of the backseat. She fumbled briefly for her keys, then let them into the house. The front room was dark except for the steady red blink of the light on Marie's answering machine on the table by the door. "Don't turn on the light," Keller whispered. "You'll wake him up."

"I still need to get him into his pajamas," Marie said. "But go ahead and put him in his bed. I'll be in as soon as I check messages."

Keller navigated by memory through the darkened living room, down the hallway, into Ben's room. He laid the boy down on the bed and pulled a blanket over him. Ben yawned, then rolled over on his side and curled up. Keller stood looking down at him for a moment. He reached out as if to stroke the boy's hair, then pulled his hand back. He turned and walked out of the room.

When Keller reentered the living room, Marie was standing by the answering machine. She still had the backpack slung on her shoulder. She had turned the light back on, and Keller could see an angry frown on her face. "Trouble?" he said.

"Message from my ex," she replied. "Guess the FBI's gotten

to him about me. He's not exactly happy." She pushed the button. The voice that came out was pure country, thickened with anger. "God damn it, Marie," the voice said. "I don't know what the hell you got into this time, but a coupla FBI agents just left here askin' about you and that damn boyfriend of yours. I'm talkin' to my lawyer in the mornin'. I need to get my son outta that house." There was a click. A mechanical voice announced "Sunday. Twelve. A.M."

"I see you still haven't learned to set the clock on that thing," Keller said.

"Don't make jokes, Keller," she said wearily. He held out his arms and she came into them, letting Ben's backpack slide to the floor. Keller held her tight. Finally, he said, "It'll blow over. You said he gets like this every now and then."

He felt Marie nod against his chest. "Every chance he gets these days. 'I'm gonna get my lawyer and take my son back,'" she said, her voice a practiced imitation of the one on the machine. "He goes in, the lawyer tells him it's going to cost some money he doesn't want to spend, so he satisfies himself by talking ugly to me for weeks." She sighed. "I am so fucking tired of this, Jack."

"I know," he said. Suddenly he remembered the Taurus. "I think they were outside," he said.

She pulled back and looked up at him. "Who?"

"The FBI. There were two people in a rental car parked across the street. When I noticed them, they drove off fast."

Her face darkened with anger. "They're watching my house?" She stepped away. "Jesus!" she fumed. "Who do these bastards think they are?" The look on her face turned to uncertainty. "What's going on here, Jack?"

"I don't know," he said grimly. "But Angela's talking to Scott McCaskill. You get hold of Tammy Healy and let her know. I'll

46

have a talk with this agent Wilcox and see if he's the one that
sicced the Feebies on us. We'll put a stop to it."

She nodded. "In the meantime," she said sadly, "I don't think
it's a good idea for you to stay here tonight, Jack."

He started to protest, then shut his mouth. "Okay," he said
after a moment.

She came back into his arms. "I want you to," she said against
his chest. "God knows I need you. And I dragged you all the way
here . . . But if somebody's still watching . . . and this thing with
my ex . . . you understand."

"Yeah," he said. "Ben's got to be your priority."

She looked up at him. "You're upset," she said.

"Yeah," he said again. "I am. But not with you."

She buried her face in his chest again. "I love you, Jack," she
whispered.

"I love you, too," he said. He rested his chin on the top of her
head for a moment. Then he broke the embrace. "I'd better go,"
he said.

She smiled. "You better," she said, "before I change my mind."

He drove away, down the darkened streets. Through the windows he saw the lights of houses, the soft blue glow of televisions.
He wondered at the lives of the people in those houses, wondered
what it would be like to lead a normal life. The thought of driving
back to Wilmington and spending the night in his empty house
depressed him even further. He turned on the radio.

He wanted the people he loved to be safe. But life seemed to
have other ideas. It had been easier when there was no one to
care about, he thought. After losing his men in Saudi to friendly
fire, he had drifted through life, not giving much of a damn
about himself or anyone else. Then he had started working for
Angela. His lack of concern for himself made him fearless in the
takedown. He would go places and take risks that other bounty

hunters wouldn't. But as he and Angela got to know one another, he found himself admiring her quiet strength and her particular brand of courage. Before long he had found himself falling for her. She had gently turned him away, the pain of her own experience making her fearful of ever becoming emotionally dependent again. Then he had met Marie. And Ben. Angela had found Oscar. And now everything was complicated. He had lost all sense of fear for himself, but fear had found him again, not for himself, but for the other people in his life. And the fear hurt. It was like broken glass in his stomach sometimes.

He realized that his aimless driving had taken him to the neon strip of Bragg Boulevard. The bars were crowded, even on a weeknight. He picked one at random.

The place was smoky and noisy. The tables were full, and it was standing room only at the bar, which seemed evenly divided between couples trying to have earnest conversations and solitary drinkers staring morosely into half-empty glasses. At the back of the room a band with an aging and paunchy lead singer was grinding out a flaccid version of "Honky Tonk Women."

Keller insinuated himself between two bar stools and ordered a Jack Daniel's on the rocks. The drinks from dinner had lost their effect, and Keller wanted it back.

"Well," a voice said, "look what the cat dragged in."

He turned. Carly Fedder was standing behind him, a lopsided smile on her face. She was dressed in white slacks that hung low on her hips and a red midriff-baring top. She gestured to the bartender. "Put this one on my tab, Roger," she said. Her voice was slightly fuzzy. Roger nodded, his face carefully expressionless.

Carly slid into the space between the bar stools with Keller. There wasn't enough room, and the guy on the stool next to her had to shove over slightly, giving her a dirty look as he did so. She ignored him. The narrow space forced her up against Keller, the length of her body pressed against his, her face inches away. She smiled at his obvious discomfort. "So," she said casually, "finding anything out?"

Keller took his drink from the bartender. He gestured with it at the crowd. "You want to talk here?"

"Good point," she said. "C'mon," she took his arm and led him away from the bar. In a corner near the front windows, a wooden bench that looked like an old church pew ran along the wall. There were a few couples and small groups there, but Carly found them a seat that wasn't too close to anyone else. The band finished "Honky Tonk Women," paused briefly, and lurched into "Brown Sugar."

"So," Carly said. "Report to me, Mr. Detective." She was so close that Keller could smell the liquor on her breath.

"Maybe we should wait until you're a little more sober," Keller said.

Anger flashed briefly in her eyes, but she smothered it quickly. She arched an eyebrow at him. "You've been drinking iced tea all night, I guess."

Keller sighed. He wasn't in the mood to fight with her. "Okay," he said, "have it your way." He took a sip of his drink. "Dave Lundgren's AWOL. The reason the Army isn't telling you where he is, is that they don't know."

She snorted. "Yeah. My lawyer told me you'd left a message. I don't believe it."

"Well, you might find it more believable when I tell you this. There's been a couple of FBI agents asking around, trying to find out what we know."

Her eyes widened. She sat up, tossing off her drink in one swift gulp. "FBI?" she said. Suddenly the brittle facade was gone. Her hand was shaking. "They must think something's . . . oh my God . . ." The shaking became worse. She had gone pale.

"Please," she said in a small voice. "Can you please get me out of here?"

Keller stood up. She got up with him and leaned on his arm. "Please," she said again, "I have to go now."

"Okay," Keller said. They made their way toward the door.

"Hey!" a voice cut through the din. Keller looked back. Roger the bartender had picked a piece of paper off the bar and was waving it at them. "Your tab?" he hollered.

"Oh," Carly said. "I'm sorry . . . I'll . . . I'm . . ." she seemed totally out of it.

"Stay here," Keller said. "I'll take care of it." He left her leaning on the wall by the door while he worked his way over to the bar. "Thirty-five seventy," the bartender said. He shrugged at Keller's surprised look. "She's been here since five-thirty, man." Keller took a pair of twenties out of his wallet and handed them across the bar. The bartender grinned. "Carly strikes again," he said.

"What do you mean?" Keller said.

"Got someone else to pick up her tab." The grin grew wider. "Don't worry, buddy, it's worth the investment. For a while."

Keller turned and looked at Carly. She looked ready to collapse. When he reached her, she slipped an arm around his waist as if for support. His arm automatically went around her shoulders as they left.

It was a warm summer evening, but a light breeze was blowing and cooled things off a bit. The fresh air seemed to enliven Carly somewhat. She straightened slightly, no longer sagging against Keller.

"Where's your car?" Keller asked.

"Hmm," she said, considering the question. She gestured vaguely down the street. "Down there, somewhere," she said.

Then she began to sing in a surprisingly clear soprano. "Some-wheeeere . . . out theeere . . ." She laughed. Then she looked at him. "I don't think I should be driving, do you?"

He sighed, but she had a point. "Okay," he said. "I'll drive you home."

"What about my car?" she said. Her voice was playful as she added, "Will you bring me back in the morning to get it?" The hidden meaning was anything but.

"I'm not staying the night," he said. "Come on." He led her down the street to his car. She was silent as she got in.

"If you don't like me," she said as Keller started the car, "why are you doing this?"

"I didn't want you driving," he replied. "If you'd gotten into a wreck . . ."

"Bullshit," she said. "I could have gotten a ride from any of a dozen men in there. You could have walked away. Why didn't you?"

He had put the car in gear, preparing to pull away from the curb. He put it back in park. "You asked for my help," he said. "If you don't want it now . . ."

"Aha," she said, smiling triumphantly as if he had confessed to something. "So that's it. That's what makes Jack Keller tick. You want to hellllp." She said the last word in a drawn-out, mocking singsong.

"Okay," Keller said through clenched teeth, "I think . . ." He turned back toward her. She had leaned over so her face was inches from his, her eyes half-closed. "Help me, Jack," she whispered. "Help me . . ." She kissed him. Her lips were soft and demanding at the same time. She placed one hand on his thigh below the knee, then slid it up in a bold caress. Keller felt his body respond instantly as her fingers traced his outline

51

beneath the fabric of his jeans. "Mmmmm," she murmured. "So strong . . ."

He broke the kiss and tore her hand away. "Cut it out," he growled.

She didn't back off, but she didn't resume the kiss. Her eyes held his. "I need someone tonight, Jack," she whispered. "I don't want to be alone. You can help me."

"You don't want help," he said. "You want to prove something. God knows why, but you were looking for a button to push. The minute you found it, you pushed it."

She pushed herself away from him. "You think you're so god-damn special," she spat out. "A regular knight in shining armor. But I know how much you wanted me. You think I couldn't feel it?" Her smile was as cold and sharp as a razor. "You're no different than any other man."

"Then I guess you proved your point," he said. "And you didn't even have to fuck me to do it. I'd call that a win-win. For both of us." He put the car in gear and pulled away from the curb. She maintained a tight-lipped silence until they reached her apartment. She opened the door and prepared to get out. As she did, she turned back toward him.

"I'm calling my lawyer tomorrow," she said. "I'm telling her to hire someone else. You and your girlfriend are fired." She slammed the door without waiting for a reply. It was just as well, Keller thought; he couldn't think of anything more original than "You can't fire me, I quit."

seven

First thing Monday, Marie called Tammy Healy. "We need to talk," she said.

"I agree," Healy said. "Carly Fedder was on my answering machine this morning, screaming mad. She was telling me to fire you and, and I quote, 'that sonofabitch boyfriend' of yours."

Marie felt a tightening in her stomach. "What happened?"

"She wasn't specific, but apparently your friend Keller got into some kind of argument with her last night."

"That's impossible," Marie said. "He was with . . ." She stopped. She didn't know where Keller had gone after leaving her. She swallowed. "So am I fired?"

"I don't fire anyone, Miss Jones, until I hear their side of the story. Can you be here at ten o'clock?"

"I'll be there," Marie said.

. . .

It took Keller almost ten minutes to fight through the secretary's attempts to divert him from Wilcox. Finally, the CID man came on the line.

"You asshole," Keller said. "You mind telling me why you sicced the FBI on me?"

"Hold on a second, Keller," Wilcox began. "Just calm down."

"I will *not* calm down, goddamn it!" Keller yelled. "Two agents showed up at my office yesterday and tried to threaten my boss. They're watching my girlfriend's house. Now tell me what the hell's going on!"

There was a pause. Then, softly, "You found the kid yet?"

"No," Keller said. Something in Wilcox's voice sent a chill down Keller's spine. "Why?" he demanded. "Do you think she might be in danger?" Silence. "Damn you, Wilcox, talk to me!"

"Not on this line," Wilcox said. "I'll meet you. You still in Wilmington?"

"No," Keller said. "I'm in town. I can be at Bragg in about a half hour."

"Not at my office, either," Wilcox said. "Meet me for lunch. You like Chinese?" Keller said yes. Wilcox gave him the name of a restaurant near Cross Creek Mall. "Twelve thirty," he said.

"Twelve thirty," Keller agreed. He hung up, more baffled than ever.

The plastic sheeting had most likely kept any traces of blood or tissue from the floor, but DeGroot was a careful man. He scrubbed the floor thoroughly with soap and brush. Burning the abandoned old house to the ground might have done a more thorough job of eradicating any evidence, but it would have attracted attention, even in this secluded area. Plus, an empty house far away from prying eyes or ears was a resource a man like DeGroot didn't waste lightly. He had a number of these personal safe houses scattered at various places around the globe, purchased through a variety of aliases and shell companies. The things that made such places useful to DeGroot made them unattractive to most people, and therefore cheap.

He stepped out onto the house's tiny back porch and lit a cigarette. He looked at the neatly wrapped plastic bundle lying by the steps. He sighed. It had been a chore wrestling Lundgren's body out the door, and getting him into the trunk of the car wasn't going to be any easier, especially considering the things that were already packed there. He had decided to abandon this safe house, but he had a lot of gear stored here; weapons, explosives, and the other tools of his trade. He didn't want to leave them behind where someone could stumble across them, and they very well might come in handy on his quest. But now, with a body to dispose of, he'd most likely have to move some of the bulkier items around. He decided to take a break beforehand. He sat down on the steps and took a drag off his cigarette. It was clouding over, with the faint smell of rain on the wind. DeGroot savored the moment.

He had to admit, he liked it here. The area where he had grown up had been hot and dry. The scant rainfall and lack of major rivers had made drought a constant and lurking specter. But the land here was rich, and webbed with creeks and small rivers. He turned them over in his mind, considering their suitability for what he had to do next. While he thought, he picked up a pair of pants from the neatly folded pile on the steps. He pulled Lundgren's wallet from the back pocket and flipped it open. He removed the small amount of cash from it. He flipped idly through the plasticine folders one last time. Military ID, PX card, driver's license.

The wallet had produced nothing particularly useful before,

and he didn't expect anything different now. He was, he admitted to himself, just stalling. He pulled the cards out, one by one. He'd scatter them randomly at various places away from the body. As he pulled the cards out, a small card fell from between them. DeGroot picked it up. It was a business card, a fancy one. The raised lettering read "Black, Diamond, and Healy, Attorneys and Counselors at Law." In smaller letters beneath were printed a name and phone number.

"Tamara Healy," he said out loud. "Now who might this be?" When he flipped the card over, he got his answer. Scrawled on the back of the card in blue ink was a note: "Talk to my lawyer. C."

"Hmmm," said DeGroot out loud. "I might just have to do that." He stood up. "Okay, *tjommie*," he said to the body. "Time to get back to work."

eight

Marie sat in the waiting room of Black, Diamond, and Healy, leafing through a magazine without actually looking at it. She wondered if Tamara Healy would make an issue out of paying her for the time already expended. She wondered how long her rapidly dwindling savings would hold out. She wondered what it was that Keller had done to piss the client off.

"Damn it, Jack," she whispered under her breath. She had already halfway decided that she was going to drop the case after what she had found out about Carly Fedder. But when she found out that Keller had gotten them fired, the cold feeling of financial panic she had experienced made her wonder if she had ever intended to go more than halfway. Part of her didn't like the feeling that she would continue working the case, even against her better judgment. Another part of her, fiercer and more primitive, defiantly told her that she would do anything to keep a roof over her and her son's head.

Marie sighed. Being a cop had had its share of ambiguities

and gray areas. But it had been nothing like this. As a police officer, she had been part of a community. There were people she could turn to, who could give her some feedback as to right and wrong. But she had been severed from that community forever. She knew now the way her fellow cops had turned away from her demonstrated their ethical guidance may have been suspect, to say the least. She still missed it.

Tamara Healy interrupted her reverie by breezing into the waiting room from the hallway leading back toward the offices. She clutched a sheaf of phone message slips in one hand and motioned Marie into the hallway with the other. "Sorry to keep you waiting, Marie," she said over her shoulder as Marie followed her. "Mondays are usually kind of a zoo around here." She led Marie into a small conference room. "Coffee?" she said. Marie shook her head no.

"So," the lawyer said as she sat down at the head of the table. "Before we discuss this little friction between our client and Mr. Keller, tell me what you've found out."

Marie took a deep breath. "You may not like it," she said.

Healy smiled grimly. "Maybe," she said. "But I like surprises even less. Especially when they happen to me in court."

"Okay," Marie said. She told Healy about her interviews with the day-care personnel. The lawyer listened without expression, asking a terse question here and there. Marie finished by saying, "I don't know if Carly Fedder is the right person to have custody of Alyssa."

Healy arched an eyebrow at her. "Oh?" she said. "And the better choice would be the absentee father that she barely knows? The one who barely showed an interest for the first five years of the girl's life?" She held up her hand and stopped Marie's answer. "We don't get to make those choices, Marie. That's why we have the folks in the black robes. All I do is present my client's side. Something Dave Lundgren never gave my client . . . our client . . . a chance to do." Marie must have still looked doubtful. Healy leaned forward, her eyes locked earnestly on Marie's. "Think about it this way," she said. "You used to be a cop. And a good one, from what I hear. Did you like it when people took the law into their own hands?"

"I didn't," Marie admitted.

Healy's voice picked up intensity, as if she were building to the climax of a closing argument. "Well, that's exactly what Sergeant David Lundgren did, Marie. He didn't give the law a chance to work. He just grabbed that girl and took her away from the only home she ever knew. It may not have been perfect, but it was her home. And now she's God knows where, with no way to know if she's safe or not."

"Wow," Marie said. "You're pretty good."

Healy looked startled for a moment, then grinned. "Sorry," she said. "I get a little carried away." She leaned back. "Anyway," she said, "let's move on. I had a message this morning that a couple of FBI agents dropped by, wanting to see me."

"Did you talk to them?"

"Hell, no!" Healy said. "And you don't, either. Anything I know is covered by attorney-client privilege. And since you work for me, so are you."

"They're looking for Jack . . . Mr. Keller, too," Marie said. "And he thinks they're watching my house."

For the first time, Healy looked concerned. She chewed her lip thoughtfully. "Him . . . I don't know. He's not really officially an employee. I could argue that he's covered by privilege, but it's not a slam dunk."

Marie smiled wryly. "It won't make any difference to him if he's covered or not. If he doesn't want to talk, he won't. And he's not happy with the FBI right now."

"Still," Healy said, "I want to cover the bases here. We'll put him on the payroll. Special consultant or something. Ask him to call me."

"What about the client?" Marie said. "She wants us fired."

"Don't worry about Carly," Healy said. "I'll straighten it out. But it might be better to just let me deal with the client from now on."

Marie stood up. "Thanks," she said.

Healy stood up as well. "I'm not just being nice," she said. "It's better to have you two inside the wire rather than out."

Marie pondered that. "Thanks anyway," she said.

Healy shook her hand. "Don't mention it."

It wasn't until she was on her way out the door that Marie realized she had talked herself back into remaining on the case. She laughed ruefully to herself. "Played again," she muttered.

The Chinese restaurant Wilcox had picked out had a railroad theme, with the dining area divided into long, narrow rooms like dining cars. Booths ran down either side of the central aisle. The booths had high backs that blocked off sounds of conversation. "You having buffet?" the slender waitress said in heavily accented English as Keller slid into the booth.

"I'm waiting for someone," Keller said. "Give me a few minutes."

The waitress looked baffled for an instant, then smiled broadly. "Okay," she chirped. "Something to drink?" It was obvious that she had exhausted her entire stock of English. Keller ordered a beer. The girl nodded and walked off.

Wilcox arrived at the same time as the beer. He was dressed in civilian clothes, a cheap off-the-rack suit that had seen better days. From his haggard, baggy-eyed look, so had Willcox. "You having buffet?" the girl repeated. Wilcox nodded and ordered water.

"So," Keller said after they had filled their plates. "The FBI. What's the deal?"

Wilcox pushed some rice around on his plate. "It's not just Lundgren," he said. "There are two others missing."

"All Deltas?" Keller asked.

Wilcox nodded glumly. "All from the same unit."

"And all just back from Afghanistan," Keller said.

Wilcox nodded again. "The two FBI agents—Gerritsen and Rankin—are from a Bureau task force. They're working the terrorist angle."

Keller shook his head. "That doesn't make sense," he said. "Terrorists would want to make an example. They wouldn't disappear these guys. They'd blow them up."

"That's what I keep trying to tell them," Wilcox said. "But anything that could even remotely be terrorist related has them all jumping at shadows. Now they're even doing background checks on all three, seeing if maybe they might have crossed over."

"What, you mean defected?" Keller snorted in derision. "Right. These guys are motivated. They'd cut their own nuts off before they'd join the other side."

Wilcox's jaw tightened. "I know that, and you know that," he said. "But the Bureau doesn't know that. And let's be real. There's a lot more corners here than you realize. Hell, they may have formed their own side."

Keller considered that for a moment. Then he looked at Wilcox and spread his hands. "So why are we here?"

Wilcox took a deep breath. "We're here to pool information," he said. "Maybe something you know will fit with something I know that makes sense."

"And if it doesn't?"

Wilcox gave him a humorless smile. "Then we've both wasted our time, and if someone learns about this, my career is over, probably worse. The only consolation I have is that you'd probably end up in the same prison as me."

"Got it," Keller said. "I don't like you; you don't like me. But we have to work together. Eddie Murphy and Nick Nolte will end up playing us in the movie."

"I'd rather be played by De Niro," Wilcox said.

"With my luck, it'll end up being Adam Sandler and Whoopi Goldberg," Keller said. "But why are you really here?"

"There's a child involved. I didn't know that before. Neither the FBI nor the Special Ops types thought that was important enough to fill me in on. I happen to think that's pretty damn important."

"You have kids."

"Yeah. Two."

"Okay," Keller said. "Fair enough." He filled Wilcox in on what he and Marie had learned so far. Then he leaned back and took a sip of his drink. "Your turn."

Wilcox hesitated, then took a deep breath. "The two other guys that disappeared at the same time as Lundgren were named Mike Riggio and Robert Powell. They went through training together. Hung out together off duty."

"They were tight."

"All those types get pretty tight with one another. Comes with the territory. But yeah, they were buddies. For one thing, they were the only unmarried guys on the team. They didn't have any close family connections. Riggio's parents were both dead, and Powell's were divorced. His psych profile said he wasn't close to either of them. Didn't say why."

"They were the only family each other had," Keller said.

"Yeah. Some guys, the Army becomes their family, you know?"

"Yeah," Keller said. "I know."

He remembered faces, looking at him in the dim glow of a chem-lite, huddled close in the confines of a Bradley fighting vehicle. Looking to him to get them home. "Where we at, Sergeant?" a voice spoke up. It was Michaels, the guy from Louisiana they had nicknamed "Forty Mike" because of his talent with the 40-mm grenade launcher. Michaels could drop a grenade within an inch of anywhere you cared to point out.

"Dunno, Forty," Keller had said. "The GPS is deader'n shit. I'm going outside to take a piss and look around. Maybe get a fix on the stars." The answer seemed to satisfy them. They slumped back in the web seats. Some of them pulled their helmets down over their eyes to sleep. In truth, Keller could no more navigate by the stars here than he could sprout wings and fly. But he had to say something. They trusted him. He exited the vehicle through the rear hatch and stretched. He walked a few feet away, unzipped, and took a piss on the desert. When he was done, he heard the sound of rotor blades. It had to be one of the good guys. The bad guys no longer had an air force to speak of. He raised his hands and started waving. It was a stupid gesture in the dark, but he couldn't think of anything else to do. "Hey!" he yelled. "Hey—"

A Hellfire missile homes in on a laser beam focused on a target from a ground observer or from the launching aircraft itself. It is primarily intended to pierce the heavy armor of a main battle tank. Against a lightly armored target

like a Bradley, the effect is devastating. Keller saw the
trail of the missile's rocket motor like a bolt of white light
from the sky. It touched the Bradley and the world seemed
to explode. Keller was knocked to the ground by the blast.
Then he heard the screaming as the Bradley caught fire.

"You okay, Keller?" Wilcox was saying.

Keller shook his head to clear it. "Yeah," he said. "I'm okay."

"You don't look it," Wilcox said. "You look like you just saw a ghost."

"I'm fine," Keller said.

Wilcox's cell phone rang. He continued to regard Keller with a doubtful expression as he pulled it out. "Wilcox," he said. Then the blood seemed to drain from his face. "When?" he snapped. "How long had he . . . okay. I'll be there. Don't do anything . . . *Damn* it!" The person on the other end had obviously hung up the phone. He snapped the cell phone shut and looked at Keller.

"The Hoke County Sheriff's Department just found David Lundgren's body in Drowning Creek," he said.

"The little girl?" Keller asked.

Wilcox shook his head. "No sign of her." He stood up. "You'd better come with me, Mr. Keller," he said. "I'll need to ask you some questions on a more official basis. And your girlfriend."

"Wait a minute," Keller said. "I thought we had an understanding."

"We did," Wilcox said. "But that was before this became a murder investigation. And the terrorist angle is looking a lot more plausible." He paused. "It looks like Lundgren was tortured before he was shot."

●　●　●

Alyssa stared. The deer was standing not more than twenty feet away. It seemed wary, but not afraid. It was a fawn, like the picture of Bambi on the wall at Miss Melanie's. But this one was real. She realized her mouth was open and closed it. "You stand there with your mouth open," Miss Violet always said, "an' birds might just nest in it." Alyssa was pretty sure that Miss Violet was teasing, but there sure were a lot of birds up here, so she decided to play it safe. As she watched the fawn intently, a doe stepped out of the woods behind it. It must be the fawn's mommy, she thought. She wondered what her own mommy was doing right then. She wondered where her dad was. Then it hit her. "I'll bet Dad is going to get Mommy and bring her up here," she said out loud. The sudden outburst shattered the silence in the clearing and the doe bounded away, followed closely by the fawn. Alyssa was disappointed for a moment, but the thrill of the idea that her mommy and her dad were going to come up here together blew the disappointment away like a morning fog. She scooped up FredtheFrog and looked him in the eye. "That's it," she told the frog decisively. "We'll all be together, and Mommy won't be so sad and tired all the time, and we'll see deer every day." FredtheFrog wisely said nothing. Alyssa looked around. The cabin where her uncles had taken her sat just below the crest of a heavily wooded mountain. There were other mountains all around, but this was the best one because it was higher. You could see forever from up here. Mommy was going to love it.

There was the heavy thunk of a vehicle door slamming, and Alyssa's heart leaped. Maybe that was them now. She ran toward the tiny cabin, holding FredtheFrog by one leg. But it was only Uncle Mike. He had an armful of groceries in a brown paper sack. He looked upset. She ran up to him anyway. "Did you see my dad?" she asked. He looked even more upset. "What's the matter?" she asked.

"Nothing, honey," he said. "I need to talk to Uncle Bobby, okay? Can you stay out here for a few minutes?"

"Okay," she said doubtfully, then brightened. "I saw a deer," she said.

"That's nice," Uncle Mike said absently. He went into the cabin.

Alyssa sat down on the steps. She felt deflated, like an old balloon. She looked at FredtheFrog. She ran her finger over the frog's tummy, feeling the outline of the secret beneath the felt. Maybe FredtheFrog wasn't talking because he had a tummyache. She was starting to get one, too.

nine

"Kak!" DeGroot spat out the expletive as he read the words in the file.

"Sir?" the court clerk said.

He looked up and gave her what he thought was an ingratiating smile. "Sorry," he said. He closed the file and handed it back across the counter. The file was labeled on the front in black Magic Marker. Fedder, Carlotta J. vs. Lundgren, David M. *"Dankie* . . . ah, thanks," he said.

"You're welcome, sir," the clerk said. As he was leaving, he noticed the framed needlepoint on the wall behind the counter: WHEN GOD CLOSES A DOOR, SOMETIMES HE OPENS A WINDOW.

"I like your sign," he said. The clerk looked confused for a moment, then glanced back at the wall. She was smiling as she turned back. "Thanks," she said. "You have a blessed day, now."

"You, too."

The clerk's office was bustling with people, so DeGroot kept his face impassive as he walked out. His mind was racing, however. A child, he thought. He went after his child. After looking up the name of the lawyer on the card he had found, he had surmised that there was some legal action pending. A few moments with a helpful clerk in the lawyer's home county had showed him how to look it up in the public records. And it had all been there in the dry archaic language of court filings. A custody dispute, an appeal for a court order after the child had been taken. So that's what you were protecting, DeGroot thought.

Lundgren had taken a side trip to fetch his daughter, but he didn't want DeGroot to know about it. Stupid, DeGroot thought. If he'd have just told me . . . then he reconsidered. If I was him, DeGroot thought with a cold, inward smile, I wouldn't want me to know I had a child, either. Children were leverage. One had only to apply slight "pressure" to a child to get a parent to do whatever was needed. He had proved it enough times. A subject who had stood up under days of "pressure" without saying a word would start singing like a bird once you brought their child into the room. Often, no more was needed than a threat, which was fine with DeGroot. It was the result that mattered, not the process.

He took the elevator down to street level and stepped out of the building. It was late afternoon, and the big courthouse cast the street into shadow. DeGroot sat down on a concrete planter on the sidewalk and contemplated his next move. He needed Lundgren's key. Lundgren hadn't had the key on him. From the tone of the court filings he had just read, it wasn't likely that he'd given it to the Fedder woman, the child's mother. He'd probably left it with his buddies, Riggio and Powell. But Lundgren had declined to tell him where they were and DeGroot hadn't taken enough time to persuade him. Which most likely meant that the child was with them as well. And, of course, so was the key that they held. And he needed them both to unlock his future.

So. Find the child, find Riggio and Powell, get the other key. He'd probably have to kill them. They weren't likely to be cooperative after Lundgren had tipped them off. Once he had the other key he'd have what he needed to finance his long-awaited and, to his mind, richly deserved retirement. Someplace warm, with a beach. DeGroot had waited a long time for an opportunity like this, and there was no way he was going to just give up now.

He considered the child. She was no threat, and applying "pressure" to her probably wouldn't have the same effect on Riggio and Powell. Still, one never knew. People got attached. He mentally filed her under the category of things that might be handy later. But how to find her? Unless the police found Lundgren's body, they were liable to give searching for her a low priority. So far, for all they knew, it was a family squabble. But the lawyer . . . Ah, the lawyer probably had people looking. He'd try to find out what they knew.

With that thought, and with a plan forming in his mind, DeGroot stood up. It was good to be back on the hunt.

ten

The last time Marie had talked to an FBI agent, she was being debriefed as a witness. The interrogation had been so exhaustive she wondered how the Bureau acted when they didn't think you were on the same side. Now she was finding out, and she wasn't liking it a bit.

"For the last time," she said. "I work for Tamara Healy. She's a lawyer. Everything I know is covered under attorney-client privilege. If she gives me the okay, then I'll be glad—"

"How long have you had that PI license, Ms. Jones?" asked the male FBI agent—was it Rankin or Gerritsen? Marie couldn't remember.

"Four months," she said. "Look, do either of you know what time it is? I have to make arrangements for my son."

They ignored her. "And you'd like to keep that license?" the female agent said.

"Yeah, I would. It's my job. And I haven't done anything wrong."

"Some people might think obstructing a federal investigation—"

"I'm not obstructing anything, damn it!" Marie exploded. She stood up. "I want to help you. There's a little girl out there who's still missing, or have you two forgotten that? All I need to do is talk to my client and get her okay—"

"Sit down, Ms. Jones," the male agent said.

She cocked an eyebrow at him. "Or what? You're going to get my PI license revoked for standing up out of turn?" She started to walk toward the door. The female agent got in her way. Marie stopped. "Am I under arrest?"

"Why would you be under—"

"Oh, for God's sake, honey," Marie said wearily. "Don't run that game on me. I used to be a cop, remember? I know what you're up to, because I've done it myself. But I'm asking you point-blank. Am I under arrest or not? If I'm not under arrest, then get the hell out of my way. If I'm under arrest, tell me what for and get me a lawyer. I use Scott McCaskill in Fayetteville."

"I don't think you quite understand how the landscape has changed since September eleventh," the male agent said.

Marie turned to look at him. "Oh really?" she said. "Well, Agent Rankin," she said, taking a guess, "I'm still an American citizen, last I checked."

"I'm Gerritsen," he said.

"Sorry. I'm tired," Marie said as she turned back to Rankin. "So what's it gonna be, Rankin?" she said. "Am I going home or am I waiting for my lawyer?"

Rankin's response came out of left field. "Did you know Jack Keller was romantically involved with your client?"

Marie felt like she'd been punched in the stomach. "What the hell are you talking about?" She turned to look at Gerritsen. He was pulling some photographs out of a file folder. He laid them on the table. Marie moved slowly, almost unwillingly, toward the table. There were several eight-by-ten photos spread out there. They showed two people walking down the street, arms around each other. She spotted Keller's long blond ponytail right away. It was harder for her to make out the other figure because her face was turned away, but the slender form could easily be Carly Fedder's. The next shot showed them seated in a vehicle. They were kissing.

Marie sank into the chair. She saw Gerritsen shoot a triumphant look toward Rankin. She hated him for that look.

"These are surveillance photos we took the other night," Rankin said.

"Okay," Marie said. "You wanted to shake me up, you got your damn wish." There were tears in her eyes as she looked up. "But I'm still not saying anything until I talk to Tammy Healy. Or my own lawyer."

"If Jack Keller was involved with Carly Fedder, wouldn't that give him a plausible motive to kill the other man in her life? The man who had taken her child and caused her so much pain?"

Marie shook her head. She was still numb with shock. "No," she said. "Jack Keller's not a murderer."

"Really?" Gerritsen's voice was almost, but not quite, a sneer. "Six months ago, Jack Keller forced his way into a hostage situation and nearly killed a suspect in cold blood. Before that, he was involved in a pair of shoot-outs that left Fayetteville looking like downtown Fallujah. He was discharged from the Army after losing his shit and firing on one of our own aircraft. This guy's no Boy Scout, Ms. Jones."

"There's a problem with your theory," Marie said. "If Keller killed Lundgren, where's the little girl?"

"Good question," Rankin spoke up. "Maybe Keller knows. Maybe that's why Lundgren was tortured. Maybe Keller took things into his own hands and tried to get it out of him."

Gerritsen sat down in the seat across from her. "So you don't want to talk about Carly Fedder," he said. "Let's talk about Jack Keller."

"You cannot *be* this stupid, Wilcox," Keller said. He was seated at the table in one of the interrogation rooms. "Why the hell would I kill Lundgren?"

"Why the hell would you not tell me you were romantically involved with Carly Fedder?" Wilcox shot back.

"What?" Keller said.

"The FBI showed me some very interesting photos a few moments ago. You appeared to be getting pretty friendly with your client."

"They were following me," Keller said. "Even before—" He shut up.

"Before what?"

Keller considered for a moment. Then he said, "I saw them at Marie's . . . Ms. Jones's . . . house the other night. It didn't occur to me that they were tailing me afterward."

"Yeah, well," Wilcox said. "They've been taking this very seriously, Keller. So maybe you better start doing the same. What was going on between you and Carly Fedder?"

Keller shook his head. "Nothing. I ran into her in a bar downtown. She was wasted. Drunk off her ass."

"The bartender says you paid her tab."

"She'd been drinking for a while. She walked out without paying, and the bartender was making an issue of it. She was getting ready to try to drive home. It wasn't a good idea. So I gave her a ride." He sighed. "She made a pass. I turned her down. End of story."

"Maybe," Wilcox said. "Maybe not. The FBI still wants to talk to you."

"So what are you," Keller snapped, "their errand boy?" The way Wilcox's face reddened told Keller he'd landed a blow with that one. He considered adding something even more cutting, but pulled back at the last minute. Wilcox had been an ally. He could be again. "Look," Keller said. "You know this is bullshit. I know this is bullshit. So how do we convince Heckle and Jekyll in there that it's bullshit?"

Wilcox sat down in the wooden chair opposite Keller. "You're on your own there, Keller," he said. "They don't . . ." He shook his head as if reminding himself not to say too much.

"So when do I get to talk to them?" Keller said.

"The agents will be with you as soon as they get done talking to Ms. Jones."

Keller stood up. "What? Marie's here?"

Wilcox stood up as well. "Whoa," he said. "Hold on a minute."

"Fuck that," Keller snarled. "Where is she? Are they telling her . . ." He felt a sick sensation, as if his stomach had just fallen through the floor. "Sure they are. They're spinning her this same line of bullshit about me and Carly Fedder. Trying to shake her up." He moved to the door. Wilcox got up to stop him. Keller's arm shot out and caught Wilcox in the chest. He slammed backward into the wall. "I swear to God, Wilcox," Keller said in a low, deadly voice, "if you and those Keystone Cops in there are—" The door swung open wide. Tamara Healy was standing there, flanked by a uniformed sheriff's deputy. "Am I interrupting anything?" she said.

"No," Keller said. "I was just leaving."

"Like hell . . . ," Wilcox began.

"Actually," Healy said, "he is. Unless you arrest him."

"He's a material witness in a federal investigation," Wilcox said.

Healy regarded him coolly. "And where's your material witness warrant? Where's the affidavit?" She waved off his answer. "Don't bother," she said. "I know you don't have one. I, however, have this." She pulled a document out of the folder. "*Habeas corpus* writs, signed by Judge Longtry. One for Mr. Keller, one for Ms. Jones." She handed it to Wilcox. "Mr. Keller and Ms. Jones will be available for deposition at the government's convenience. They'll be glad to answer your questions then. Subject, of course, to attorney-client privilege." Wilcox took the paper and read it. Healy waited patiently. He handed it back, looking subdued. "Now," Healy said sweetly, "where can I find Ms. Jones?"

Keller waited in the hall until Healy exited from another interrogation room. Marie was behind her. She didn't look at Keller. They were followed by the two FBI agents, who looked ready to explode. Healy put one arm around Marie's shoulders, another around Keller's. "Now," she said, "let's go." They walked toward the doors of the Sheriff's Department. "Brace yourselves," she said in a low voice. "The press is here."

"Fuck," Keller muttered.

"Don't be too pissed off," Healy said, "They have their uses. It's part of the reason we were able to get the writ. Longtry hates bad publicity." They were approaching the glass doors. Keller could see the crowd milling around outside. "Eyes front," Healy said. "Don't make eye contact, and for God's sake don't say anything."

Walking through the glass doors was like being suddenly caught in a breaking wave. There was a roar of questions being shouted and a rapid-fire barrage of lights exploding. Keller put his head down and pushed his way through as questions were hurled at him from both sides.

"What do you know about the soldier found dead this morning?"

"Is it true his body was mutilated?"

"Are you a suspect in the murder?"

"Are you free on bail?"

Then, out of the crowd, Keller heard his name being called.
"Mr. Keller! Mr. Keller!" He jerked his head up in shock. The
crowd parted slightly as reporters in the crush turned to look at
the person who seemed to know more than they.

A petite Asian woman with short, perfectly coiffed hair
pushed her way through the crowd, trailed by her cameraman.

"Oh, shit," Marie said.

"Mr. Keller, Grace Tranh from Fox Investigative Reports," the
woman said crisply, sticking out her microphone as the cameraman raised his lens to fix on them. "Can you tell us what your
connection is with the murder of the Special Forces soldier found
dead this morning?" The noise of the reporters subsided. No one
else had known that the dead man was with Special Forces.

"No comment," Keller said through clenched teeth. He tried
to push forward, but she stood her ground.

"Are you a suspect because of your involvement in the hostage
crisis in Wilmington a few months ago?" Tranh persisted.

"No comment," Keller said again, and pushed past her.

"You know each other?" Tammy Healy asked.

"You could say that," Keller grunted. They made their way to
Healy's Ford Expedition parked at the curb. Healy took the driver's seat. Keller turned to Marie. "Front or back?" he asked.

Marie still didn't look at him. "I don't care."

"Marie!"

She looked at him. Her blue eyes were flat and dead. "Jack,"
she said, "I'm not going to talk about this here, okay? Not here,
and not now." She savagely yanked the back door open and got in.

Keller climbed into the front. Healy had already started the vehicle and was moving forward, the crowd of reporters parting reluctantly. They pulled onto the highway and headed for Wilmington.

"Thanks for getting us out of there," Keller said.

"Thank Scott McCaskill," she said. "He's the one who knows
all that criminal stuff. I'm a family lawyer. I couldn't figure out
how to get a *habeas* writ if you held a gun to my head. I just
came down to deliver it because Scott was tied up."

"You sure acted like you knew what you were doing," Keller
said. "You learn that from Scott?"

She laughed. "No, Jack, bluffing he learned from me." She
gave a little secret grin. "Among other things." Keller glanced
back at Marie. She was staring vacantly out the window. He
caught Healy glancing at her in the rearview mirror. "How you
doing back there, Marie?"

"Fine," Marie said distantly.

Keller took a deep breath. "Ms. Healy—"

"Tammy," she said.

"Tammy," Keller said, "the FBI made a couple of accusations
back there, some accusations you need to know about."

"Anything they can back up?" Healy said calmly.

"Not with anything real, no. But there are a couple of photographs."

"Jack," Marie said.

"She needs to know, Marie."

"I assume this has something to do with the tension between
you two."

"Yeah," Keller said. "They think I was involved with Carly
Fedder."

She didn't react. "Go on."

"I ran into Fedder a few nights ago downtown. She was
drunk. I gave her a ride home."

"Ah."

"The Feebies were tailing me at the time, or maybe it was her. Anyway, they took a picture of her making a pass at me." He looked back at Marie. "I turned it down. But the picture—"

"You turned her down?" Healy said.

"Yeah."

They had pulled up to a stop sign. Healy looked him up and down. Then she grinned again. "No wonder my client's so pissed off." She spoke over her shoulder to Marie as they pulled away from the sign. "I know it's none of my business, hon," she told Marie, "but I tend to believe him. I heard Carly Fedder the day after. And if there's one thing I know, it's the voice of a woman scorned."

Keller looked back again. Marie was still looking out the window, not responding. They drove like that for a few minutes. Finally, Keller said, "So what do we do now?"

"*We* don't do anything," said Healy. "Lundgren's dead and the child is missing. It's a law enforcement matter now. Let them handle it."

"Those idiots?" Keller said. "They act like they've forgotten the kid's even alive."

"Jack," Healy said, "she probably isn't. And if she's in the hands of whoever did that to David Lundgren . . . it might be better if she isn't." No one said anything after that. They pulled up in front of the restored Victorian that housed Healy's offices. As they got out of the car, Keller turned to Marie. "Marie . . . ," he began.

"Jack," she said wearily, "I don't want to talk now. I'm exhausted. I just want to go home and be with my son." She walked away toward her car without looking back. Keller stood and watched her go. Healy came and stood beside him.

"Just let her rest, Keller," she said. "She'll come around."

"And if she doesn't?" Keller asked.

"Then look me up," she said. "I'm in the book." At Keller's look, her smile vanished. "Joking," she said. "Sorry."

Keller looked over her shoulder. "They're back," he said.

She glanced behind her. A nondescript rental car was parked across the street. "Those same people that were tailing you the other night?" she said.

He shook his head. "Different car. And this is only one person." As he spoke the car started up and began pulling away. Keller caught a glimpse of a lean, hard face below a military-style short haircut. Then the car was gone.

"Jesus," Healy said. "What the hell are they trying to accomplish?"

"I don't think that was the FBI," he said. "That guy looked military."

"Wonderful," Healy said. "I'll call Wilcox tomorrow and let him know if he keeps harassing me, he'll be hearing from the judge again. And that includes harassing my people."

Keller cocked an eyebrow at her. "Your people?"

She grinned. "We're all in this together, Jack," she said. "One big happy family."

When the brown-haired woman's car pulled away, DeGroot had to make a choice. Stay with the lawyer or follow the employee. When the blond man had noticed his presence, the choice was made. The traffic impeded her enough so that he was able to catch up. He followed her until she turned into a quiet residential neighborhood. The traffic there was lighter, and DeGroot feared she'd notice him, so he broke off and turned the other way. After a short interval he headed back. It took about a half hour, but he eventually spotted the car parked in a driveway. There was a mailbox at the end of the driveway, marked "M. Jones." There was a scattering of children's toys in the front yard. He made a mental note of the address. He felt a lifting of the gloom that had clamped down on him earlier. He thought about the plaque he had seen in the clerk's office: When God closes a door, sometimes he opens a window. It had been a long time since he believed in God. But he did have to admit, new opportunities seemed to be opening up every moment. He slowed for a moment to observe the place, his experienced eye checking for routes of ingress and egress. It was then that he noticed the police car coming down the street, followed by a large pickup truck. He slowed for a moment, watching as the vehicles pulled in to the driveway of the house he had just been watching. Then he accelerated away.

eleven

When Keller pulled up to the house, he wasn't able to park in the driveway. There was no room. There was a red, new-looking pickup parked in the second space, and a police car parked behind it, its rear end partially in the street. Keller parked on the street across from the house and got out slowly. He could hear the sound of raised voices as he approached the open door. A uniformed patrolman came out. He looked unhappy. He was followed by a man, in blue jeans and a red T-shirt, who was holding Ben in his arms. The boy was silent, but his eyes were wide and he had his thumb stuck in his mouth. Keller couldn't remember ever seeing Ben suck his thumb before. Marie came last. Her eyes were red and tears streaked her cheeks. Keller stopped. "What's going on?" he said.

The man holding Ben looked over at Keller. His eyes hardened. He was short and broad. He wore his dark hair in a short military-style brush cut. His face was square, with a slight dimple in the chin.

"This ain't none o' your business," he said.

"Who the fuck are you?" Keller demanded.

"Easy, sir," the officer interjected.

"I'll take it easy when I find out—"

"No, sir," the officer said, reaching down to the container of Mace on his belt. "You'll take it easy now. Back up, and leave this—"

"I got a court order," the man broke in, to the annoyance of the officer. "So you just back off." He carried Ben to the truck and opened the door. There was a car seat in the back of the King Cab.

Keller looked at Marie. She was watching the man strap her son into the car seat. She looked shattered. "Marie?" he said.

Fresh tears spilled down her cheeks. She tried to speak, but choked on the words. The man finished tightening the belts and closed the door. He turned to Keller. "You must be the guy she's been fucking," he said. "Take her back inside for a quick one. That usually makes her forget about our son."

Keller started for him, but the officer interposed himself firmly. "Get in the truck, Mr. Forrest," he said over his shoulder. He turned back to Keller. "And you, sir," he said, "you just—"

Keller ignored him. He turned away and went to Marie, who was standing on the porch. He tried to take her in his arms, but she shook her head. "Not here," she said. "Not now." She stumbled back through the door. Keller heard the truck's engine start as he followed her. There was a thick sheaf of papers lying on the table next to the door. The page on top was yellow and bore the title "Civil Summons." Bold black letters announced that "A CIVIL ACTION HAS BEEN COMMENCED AGAINST YOU." The sound of Marie's weeping came from the bedroom. He wanted to go to her, but the way she had pushed him away made him stop. He thumbed through the papers instead. Through the fog of legalese, phrases snarled out at him. "Unstable lifestyle." "Association with violent individuals." "Immediate and imminent risk to the minor child of abuse and neglect." The final page was a "Temporary Emergency Custody Order" giving custody of "the minor child" to his natural father, Carson Treadwell Forrest. A hearing was set for the following Monday. Keller went into the bedroom. Marie was facedown on the bed, her head resting on her arms. He sat down on the bed next to her. He reached out and stroked her hair gently. "I'm sorry" was all he could think of to say.

She rolled over and sat up. "I can't believe it," she said. "He never did anything but threaten before." She shook her head, her grief turning to anger. "I can't believe he'd lie like that, though."

"It's not all lies," Keller said.

"What do you mean?" she said, her face hardening.

"What he said about me," Keller said. "He's right. I haven't brought you anything but trouble since we met."

She smiled a little then. "Well, I wouldn't say that's all you've brought me."

He stood up. "Thanks," he said, "but you know I'm right. I get into bad situations. And I drag you into them. And one of these days, Ben's going to get dragged into it, too."

"Jack," she said, "bad stuff happens to people. That's not going to stop happening if you leave. It's not going to make us any safer."

"Maybe," he said, "but at least I won't be the one dragging the bad stuff to your doorstep."

"So you're walking out?" she demanded. "When I need you the most?"

"You need Ben more than you need me," he said. "And if I'm around, you probably won't get him back." He walked to the door.

"Damn it, Jack," she said. "I won't leave you because my ex can't handle the idea of us being together."

"I know you won't," he said. "So that's why I'm the one pulling the plug." They looked at each other in silence for a few moments. The buzzing of Keller's cell phone sounded unnaturally loud in the quiet. He pulled it off his belt, looked at the caller ID, then at Marie. "It's Tammy Healy," he said. He flipped the phone open. "Keller," he said.

"Jack," she said, "are you still in town?"

"Yeah," he said. "I'm at Marie's." He looked at Marie. "Her ex just came in here with an emergency court order and took her son."

There was a moment's pause. "Damn," Healy said, "Everything always happens at goddamn once." She sighed. "Okay," she said. "Does she want an appointment this afternoon?"

Keller pulled the phone away from his ear. "You want to see Tammy Healy this afternoon?" Marie looked doubtful. "You're going to need a lawyer to fight this," Keller said. "Even I'm not stupid enough to walk into a courtroom armed with nothing but the truth."

Marie nodded. "Okay."

"Yeah," Keller said into the phone.

"Fine," Healy said. "And I need to see you, too. Something's happened in the Fedder case."

"What?" Keller said.

"I'll talk to you when you get here," Healy said. "One hour." She hung up.

"She'll see us in an hour," Keller said.

Marie looked puzzled. "Us?" she said.

"She wanted to see me, too," he told her. "Something about the Fedder case."

"I thought she was off that," Marie said.

"She said something had happened."

"If it was something that made her drop everything so she could see you in an hour," Marie said, "it must be something major."

A few blocks away, DeGroot sat in his car at the curb, watching the big pickup truck go past. He caught a glimpse of a child's blond head in the passenger seat. He had circled the block after watching the truck pull in. No one had noticed him because of the argument going on in the yard. He had pulled away and parked a short distance up the street.

I scheme poor old Lundgren isn't the only one with family problems, he thought. He pulled out and followed the truck, keeping a discreet distance. The truck wound its way through the residential streets, onto the main drag. Eventually, it turned into the parking lot of a Motel 6. DeGroot made a note of the room they stopped in front of before he exited the parking lot. He looked down, noticed the gas gauge. Nearly empty. He found a gas station and pulled up to the pump. As he filled the tank of the rental, he thought over what he had seen.

The big blond fellow and the woman with the child—Jones—work for the lawyer, he thought. *The blond fellow and Jones are involved somehow. Maybe that's why the other man took the child? A jealous husband? But why didn't he leave? Puzzling. But,* he decided, *not what I came here to find out. I need to know what was going on with Lundgren. It has something to do with his child. And the one who knows that is . . .* The gas pumped clunked and shut off. *The lawyer.* He slotted the nozzle back into its holder and waited for the credit card receipt. Time to pay a visit to the lawyer.

twelve

"Thanks, Cindy," Tamara Healy said to the young blond behind the desk as she came out of her office. "I'll see Mr. Keller first. Marie, would you like a cup of coffee while you wait?" Marie shook her head wordlessly. She still had a look of devastation on her face. Healy walked over and crouched beside her chair. "It's going to be okay, hon," she said softly, taking Marie's hand. "We're going to do everything we can for you."

Marie nodded, still not speaking. Keller followed Healy as she stood up and walked into her office. She seated herself behind a large, expensive-looking oak desk and motioned Keller to an equally expensive-looking chair. She spoke before he was fully seated.

"I've gotten a call regarding Alyssa Fedder," she said.

"From who?" Keller asked.

"The people that have her," Healy said tonelessly.

Keller rubbed his chin. "You call the cops?"

She shook her head. "They made it very clear I was not to do that. They said they'd know if I did and no one would ever see Alyssa Fedder again."

"So," Keller said, "why tell me?" He was beginning to feel distinctly uneasy about the answer.

"They want to turn the girl back over to me. They gave me directions to a place near where they say they have her. It's in the mountains."

"So go," Keller said. "Or take your chances, call the cops and let them go."

She shook her head again. "I'm not stupid, Jack. I'm not going up there by myself, in the middle of nowhere, with men I've never seen. I've been called a lot of things, most of them ending in bitch, but I don't think anyone thinks I'm that crazy." She picked up a pack of cigarettes. Her hands trembled as she took one out and lit it. She offered the pack to Keller. He thought for a moment, then took it.

"I've been trying to quit," she said.

"Probably a good idea."

"So?" She took a long drag on the cigarette.

"I'll go," he said. "That's what you've been leading up to, right?"

She nodded, looking surprised. "I thought I'd have to talk you into it."

"There's a condition," he said.

She blew out a long stream of smoke and grinned at him. "If it's sexual favors, honey, you had me at hello."

"Thanks," he said, "I'll keep it in mind. But it's about Marie."

She turned serious. "You want me to take her case. For free?"

"No," he said. "She'll figure that out and she'll never accept it. But she's practically broke. Keep the price low, and let her pay it off over time. She'll do it."

"I know she will," Healy said. "You'd do this for her?"

"Yeah," Keller said.

Her smile this time was wistful. "Why couldn't I have met you fifteen years ago?"

"Because I was a complete head case," Keller said. "And I wouldn't lay odds that I'm not headed that way again. Now, how are we going to keep these guys from knowing I'm there?"

"They know you're coming," she said. "I told them I was scared to come alone. I wanted someone with me. I brought up your name, and they said okay. Seems they know you from TV."

Keller grimaced. "Great," he said.

"Well, they know for sure you're not a cop. And they know your face."

He rubbed his chin. "No way are these guys professional criminals," he said. "Pros would never agree to something like that. I figure it's Lundgren's buddies. Powell and Riggio. Lundgren took the girl and left her with them. Now Lundgren's dead, they want to get rid of her. Fast." He looked back at Healy. "He's their buddy's daughter," he said. "I don't think they're going to hurt her. Or you."

"I want you there anyway," she said. "If I bring the cops, they might run. I need to get that little girl back."

"Does Carly Fedder know what you're doing for her?" Keller asked.

"Not all of it," she said. "She just knows I'm working on something. She's sitting tight. She won't go to the cops."

"And when you get the girl back," Keller said, "you're going to hand her over to her mother." His voice was expressionless.

"Yeah," Healy said. "I am. Because that's the only choice, Jack. Her father's dead. Who else do you suggest giving her to?"

"I'm just saying," Keller said, "You need to keep an eye on your client. Otherwise . . ." He stopped.

There was a pause. "Otherwise what?" Healy said.

Keller took a deep breath. "Otherwise that kid could end up like me," he said.

"There are worse things to be," Healy said gently.

"Maybe," he said, "but I wouldn't want to meet any." He stood up. "Can I send Marie in?" he said.

She stood up and took a folded piece of paper out of her desk drawer. "These are the directions to the meeting," she said. It's at seven P.M. tomorrow, but it's a long drive. Get some sleep and meet me here at noon."

"Okay," he said. See you then."

As Keller reached the door, she spoke again. "You know, Jack," she said, "she's lucky to have you."

"No, she isn't," Keller said. "I've cost her her kid. And if I keep seeing her, that's going to be permanent. So I need to step out of the picture."

"You care about her that much?" Healy said.

"Yeah," Keller replied.

"That's what I mean," she said. "Lucky." She sighed. "Send her in."

thirteen

Working late, DeGroot thought. The law-office parking lot was mostly deserted, with only one car left. DeGroot had watched as the staff filtered out and went home. He hadn't seen the Healy woman leave, so it was a safe bet that the office light burning in the window was hers. You have to admire that kind of dedication, he thought. He parked in the tiny gravel lot behind the old house and got out. He had changed into a nondescript workman's coverall, blue ballcap pulled down over his eyes. He opened the trunk and pulled out a large toolbox. DeGroot had bought the coverall and the box at a Home Depot, but most of the tools inside were his own. The gravel crunched under his feet as he affected a weary trudge toward the back door, like a repairman called out late and unhappy about it.

"That little shit," Tamara Healy muttered as she read over the court papers one more time. "Abuse and neglect, my ass." She knew the lawyer on the other side. He'd say exactly what he needed to say to get the emergency custody order, and allegations of abuse were the biggest trump card of all. No judge would turn down a request for an order if there was a chance of actual abuse; no judge would take the risk involved. It had become depressingly routine for lawyers to throw in abuse allegations, and then, once the complaining parent had actual physical possession of the child, to dismiss them before being called on to prove them. At that point, the lawyer's argument would simply be that the plaintiff was the better parent, as shown by the fact that the child (who was suddenly the total center of attention) was healthy and happy in the plaintiff's care. And it didn't hurt that, by the time of the hearing, the parent from whom the child was snatched would usually be an emotional wreck, liable to blurt out anything on the stand. Marie Jones was no exception.

Healy sat back in her chair and rubbed her eyes. She had accepted working nights and weekends as the consequence of being a domestic lawyer, and most of the time she could insulate herself from the emotional ups and downs. But she couldn't help liking Marie Jones. She knew from the way Jones spoke of her son that the woman was a good mother, and she didn't deserve what she'd been through.

Healy ground out her cigarette in the ashtray. She thought about Jack Keller. He had gotten to her as well. It wasn't just that he was good-looking, although he was certainly that. But there was an intensity about him that both thrilled and scared her at the same time. There'd be no half measures with that one, she mused. She shook her head. *No use wondering about it,* she thought. *He's off limits. For a lot of reasons.* She picked up her pen and started working on her notes for her cross-examination. Marie had given her a lot of information about her ex to work with, and if Healy could drop the right bombs at the right time, she was reasonably sure she could get Marie her child back.

There was a sound from outside her door. She looked up and frowned. She thought everyone had gone home. "Hello?" she called out. There was no answer. She got up and walked out into the front office. It was dark except for the dim illumination of her legal assistant's computer monitor. "Hello?" she said again. She heard a sound behind her. Before she could start to turn, a damp rag was clamped over her face and mouth. An arm snaked around her throat to hold her fast. There was a strong gagging chemical scent in her nose and throat from whatever the rag was soaked in. She struggled against the restraint, but the darkness closed in on her, overwhelmed her, and took her down.

She came back to consciousness slowly. She couldn't seem to open her eyes. She tried to lift her hands to rub her eyes, but the effort sent a lightning bolt of pain shrieking through her wrists and up her arms. The pain shocked her back to partial con-sciousness. Her eyes snapped open. She was looking down at the top of her desk. Her hands were resting on the desktop. There was blood on them. *Why do I have blood on my hands?* she thought muzzily. She tried to move her hands again, but the pain nearly sent her back into unconsciousness. It was then she no-ticed the small silver discs that protruded slightly from the tops of her wrists.

Her hands had been nailed to the desk.

She tried to scream, but there was something blocking her mouth, something sticky. Her mouth had been sealed with duct tape. She felt a hand grab her hair and pull her head back.

"None of that, now," a strangely accented voice whispered in her ear. "When you're ready to be a good *stukkie* and tell me what I need to know, then the tape comes off. Tune me grief and try to scream, and it stays right where it is, you check?" She could only moan in terror. He gave her a savage shake by her hair. "I said, you check?" She nodded frantically, not sure of what he meant, but terrified into agreement.

"Good," the voice said. The hand let go of her hair. Her head fell forward. Out of the corner of her eye, she saw a hand come into view and pick up the pack of cigarettes lying on her desk. She couldn't see what was going on, and the unknown terror behind her sharpened her hearing. She heard the click of a cigarette lighter, then the long intake of smoke. She whimpered as she felt the heat of a cigarette pass lightly within an inch of the skin on the back of her neck.

"Now," the voice said. "The little girl. Where is she, and who has her?"

Keller lay on his back, staring at the rough, pebbled texture of the ceiling. Get some sleep, Healy had told him, and he had honestly intended to try. He had checked into this Motel 6 for just that purpose. But it was looking like another night with his ghosts. Suddenly the room seemed to tilt. He wasn't looking up at the ceiling any more, he was looking down on a white landscape dotted with small pebbles. He was looking down on the desert.

He sat up and rubbed his face. He had always been able to sleep at Marie's, but that was over. He was alone again, and the realization gnawed at him like a hungry animal in his vitals. But it was all right. The numbness would return soon enough. He had faith. His cell phone rang. He checked the caller ID. The last few calls had been from Marie. He had stared at the number but he hadn't answered. The number this time was different. He snapped the phone open. "Keller," he said.

"Jack," Angela said. "Jack, where are you?"

"I'm still in Fayetteville," he said.

"Marie called here," Angela said. "She says you won't answer your phone. She needs to talk to you."

"No, she doesn't," Keller said. "She needs me to stay the hell away from her."

"Jack," Angela said.

"She told you what happened?"

There was a pause. "Yeah."

"So," he said. "Knowing what this asshole ex-husband of hers is using to take her kid away, you really think she needs to be talking to me right now?"

"It's that easy, then?" she demanded. "You just walk away?"

"I didn't say it was easy," Keller said.

"Come home, Jack," Angela said. "Come back to Wilmington. Be with your friends if you can't be with Marie."

"I've got something I have to do first," he said. "I should be back in a day or so."

"What is it?" Angela said. "Where are you going?"

"I'll tell you when I get back," he said.

"And what are you going to do then?" she said.

"I'm not really thinking that far ahead."

"Jack," Angela said. She sounded alarmed. "For God's sake, don't do anything to hurt yourself. Call Lucas. Talk to him."

"Don't worry," he said. "I'm not planning to do myself in."

"I am worried," she said. "And I'm going to worry about it till I see you again. Please tell me where you're going."

"Just somebody I need to go pick up," he said. "It's a favor for a friend."

"Marie?"

"In a way, yeah," he said.

"Then please be careful," Angela said.

"Don't worry," he said again. "I'm not expecting any trouble."

. . .

"You've got nothing to be ashamed of," DeGroot said to the woman. She didn't answer; he had replaced the tape over her mouth after she had finished telling him what he wanted to know. "You did well. I was surprised, actually. At how long you held out, I mean. After all, what are these people to you?" Her shoulders convulsed softly. She was crying. "*Ag*, well," he said, "we've all got things we feel like we need to do, hey?" He drew a silenced pistol from the toolbox and placed it to the back of her skull. "But in the end," he said, "it's what I need that matters. My job is to make what matters to me matter to you. And I did, didn't I?" He pulled the trigger.

Afterward, he picked the line of cigarette butts, six in all, off the corner of the desk and dropped them into a small plastic bag. He stashed the bag in the bottom of the toolbox next to the gun. He knew that even the police in this backwater city had access to technology that could extract his DNA from the filters. Most likely, he didn't have anything on file to match it with, but you never knew. He shook his head. "Six," he said, looking at the bag of used cigarettes. "*Ag* shame, you were a tough old bitch." He patted the dead woman on the shoulder, almost fondly. "Don't get up," he said. "I'll let myself out."

He drove through the streets, turning the information he had gathered over in his mind. He now knew where to find Powell and Riggio, or at least where they were going to be at a specific time and place. But they weren't stupid. They'd have put safeguards in place. He couldn't bet on just showing up at the meeting place, taking them down, and retrieving the key.

He sighed. Bringing the three Deltas into his plan had been a risk. But he needed their silence, and buying it had seemed preferable to trying to take all three of them out. They were good, the best the Americans had. Even if he'd succeeded in neutralizing them, there'd be questions if they failed to return from the badlands. Investigations. Searches. "Leave no man behind," they always said, and the silly buggers actually believed it. In his worldview, if a man was dead, that was the end of it, and going back into the *kak* to retrieve his torn carcass was lunacy. You could raise a glass to him later if you wanted to honor him. He shook his head. *Americans,* he thought. *Killers and romantics in the same skins, and you never know which one you'll end up dealing with.* Which led him back to the original problem. He had faith in his own capabilities, but two against one was not the kind of odds he played if he could help it. He needed an edge. He needed them off their guard. He sat at a traffic light and tapped his fingers on the steering wheel. They'd be expecting the lawyer and the big fellow, Keller. But they wouldn't necessarily know what the lawyer looked like. A man and a woman, then. He thought of the woman he had seen earlier. Jones. And then he knew what he needed to do.

It took him a few minutes to find his way back to the motel where he had followed the man and the boy. He cruised the parking lot slowly, looking for the truck he had seen. When he found it, he parked in a vacant space nearby. He looked at the doors of the rooms on this side of the motel. There were lights behind the curtains of three of them that he could see. He sucked air through his teeth as he thought. They were probably in the room right where the truck was parked. But the rooms were small and close together, and it could be any of the rooms on either side. He'd like to be seen by as few people as possible, and knocking on the wrong door meant someone else might see his face. He shifted in the seat and reached under it for the silenced pistol. He pulled it out, never taking his eyes off the doors. A slim leather case was next, and that went into the pocket of his leather jacket. One of the doors swung open and the man he had seen earlier walked out onto the sidewalk. DeGroot smiled. That one, then. He continued to watch. The man walked toward the office at the front of the motel, where the office was.

DeGroot waited. The man bypassed the office and walked across the front parking lot toward the street. DeGroot remembered there was an all-night convenience store across the street. He waited until the man was out of sight, then opened the door and slid out of the car. When he got to the door he looked around for possible observers, then put his ear against the door. There was a TV on in the room. He stepped back and knocked softly. There was no answer. He knocked again, more firmly. After a moment, a small voice said, "Hello?"

"Front desk," DeGroot said. "I have those extra towels you asked for."

There was a pause. "I'm not s'posed to let anyone in."

"Come on, kid," DeGroot said in as reasonable a voice as he could muster, "Your dad asked for extra towels. I may get busy later and not be able to get back. Just open the door and I'll hand them to you."

Nothing happened for a moment, then the door cracked slightly. DeGroot put his shoulder against it and shoved his way into the room. The little boy stumbled and fell backward onto his rump, looking up at DeGroot with huge eyes. His mouth hung open in shock. "Shhh," DeGroot said, his finger to his lips. "I've come to take you home. To your mum."

"Mom?" the boy said. "Where is she? Where's my mom?"

"Waiting for you," DeGroot whispered. "Come on. We have to hurry."

"My dad said to stay here," the boy said.

"Right," said DeGroot, "But you want to go home, right? I mean really, *booitje,* do you like it here?"

The kid shook his head. "I want to go home."

"Of course you do," De Groot said. "Your mum misses you. She really wants to see you."

The kid still looked doubtful. DeGroot was running out of time. "There's something we have to do first, though," he said. "Here. Sit up here." He patted the mattress. Still looking wary, the boy sat on the bed. DeGroot reached into his jacket pocket and took out the leather case. He flipped it open and took out a hypodermic needle. It glinted in the light of the room. The boy's eyes widened. "What's that?" he said.

"Something to help you sleep," DeGroot said. "We've got a long trip ahead."

"I don't want to get a shot," the boy said. "No." He started to cry. He tried to climb off the bed but DeGroot knocked him backward with a forearm, pinning him down.

"No!" the boy said as DeGroot plunged the needle into his arm. "Stop! Owwww! *Mom!*" He continued to struggle. DeGroot dropped the hypodermic and covered the boy's mouth with his hand. "Shhhh," he said. "Shhhhh." In a few seconds, the boy's thrashing grew weaker, then he lay limp. DeGroot stood up. He heard the rattling of the doorknob. He stepped back into the darkened bathroom and drew the pistol. The outside door opened, then closed. "Hey, sleepyhead," he heard the man say. "Crashed on me already, huh? Let's get you into—"

DeGroot stepped out of the bathroom. The man turned from where he was leaning over the boy. He held a pack of cigarettes in one hand. It fell to the floor as he put his hand up. His mouth dropped open, just as the boy's had. DeGroot was chuckling to himself at that as he put two bullets into the man's chest.

fourteen

The sharp chirring sound of his cell phone jolted Keller out of the light doze he'd fallen into. He was lying on the bed, on top of the covers, still fully clothed. He groaned out loud as he saw the time. Nine A.M. He picked up the phone and held it to his face, looking at the number that glowed on the display screen. Angela again. He opened the phone, still lying on his back. "Yeah," he said irritably.

"Jack," Angela said, "you need to call Marie."

"We've been over this."

"Jack," she said, "something's happened to Ben."

He sat up. "What?"

"I don't know," Angela said. "But she sounded . . . Jack, call her."

There was no arguing with the tone in her voice. "Okay," he said. "Okay."

"And call me back as soon as you can."

"Yeah," he said. "I will."

He punched the button to end the call, then the button for speed dial. The phone barely got through half a ring before it was snatched up. "Jack?" Marie said. She sounded on the ragged edge of hysteria.

"What's wrong?" he demanded.

"Jack," she said, "get over here. Please. Get over here as quick as you can."

"What's happened?" he said. "What's going on?"

"Someone called me," she said. "A man. He said he had Ben."

"Did you call—"

"I tried to call Carson. And he doesn't answer."

"The guy who called you," Keller said. "What did he say?"

"He said he wants to talk to us," she said. "Both of us. He said he was going to call me back at ten. And if we weren't both there, or if I called the police, he was going to . . ." She choked. "Just get here, Jack. Please. Please."

"Okay," Keller said. "I'm on the way." He snapped the phone shut and took a deep breath. He pulled his boots on.

The sun was well up, promising a scorching day as he walked out to the Crown Vic. He popped the trunk and looked down into it for a moment before reaching in and pulling out the shotgun. The box of shells came next, and he rested it on the bumper as he loaded the weapon, sliding each round into the magazine tube under the barrel with calm deliberation. When he was done, he racked the slide, the *clack-clack-clack* of the action sounding loud in the morning quiet. It was only then that he noticed the man standing by the drink machine. It took Keller a moment to recognize the desk clerk that had checked him in earlier. He was a young guy, already pale and paunchy from nights sitting behind the desk. He was holding a can of Dr Pepper. His mouth hung open in surprise. Keller rested the butt of the shotgun on his hip and fished the room key out of his pocket. The motel was still using the old-style key. He tossed it to the kid, who made an ineffectual grab at it. The key fell to the ground at his feet. "Checking out of 105," Keller said. He slid behind the wheel. The Crown Vic was an ex-police cruiser and Keller had left the upright weapon rack installed by the front seat. He slid the shotgun into the rack and started the car.

When he reached Marie's house, it was quiet. She opened the door before he reached it. There were dark circles of fatigue under her eyes. He took her in his arms. She rested her head against his chest for a moment, gave him a quick squeeze, then pulled away and walked back into the house. He followed her into her living room. She was pacing back and forth.

"Have you heard from him?" Keller began.

"No," she cut him off. She looked at the clock. Nine-forty-five.

"Tell me as much as you can remember," Keller said. "What he said. How he said it."

"He sounded . . . He had a funny accent. I couldn't place it. Kind of . . . I don't know."

"What did he say?"

"Oi hev yer boy," she mimicked. "That's how it started. I thought at first it was Carson, calling to gloat. But then he said that I had to do exactly as I was told or he— Jack, he threatened to cut one of Ben's fingers off."

"Did he let you talk to Ben?"

She nodded, tears brimming in her eyes. "Yeah," she said. "For a second. He was . . . It was like Ben was drunk. He only said a few words, but I could tell it was him. When the man came back on, he said that Ben was going to sleep for a while."

"The guy drugged him, maybe."

She shook her head. "Jesus, who'd do that to a little boy?"

"Somebody who wants to keep him quiet," Keller said. "That

may mean he's near somewhere public. Someplace he's afraid of making a fuss."

Marie grimaced. "Nice that you can be so analytical."

He shrugged. "I'm just trying to help."

"I know, Jack," she said. "I'm sorry. I'm just on edge here."

"Yeah," Keller said. "I don't blame you."

They waited the next few minutes in silence. The digits on the clock seemed to take an eon to change. When it clicked over to ten, Marie made a small sound in her throat and looked at the phone. It remained silent.

"Easy," Keller said. "It's not like you synchronized watches. And he may be trying to fuck with you. Make you wait. Just try to stay—"

The phone rang. Marie crossed the room in a few strides and snatched it up. "Hello . . . Yes. He's here." She looked at Keller. "There's an extension in the bedroom. He wants to talk to both of us at the same time."

Keller went into the bedroom, picked up the phone on the bedside table. "Keller," he said.

"You had a meeting set up for later today," the voice said. Keller picked up on the accent right away. *You hed a meeting sit up for lighter todye.*

"Yeah," Keller said.

"With the lawyer," the voice said. "She won't be able to make it, I'm afraid."

Keller felt a sinking feeling in his gut. He kept his voice calm. "And why is that?"

"She's a little under the weather right now," the voice said. "And the boy will be joining her, unless you do as you're told."

"What do you want?" Marie's voice quavered on the other extension.

"I want to have a meeting with the same people," the voice

said. "I want to straighten out some misunderstandings we've had."

"Like you had a disagreement with David Lundgren?" Keller said.

There was a silence on the other end. "Poor David," the man said. "If he'd just been honest with me, he could have saved himself a lot of pain. A. Lot. Of. Pain." He spoke the last words with heavy and unmistakable emphasis. Then his tone turned businesslike. "I want to keep the same thing from happening again. But I don't think my former partners trust me anymore."

"I wonder why," Keller said.

The man chuckled. "Well, you can help me fix that. They'll show up and see you there. They trust you."

"They asked for Tammy Healy," Marie said.

"But they've never met Healy. They'll think you're her. They'll give you the little girl, I'll give you your boy, then my *brus* and I will have a chat and get everything straightened out. Everyone wins."

Except you'll kill us all the minute you get the chance, Keller thought. The man on the other end sensed his hesitation. "Tune me grief," he said harshly, "and that little boy will wake up to the longest and hardest day of his life. Also the last one. Unless I decide to take my time and get creative. Then his dying could take a lot longer."

"Okay," Keller said. "How do we work this? Do we meet you somewhere?"

"I know where the meeting place is," the voice said. "I'll see you all there. Don't be late." There was a click as he broke the connection. Keller hung up the phone. He walked back into the living room. Marie was standing there, the phone still in her hand. She was looking down at an object on the phone table. Keller walked over and looked down. There was a dimly glowing

LED screen on the base of the phone. There was a name displayed in dark gray letters against the green background.

"The caller ID says that that call came from Tammy Healy," Marie said.

"Healy's dead," Keller said. "He got the information he needed from her and then he killed her. He probably has her cell phone."

"What information?" Marie demanded. "What's going on?"

Keller told her about the phone call and the meeting that had been set up to return Alyssa Fedder. "Tammy was nervous. She didn't want to go alone."

"And she trusted you," Marie said. "And this," she said slowly, "explains why one of the most expensive divorce lawyers in town is willing to take my case for peanuts. And to wait for the peanuts."

"It seemed like a reasonable trade," Keller said.

She didn't say anything for a few moments. Then she turned away. "I guess I should thank you, Jack," she said.

"We'd better get going," he said. "It's a long drive."

"Where are we going?" Marie said.

"The Blue Ridge Parkway. Near the Tennessee border."

Marie took a few moments to throw some clothes into a gym bag for Ben. "Put your weapon in there, too," Keller said. "Just in case."

"But . . . ," Marie started. Then she fell silent. She went into the bedroom. When she came out, her face was grim. "Got it," she said. They heard the sound of a car pulling into the driveway.

Keller went to the window and looked out. "Damn it," he muttered. "It's Wilcox."

"What the hell does he want?" Marie asked.

There was a knock at the door. They looked at each other. "Both our cars are in the driveway," Marie said. "It's no use pretending we're not home."

"Fuck," Keller growled. He went to the door and opened it. "You're up early," he said to Wilcox. He didn't stand aside to let the CID man in.

"You're probably going to have a lot more company pretty soon," Wilcox said.

"What do you mean?"

"Tamara Healy was murdered last night. The local cops are just finishing up at the scene. I imagine they'll want to talk to the two of you."

Marie came to stand behind Keller. "What happened to her?" she asked.

Wilcox looked at her evenly. "You're saying you don't know anything about it?"

"Neither of us is saying anything," Keller said, "without a lawyer. She's just asking."

Wilcox spoke slowly, unemotionally, his eyes gauging their reactions. "Healy was in her office," he said. "Some unknown person or persons entered by picking the backdoor lock. They nailed her wrists to her own desk. Then they tortured her with a lit cigarette, possibly for several hours, before shooting her in the head."

Keller looked at Marie. She had gone white, her hand covering her mouth. He looked back at Wilcox. "Any suspects?"

Wilcox shrugged. "Maybe, maybe not. They just let me know about it because it might intersect the Lundgren investigation."

"Well, thanks for the heads-up," Keller said. He made as if to close the door. Wilcox blocked the closing door with his foot. "You folks going somewhere?" he said.

Keller looked back at Marie. She was holding the gym bag. She glanced down at it, then back up, a look of guilt on her face.

"I think you two need to stay right here," Wilcox said firmly. He pushed against the door. Keller pushed back. "You need to leave," Marie said, her voice cracking with strain.

"What's in the bag, Ms. Jones?" Wilcox demanded. With a sob, Marie stuck her hand inside the bag. Wilcox went into his coat and swiftly drew his own weapon. He stepped back, holding the pistol in front of him, moving it back and forth from Keller to Marie. "Take your hand out of the bag," he commanded, "And put it on the floor. *Now!*" He barked the last word. A tear ran down Marie's face as she dropped the bag. "Please," she begged, "just let us go. It's important."

"No one goes anywhere," Wilcox said, "until I find out what's going on. Hands on top of your heads. Both of you." They complied. "Back away from the door, Keller," Wilcox said. "You too, Jones. Leave the bag on the floor." They complied slowly, Marie moving like a sleepwalker. Wilcox came into the house. "Back against that wall," he said.

Keller calculated his chances of getting the gun away from Wilcox. Not good. He joined Marie against the wall.

Never taking his eyes from them, Wilcox walked to the bag. He was crouching down to pick it up when the soft burr of a cell phone sounded at his belt. Without taking the gun off Keller and Marie, he straightened up, pulled the phone out and flipped it open. "Wilcox," he snapped. A look of shock crossed his face. The gun never wavered, however. "What?" Wilcox said. "How do you . . . They . . ." His face became angry. "Like hell," he snarled. He listened for another few seconds, then shut the phone with a savage gesture. He stared at them for a few seconds, his face expressionless. Then he lowered the pistol and slid it inside his coat. "We've just gotten a new lead in the case," he said. "I need to get back. Sorry to bother you." He stepped back through the open door and pulled it shut.

They stood for a moment, totally dumbfounded. "What the hell just happened?" Marie said.

"You think they got the guy?" Keller said.

"If they did . . . then maybe they have Ben."

"Why wouldn't he just say that, then?"

Marie shook her head. "What do we do now?" she said.

Keller thought for a minute. "Only safe thing to do is keep the appointment until we hear something definite. I'll call Angela from the road and ask her if she can find out what's going on." He picked the bag up off the floor. "Let's go."

fifteen

The Blue Ridge Parkway winds for nearly five hundred miles along the crests of the Southern Appalachian Mountains in western Virginia and North Carolina. It passes through no towns. It was built as a scenic route, so it is mostly tourists who drive slowly along its narrow roadway and gaze wide-eyed at the ever-changing panoramas that explode into the eye seemingly around every curve. The heaviest traffic is in the fall, when the dying of the leaves turns the hills ablaze with oranges, reds, and yellows, like the final defiant flare of stars as they expire into the cold and dark of winter. In spring and early summer, flowers cover the upland meadows: rhododendron, Queen Anne's lace, mountain laurel. There are also plants with odd and evocative names: witch hobble, Solomon's seal, Dutchman's-breeches. Now, in midsummer, most of the flowers had gone, their short lives given to the task of fertilization and reproduction. Now the views were of mile after mile of rugged mountains, like titanic knees propped up under blankets of hardwood forest, the green of the trees turned to a sapphire by the ever-present haze.

Night comes early to the Parkway, even in summer, as the evening sun slips behind the shoulders of the mountains. As the views fall into shadow, the tourists descend the long exits off the Parkway, heading for restaurant meals and motel beds in the old towns nestled in the valleys that live by their trade. In the gathering gloom, Keller and Marie saw almost no other vehicles as they made their way up the Parkway. Marie had to strain to make out the wooden mile markers that ticked off the approach to their destination. Their ears popped with the changes in altitude as they went up and over the ridges and down into the saddlebacks between them.

"I can't see shit," Marie muttered. She leaned forward and peered out the windshield.

They had said little on the long drive from Fayetteville. Marie had huddled in the passenger seat, her arms crossed across her chest, wrapped around her anxiety. Keller had struggled to find words to reassure her, but anything he considered sounded empty and foolish. They were there because it was their only chance, and that chance wasn't much.

Every few miles, where the views were particularly striking, the Park Service had built overlooks. Some were just tiny spaces where one or two cars could park and their drivers could get out to admire the scenery. Some were larger, with space for a dozen or more cars, and equipped with picnic tables and the beginnings of trails for hikers. Most of the overlooks were deserted; there was little to see. The valleys were in shadow, with only the tallest peaks catching the last of the summer sun. It was as if the darkness was rising like a tide, up from the lowlands, to drown the peaks in night.

They passed an overlook on their left. There was a single

vehicle parked there. No one was outside to watch the stars come out. It was the only vehicle they had seen in the last fifteen minutes. Marie looked back at the vehicle as they passed, turning around in the seat to watch. "That could be him," she said.

"Or the people we came to meet," said Keller. "Is he starting up?"

She craned to look harder. They went around a curve and the vehicle disappeared. She slumped back in the seat. "Probably some guy taking a leak in the woods," she muttered.

"Just a couple more miles," Keller said. They passed a brown wooden sign made to look rustic. PINEY POINT OVERLOOK, the sign said. 1.5 MILES.

"That's the one," Keller said.

"You think they're already there?"

Keller shrugged. "Don't think too much about what might happen," he said. "Imagination can hang you up in a situation like this."

She caught a glimpse of his face in the dim light of the dashboard. There was a look there she'd seen before, a hardening of the muscles around the jaw, a tightness about the eyes. She felt a chill go up her back. There was no mercy in that look. There was no trace of the man she loved there.

Someone is going to die. The thought came unbidden to her. She shook her head as if to deny it, but it came back almost immediately.

When he gets that look, someone is going to die, the voice insisted. He turned to look at her and she almost flinched, praying that that look wouldn't be turned on her. But when he looked at her, it was with concern in his eyes. "Stay with me, Marie," he said softly. "Keep it together." He turned back to the road. She put a hand on his biceps. "Thanks for coming, Jack," she said. "I'm glad you're here for me."

"No problem," he said. As they came around a sharp curve, they saw the overlook.

It was one of the bigger ones, with a parking lot on one side that could hold a dozen cars. There was a waist-high stone wall to keep the sightseer from tumbling over the sheer slope that fell away from the side of the parking lot. On the other side of the road was a smaller lot at the edge of a heavily forested slope. Marie could make out a few picnic tables just beneath the overhang of the trees. There was a large wooden signboard near the tables, with some sort of map fastened to it. The only vehicle in the lot was a Jeep Cherokee parked at the last space in the row. As instructed, Keller pulled the Crown Victoria into the space on the opposite end of the parking lot. He killed the lights, then the engine. They waited.

Across the parking lot, they saw the glow of the Jeep's interior light come on. Marie caught a glimpse of a dark-haired man behind the wheel. A figure exited the other side of the Jeep. A tall man and a child came around the front. In the dimness, Marie could just make out that both man and child had blond hair. Keller opened his door and Marie did the same. They got out and stood by the Crown Vic.

"Jack," Marie said in a low whisper, "where is he? Where's the man that called—"

"Are you Ms. Healy?" the tall man called out.

"Yeah," Marie called back. She was amazed that her voice didn't shake. The tall man bent and said something to the child. She looked up at him and said something back, just below the threshold of Marie's hearing. The man bent down and took the girl in his arms. They hugged for a moment, then the man stood up. He spoke again, and the child started walking toward them. She was holding something in her arms. A stuffed animal.

Out of the darkness, around the curve, there was a sudden blaze of headlights and the roar of an engine.

And there they are, DeGroot thought with satisfaction. *Right on time.* He turned sharply into the parking area, his wheels squealing on the pavement. In the cone of his headlights, he saw the little girl's face turned toward him, her mouth open in surprise. She dropped something she had been holding in her arms and made as if to bolt back toward the Jeep. He turned the wheel slightly and cut her off. Like a rabbit caught on the highway, she reversed course and headed back the way she was going originally. He skidded to a stop in the middle of the lot, between the two groups. The little girl was running toward the woman, her arms flailing in panic. The woman had crouched down, her arms out to catch the girl, when DeGroot came to a stop. He already had both windows open and the stubby little submachine gun pointed out the window at the woman and the girl. "All right," he called out. "Let's all be calm." He was holding the gun in his right hand, across his body, so there was a moment's awkwardness as he reached with his left to turn the car engine off. In the sudden silence, all he could hear at first was the sobbing of the little girl as she buried her face in the woman's arms. There was a tall blond man standing beside her, not moving. "You must be Keller," DeGroot called. "Step away from the car. And hands where I can see them." The man complied, more slowly than DeGroot would have liked. DeGroot cursed under his breath. The situation was hard enough to control right now without this fellow being difficult. He briefly considered shooting Keller. The more people there were, the more variables there were to deal with. He considered for a moment, then discarded the idea. Things were still too unpredictable for that. "Powell?" he called out. He didn't take his eyes off Keller. "You're there?"

"I'm here, DeGroot," he heard Powell reply.

"You see where I've got the gun pointed?"

"Yeah." His voice was calm. Good. He was staying professional. You never knew when an American was going to try something idiotic.

"Riggio's with you?"

"Yeah."

"Well, why don't we get everybody together over by the front of Mr. Keller's vehicle with their hands up. You, too, Keller. And Ms. Jones." Marie picked the little girl up in her arms and they moved to the front of the big car. DeGroot kept the barrel of the gun pointed at them. He stole a glance back at the Jeep. Powell and Riggio were walking slowly, their hands up, their eyes locked on him. He opened the car door with his left hand and slid out. In a moment, all of the targets were in his field of fire. He let out the breath he had been holding. Things would be easier to control now.

"*Lekker,*" he said. "In a moment, I'll be sending Keller, Miss Jones, and this pretty little girl off—"

"Where's Ben?" Marie interrupted.

DeGroot stifled his irritation. "He's close by," he said. "Safe."

"How do I know that?" she said. Her voice trembled slightly.

"It's not important to me that you know that, *stukkie,*" he snapped. "I'll give you directions in a minute on where to find him. Then you can all go back to your happy homes and lives while me and my *brus* here have a little conversation."

It was then he became aware of a sound at the edges of his hearing. It was a familiar sound, one he had heard so often that in most situations he barely noticed it. But here, surrounded by the silence of the mountains, it seized his attention. It was the beating of rotor blades. He glanced for a second toward the source of the noise, then did a quick double take.

Out over the yawning darkness of the valley below, he saw a pair of red aircraft running lights like angry eyes in the night. And they were headed straight in his direction.

"One and two, are you in position?" Rankin was in the front seat of the chopper. She heard the replies from the ground team crackling in the headset.

"One, ready."

"Two, ready."

Rankin turned toward the back. Gerritsen sat next to the open crew door. He was dressed head to toe in black tactical gear. A pair of night vision goggles dangled from his neck. A rifle with a night vision scope lay across his lap. Gerritsen adjusted the microphone of his own headset and gave Rankin a thumbs-up. "Okay," she told the pilot. "Light 'em up."

Helicopters, Keller thought. *It's always goddamn helicopters.* Then the brilliant cone of light caught DeGroot dead center. He threw up his hands to shield his eyes. A voice like that of God himself blasted out of the sky along with the light.

"FBI!" the voice bellowed. "PUT DOWN YOUR WEAPON!"

The combined blasts of light and sound staggered DeGroot for a second. He recovered almost instantly, however, and raised his weapon. Keller heard the crack of a high-powered rifle, almost drowned out by the thudding of the rotor blades, and a chunk of pavement flew up at DeGroot's feet.

Keller charged. He hit DeGroot with enough impact to knock

the wind out of both men for a moment and bore him to the ground. DeGroot's head hit the pavement with a sickening thud, and the submachine gun flew from his hands. DeGroot snarled and rolled, going onto his back. He brought his knee up in a vicious strike at Keller's groin. Keller turned slightly and caught the blow on the thigh. It felt like he'd been shot in the leg. He grabbed DeGroot around the throat and slammed his head into the pavement again.

"WHERE IS HE?" Keller screamed into DeGroot's face. "WHERE'S THE BOY?"

DeGroot's only response was another snarl and a punch to Keller's midsection. This one was weaker, however, and only staggered Keller slightly. The helicopter roared overhead. Keller could hear the sound of car engines, big ones, roaring into the parking lot. He slammed DeGroot's head against the pavement again. The man's struggles grew weaker. Keller felt a hand pulling at his shoulder. He reached up and brushed it off. He reached down with his free hand and placed his thumb against the socket of DeGroot's eye.

"Tell me where he is," Keller said, "Or so help me God, I'll put your fucking eye out."

"No, you won't, Mr. Keller," a familiar voice said. He felt the coldness of a gun barrel against the back of his neck. "We have the situation under control," Wilcox said. "Now let him go."

sixteen

"You tapped my phone," Marie said.

"Not me," Wilcox said. "Our friends in the FBI."

The parking lot was full of people and vehicles now. A pair of black Chevy Suburbans were parked haphazardly in the lot. She could see Keller in the back of one of them. There was a red-haired agent in the front seat, yelling at him. Keller wasn't answering. The two men from the Jeep were handcuffed in the back of the other Suburban. Alyssa Fedder was in a third vehicle, a Taurus sedan, with two other agents, both female.

Marie shook her head. "I should have figured it out back at the house. When you just turned around and left."

"I wouldn't be complaining if I were you," Wilcox said. The chopper made a low pass overhead. He stopped talking and waited for the racket to die down before continuing. "They probably saved your life just now."

"Saved my life?" Marie's voice was a low hiss. "They used me as fucking bait, Wilcox! Me and my son. They could have picked that bastard up at any time and gotten Ben back." She glanced over to where DeGroot stood between two FBI agents. His hands were cuffed behind his back. There were already bruises rising on his neck and another beneath his eye, but he looked remarkably calm. She started toward him. Wilcox tried to block her. She shoved him aside and kept walking.

"Where is he?" she hissed as she came closer. One of the black-suited FBI agents blocked her way. The agent, a black man built like a football linebacker, didn't move when she collided with him.

"Where is he?" Marie demanded again over the agent's shoulder. Her composure snapped and she screamed at DeGroot. *"What did you do with my son?"*

The man looked at her expressionlessly. He turned to the other agent, this one a shorter white man. "I want to make a deal."

"Fuck you, shitbird," the white guy said.

DeGroot shrugged. "Suit yourself, *boet,*" he said. "But that little boy's running out of time."

"Tell us where he is, and we'll consider your request," the black guy said.

DeGroot shook his head. "Can't tell you," he said. "I'll have to show you. I have to take you there."

"Bullshit," the white agent snapped. "You can give us directions."

"Yeah," he said, "I could. But you wouldn't know how to disarm the surprise I put with him. You might figure it out. If you had time."

"Oh my God," Marie said. "What did you do?"

DeGroot smiled at her. "Made sure that you and your boyfriend wouldn't be coming after me once you found the boy." He shrugged again. "*Ag* well, that plan's buggered since this crew's rocked up. So, makes sense for me to keep the little fellow alive, hey? But this lot might fuck it up. So I have to be the one."

The two agents looked at each other. "We'll have to run this by the Agent in Charge."

"Don't be long," DeGroot said. The white agent walked away quickly. In a moment he was back. With him was a short, red-haired man with a scowl on his face. "I'm Special Agent in Charge Clancy," he said. "What's this I hear about you wanting to deal?"

Clancy, Marie thought. *Where have I heard that . . . oh, shit.* She glanced over at where Keller still sat in the back of the FBI Suburban. Keller's last encounter with Clancy had not gone well.

"Those are my terms," DeGroot was saying. "I lead two of your people to the boy. I disarm the explosive."

"And in return?"

"In return, I get a trial, not a ticket to someplace where I'll never be heard of again. And you tell whoever holds that trial that I could have killed the boy but didn't. Sounds fair, hey? All you do is tell the truth. And you'd do that anyway. Oh, and before trial, I get a phone call." He grinned. "There's someone I want you to talk to."

Clancy worked his jaw for a moment, as if he was chewing on the idea. "Tick . . . tick . . . tick . . . ," DeGroot said. The chopper passed over low again, causing everyone but DeGroot to flinch downward and cutting off all conversation. When the roar had died away, Clancy turned and shouted at an agent nearby. "Call the damn chopper," he ordered, "and tell them the area's secure. They can go home." He turned back to them. "All right," he snapped. He turned to the two agents. "Leonard. Swierczynski." He jerked his head toward DeGroot. "You go with him. Stay close." He looked at DeGroot. "So where's the boy?"

DeGroot nodded his head toward the wooded slope. "Up there," he said.

"In the woods?" Clancy said.

DeGroot nodded. "And don't think of going back on our deal," he said. "There's half a dozen trails up that mountain. Only I know the right one. Oh, if we're going to be walking in the woods together," he said, "I'll need these cuffs off." Leonard and Swierczynski looked at each other, then at Clancy.

"Fine," Clancy said. "But if you're going to be taking my people into the woods in the dark, I'm putting two more agents on you." DeGroot just nodded.

"I want to go," Marie said. "He's my son. He'll be terrified."

Clancy shook his head. "No. No way. I'm not putting a civilian into this situation. The last time that happened, things went cockeyed."

I know, Marie thought.

"Get Guthrie and Starr to go with you," Clancy was telling the two agents. He looked at DeGroot. "And if he tries to escape," Clancy said, "shoot him."

It was only about a half mile from the overlook to the peak, but the trail wove back and forth through the trees, winding its way up slowly so that the tourists wouldn't have to climb the steep slope directly. DeGroot picked his way carefully along the trail. Two of the agents, Leonard and Swierczynski, flanked him on either side. The beams of their flashlights bobbed and wavered as they tried to keep up on the uneven ground in their dress shoes. Two more, who he supposed were Starr and Guthrie, followed behind. He could hear them breathing hard.

"How much further?" grunted one of the agents beside him. It was Leonard, the big *kaffir*.

"You've been behind the desk too long, *boet*," DeGroot said. "You're out of shape. It's just a bit further." He heard the sound of running water ahead. "There's a footbridge that goes over that stream ahead," he warned them. "It's narrow. We'll have to go single file." The ground leveled out slightly as they approached the stream. Leonard took up a position ahead, with Swierczynski behind. Starr and Guthrie trailed. The crude wooden bridge appeared in the beam of the lights. "This bridge is old," DeGroot said. "It's shaky. Best we cross it one at a time." Leonard looked at him suspiciously for a moment. "Okay," he said finally, "I'll go first."

"Sure," DeGroot said.

Leonard turned to the other agents. "Watch him," he said. He turned and started across. His shoes clattered on the worn planking.

"Mind your step," DeGroot called out. "There's some boards missing." Leonard reached the end of the bridge and stepped off onto the trail. He turned and pinned DeGroot in the beam of the flashlight. "Now you," he said.

The stream was invisible in the darkness, but DeGroot could hear it chuckling over the rocks beneath. As he reached the end of the bridge, his foot caught in the gap where a plank had once been. He stumbled forward and landed full-length on the ground with a loud exhalation of breath. He lay there for a moment, groaning. He could hear footsteps clattering across the bridge. Leonard's heavy tread approached from the other direction. DeGroot rolled to one side of the trail. He groped for a moment in the leaves until he found what he was looking for, what he had left there when he prepared this ground earlier. It was a plastic grip with a trigger assembly, like a pistol without receiver or barrel. Without looking up, he squeezed the trigger.

A massive roar split the night and the darkness turned to momentary daylight. The three agents bunched together on the bridge didn't have time to scream as the pair of claymore mines

DeGroot had placed on his side of the bridge scythed them down. The hundreds of ball bearings embedded in the front of the mines blasted every living body in the kill zone into pulp. The bridge itself disappeared in a rain of splinters. DeGroot sprang upward, toward where he had last heard Leonard. The *kaffir* was standing there, his face slack in shock from the blast and carnage that had shattered the nighttime silence. DeGroot caught him in the throat with a vicious punch that fractured his windpipe. The man went down, gagging for the breath he'd never take again. DeGroot aimed a killing blow at the FBI agent's temple and the gagging stopped. DeGroot picked up the flashlight and looked around. He located Leonard's weapon on the ground by the trail and picked it up. He checked Leonard's body again to determine whether a killing shot would be necessary. It wasn't. He rifled through the agent's coat for spare ammo clips. He found two and pocketed them. He looked back down the trail. There were more agents down there, he knew, and they'd be on their way soon. He reached into the bushes where he'd hidden the trigger for the mines. He came up in a moment with a small two-way radio he had bought at Radio Shack. He turned the device on. The low hiss of static came from the tiny speaker. DeGroot keyed the mike.

"Keller," Clancy said, "Lately it seems like every time some kind of major shit starts in this state, you're in the middle of it. You got any explanation for that?"

Keller shrugged. "Just lucky, I guess." He looked over to where a group of FBI agents were clustered around DeGroot's vehicle. "Any sign of the boy?"

Clancy shook his head. "This DeGroot asshole says he's got him stashed up on the mountain. Booby-trapped."

"Who is that guy, anyway?" Keller said.

"Some kind of mercenary," Clancy said. "He was mixed up with whatever Lundgren, Powell, and Riggio were doing."

"Which was what, exactly?"

Clancy looked sour. "We don't know, and even if we did, do you think we'd tell—" He stopped short as something that sounded like a clap of thunder ruptured the night. It came from somewhere in the woods.

"Shit." Clancy yelled. He turned and bolted toward the Taurus where Alyssa Fedder sat. "Get the girl out of here! Now!" Wilcox looked as if he was going to make an argument of it, but then he looked at the girl. He started the engine. The tires spun briefly in the gravel before they caught and the car wheeled quickly onto the blacktop. It was gone in seconds. Marie was sprinting for the tree line. Keller jumped out of the Suburban and ran after her. "Get back here!" Clancy bellowed. Marie ignored him. As Keller ran past him, Clancy grabbed his arm. The momentum of Keller's rush spun him around. Clancy grabbed him in a bear hug. "Oh, no you don't," he grunted. "We're not going to—"

At that moment, DeGroot's car exploded as the other two-way radio, rigged as a detonator, set off the plastic explosive in the trunk. The agents standing by the car were killed outright. Clancy and Keller were knocked to the ground by the blast with Clancy landing hard on top of Keller. They lay there stunned for a few moments. "Clancy," Keller grunted. "Get off me." There was no response. Keller pushed, and Clancy's limp body slid off of his. Keller got to his feet painfully. He looked at Clancy.

The FBI man lay on his side on the ground, his eyes open and unseeing. A jagged piece of metal protruded from the middle of his back. Blood trickled from the corner of his mouth. Keller looked around for Marie. She was across the road, by the trailhead. She was on her hands and knees, slowly getting up. She looked at Keller for a moment, then staggered toward the woods. "Marie," Keller shouted. "Wait!" She ignored him and disappeared into the gloom. Keller swore under his breath. He ran to his car. His shotgun sat propped up in its rack on the driver's side. He pulled the weapon out and racked the slide as he headed after Marie.

"Hey!" a voice came from one of the other vehicles. "Hey!"

Keller looked over. The two men who had brought Alyssa Fedder to the overlook were raising their heads above the windowsill of one of the Suburbans. All of the windows on one side had been blown out. The two men's faces were streaked with blood, but the cuts on their faces looked minor. Shattered glass glistened like gems on their skin and in their hair.

"Get us out of these handcuffs," the blond man who had taken Alyssa from the car said. "We'll help."

"Right," Keller said. He continued across the parking lot.

"You're up against a pro," the dark-haired one called. "You're going to need all the help you can get." That stopped him. He looked at the two men for a moment, then jogged over to the black Suburban.

"Where's the handcuff key?" he said.

The blond man nodded toward the other side of the car. "The guy who was standing right over there had it," he said. "Before the car went up."

Keller rounded the big truck. One of the FBI agents, a balding sandy-haired man, was sitting propped up against the side of the vehicle. He was semiconscious, his eyes foggy.

"Give me the keys to those cuffs," Keller demanded. The man looked up at him uncomprehendingly. "What?" he said, his voice slurred. He raised his hand to his ear and smiled apologetically. "Sorry," he said in a too-loud voice. "Can't hear."

"Damn it," Keller muttered. He bent down and started going through the agent's coat pockets. "Hey," the man protested weakly. "Hey—" He reached up with one hand. Keller brushed the hand away easily. "Sorry," he muttered. "I need that key." His hand brushed across the small hunk of metal and he pulled it out.

"I think I need a doctor," the agent said calmly. "I don't feel so good." Then his eyes glazed and he slumped over. Keller bent down and felt for a pulse. Then he opened the car door and began unlocking the dark-haired man's cuffs. "Is the guy all right?" the man said.

"He's dead," Keller said. The dark-haired man slid out of the vehicle and knelt on the ground by the FBI man as Keller uncuffed the other man.

"C'mon, Mike," the blond man said. "We haven't got time."

The dark-haired man sighed and stood up. "Probably couldn't have done anything anyway," he said in a detached voice. "Overpressure like that, his insides probably look like strawberry jam." He looked at Keller and extended a hand. "Mike Riggio," he said. "My partner here's Bobby Powell."

"Jack Keller," Keller said. "We need to move. Marie's alone up there."

Powell and Riggio looked at each other. "That's not real bright," Powell said.

Keller began jogging for the trees. "Your pal said he has her kid up there," he called back. "She's going after him."

"Hold up," Riggio said. "We need to get a couple of—"

"You catch up," Keller snapped back. "I've waited long enough." He turned and headed across the road toward the woods where the blackness loomed like a wall. He barely broke stride as he reached the trailhead. Once under the shadows of the trees, however, he had to stop. He couldn't see two feet in front of him. After a few moments, he began to be able to make out vague shapes, more like slight differences in shades of black than actual objects. He shut his eyes and listened. A slight breeze was blowing up from the valley and the leaves of the hardwoods rustled nervously. The breeze died slightly and Keller could dimly make out Marie's voice, somewhere up the slope. She was calling Ben's name. He opened his eyes again. He could at least make out the trail well enough to walk. He started up the rough path. As he reached the first curve in the trail, he heard a slight sound behind him. He began to turn toward the sound. A hand was clapped across his mouth and he felt the point of a blade against the base of his spine.

seventeen

Marie stopped in the center of the trail, panting with exertion. She bent over and put her hands on her thighs, trying to catch her breath. The bullet scar on her abdomen throbbed. *I'm not going to make it,* she thought. *That bastard. That bastard's going to kill my son. If he hasn't done it already.* The thought nearly drove her to her knees. Part of her wanted to curl up on the ground in a ball and lie there until the mountain wore away. *No,* another part of her spoke up, *he may be alive. He may be hurt. If he is, he needs me. He'll be so scared . . .* She straightened up, took a deep, shuddering breath. The air was cool and dry, and the fog of fatigue and despair in her seemed to part slightly. She cupped her hands on either side of her mouth and called. *"Ben!"* The darkness seemed to swallow the words. She stopped and strained her ears, listening for any reply. None came back to her. She gritted her teeth and headed up the trail. When it seemed that she was about to run out of breath again, she caught a faint whiff of something acrid in the air. There was a dim red glimmer in the trees ahead. Something was on fire. She broke into a run.

In a moment, she reached the edge of a streambed. The slope here leveled off, and the trail cut straight across the face of the mountain. The smell was stronger here, strong enough for her to identify. Cordite. Cordite and burned meat. There were half a dozen small blazes among the trees, burning like campfires. Their incongruous light cast a glow over the clearing. There were a few boards and a post where a bridge had once crossed the stream. As she stopped running, she stumbled over an object in the trail, something soft and squishy. She looked down and a sob stuck in her throat. It was a human arm, torn off at the shoulder. A gold wedding band on one finger reflected the firelight. She looked up. She could make out shapes on the ground. Slowly, she walked to the lip of the streambed and took in the other shapes lying below. The water flowed, implacable and uncaring, over a couple of them. All of the bodies were torn and bloodied. All were larger than a child's body. *He's not here,* she thought. *He's not here.* She cupped her hands around her mouth again. "BEN!" she called out.

DeGroot heard the faint call from below and looked down at the boy. He was seated on a flat rock, his hands bound behind him, his ankles strapped together with duct tape. Another strip of duct tape sealed his mouth. A web belt was wrapped around his chest. There were small pouches hanging from the belt. The pouches were filled with the same C4 that had been in the trunk of his vehicle. The boy's eyes were wide and terrified in the darkness.

"Easy now, *boykie,*" DeGroot said in a low voice. "You don't want to be moving about too much." He looked out. His vantage point was a flat clearing at the top of the mountain. A hardy tourist who made his way up to the end of this, the longest of the trails in the system below, could enjoy a view over hundreds of square miles of these mountains. DeGroot could see the glow of lights in the valley, small towns glittering like clusters of stars in the darkness, mirroring the riot of stars strewn across the sky above. But it was the redder glow he could see closer below that concerned him most, the fires that showed where his preparations had done their work. He had no way of knowing how many variables he had eliminated. The four with him, to be sure. Probably quite a few more with the bomb in his vehicle. But there was no way to tell, and some of those men might still be hunting him, and he doubted that they would be in a mood to take him prisoner again.

The boy made a small terrified sound in his throat. DeGroot drew back his foot as if to kick him into silence. Then he stopped as he heard the voice drifting up from below. The woman's voice, calling her son's name. So she at least had survived. DeGroot looked down at the boy appraisingly. He might still have some use. He bent down and ripped the duct tape away from his mouth. "You hear your mum down there, *boykie?*" he said. The boy nodded, too terrified to speak. "You want to see her again?" Another nod, more vigorous this time.

DeGroot drew his knife. "Then scream," he said.

"For Christ's sake, Keller," a voice—Powell's—hissed in his ear. "Don't go running straight up the goddamn trail. You want to die that bad, just stick that fucking shotgun in your mouth and pull the trigger." The hand over his mouth was pulled away. So was the knifepoint in his back. Keller turned. Riggio stood a few feet away, holding a short-barreled assault rifle on his hip.

"Wish we'd have brought the night vision goggles," he said.

"We weren't expecting anything like this," Powell said. "I'll take point. Mikey, you take the rear. Make sure that bastard doesn't get behind us. And Keller, stay off the trail. He's got it booby-trapped."

From high above, a faint cry drifted down, a high-pitched wail of fear.

"Holy shit"—Keller heard Riggio's voice in the darkness—"that sounds like a kid."

"He's alive," Keller said. "And Marie's going to go after him."

"Then he'll probably kill her," Powell said. "Or worse, take her as a bargaining chip. The only reason he'd leave the boy alive is as bait. Come on." He seemed to fade into the darkness beside the trail. Keller followed.

In the army, Keller had learned the basics of moving quietly. Later, he had learned other tricks of stealth and concealment that had helped him in the hunt for jumpers. He had always thought himself capable when it came to moving without being heard. But the two men with him seemed like wraiths, moving like smoke between the trees, slipping through undergrowth without making a sound, presences that were sensed rather than seen. He felt awkward, like some huge clumsy animal blundering and crashing through the brush. Gradually, however, he seemed to pick up the rhythm and flow until he was moving up the mountainside, not quite as silently as they, but so nearly as to make no difference. He began to feel the familiar thrill, the drumbeat in his veins that came when he was on the hunt. His senses seemed honed to maximum sharpness; he could feel the slightest feather touch of a night breeze on the back of his neck, smell the scent of the forest, the dark rich smell of rotting vegetation and the sharper tang of new growth, death and life melded in one dense and complex perfume. He could hear the rustle of leaves in the slight breeze, a skittering in the underbrush as some small creature fled his approach. And, once again, over all, the faint cry of a child. He drew up short. There was another sound ahead, a faint crackling, and the faintest, throat-tickling hint of smoke on the wind. Then the fickle breeze shifted to another point of the compass, and another smell came to him, one he knew all too well, one that haunted his memories and stoked his nightmares. It was the stench of burned meat and of viscera torn open and laid obscenely exposed to the night air.

Burning, he thought, *they're burning*.

He threw caution aside and broke into a run. He heard one of his companions hiss a warning behind him. He ignored it. He burst into the clearing, screaming Marie's name.

DeGroot was a shadow among shadows, crouched in the darkness in the lee of a massive fallen tree trunk. He watched the woman sprinting up the trail. She stumbled slightly and he could hear her panting in great ragged exhalations. The child cried out again on the slope above him, and the woman stopped. She cupped her hands to her mouth and called out. "I'm coming, baby," she called out. "Hang on." She was only a few feet away, within easy striking distance. DeGroot tensed, ready to spring. Come on, he thought, just a little closer . . .

"MARIE!" a male voice bellowed from down the trail. DeGroot faded back into the shadows, cursing to himself. He calculated the odds of taking the woman before the owner of that voice could arrive. The woman would fight. Precious seconds would be lost. And then the man, or men, would be on him. A shot from his stolen pistol would be quicker but it would give away his position. It was too uncertain, he decided. DeGroot valued certainty. It was rare enough to be valued highly. He'd wait.

Another figure came pounding up the trail. It was Keller. He and the woman embraced.

"I saw the bodies," Keller said, his voice tight and breathless. "I thought—"

She cut him off. "Ben's up there," she said. "He may be hurt." She turned as if to start back up the path. Keller restrained her. "Wait," he said, "Just a second. The other two are right behind me."

Other two? DeGroot thought. He liked these odds less and less. Then he saw a man come out of the trees on the other side of the path. Riggio. Another figure appeared beside the first. Powell. DeGroot furrowed his brow. Where was the FBI? Surely they wouldn't have let these people come up here alone. He turned over all the possibilities in his mind. No FBI with them, He thought, So . . . no FBI. The little surprises he had prepared had exceeded his expectations. DeGroot bared his teeth in a quick grin, then stifled it just as quickly. He ran his thumb slowly over the edge of the knife, contemplating. There was still information to be gleaned from Powell and Riggio. He might still accomplish the mission he had set out on. But Keller and the Jones woman might pose a problem. He gave a mental shrug. He remembered a fragment of an American country song that he had heard the Delta men playing on their CD players in Afghanistan. *Know when to hold 'em, know when to fold 'em.* Time to fold them, he decided.

DeGroot didn't share the Americans' near fanatical dedication to the Mission. Not if it was likely to get him killed, or worse. Besides, there might be intelligence to be gathered down below, at the foot of the slope. If he understood the tactical situation, there was nobody down there. And considering what he had prepared for them at the top of the trail, there might soon be no one up here.

Slowly, so slowly as to seem part of the forest, he moved away from the trail. He melted into the darkness and the shadows, heading back down the slope.

"Look," Powell said. "You two need to understand something. DeGroot—the guy that's somewhere on this mountain—is a stone fucking killer. You saw the kind of shit he rigged down in the parking lot. He's probably set traps all up and down this god-damn trail, with your kid"—he looked at Marie—"as the bait. You keep running straight at him, he's going to take you down. He's going to take you down real nasty, and the boy with you. Your only chance of getting out of here, and getting the kid out alive, is to let us lead. Okay?"

"What do you care?" Marie said, her voice shaking. "I don't know anything about you. For all I know, you're working with him. How can I trust you?"

Powell looked at her for a long moment. "Lady," he said finally, "I have done some stupid shit lately. I know that. I've fucked up in ways I'm going to be paying for for a long, long time. Maybe, just maybe, if I can pull something good out of this mess, I can start finding my way back."

Another cry came to them on the wind. They were close enough now to make out the words. "MOM!" a voice full of tears cried down the slope. "MOM!"

Riggio stepped back onto the trail. They hadn't seen him go. "Trail's clear," he whispered. "Until you get to the top."

Powell looked at him. "You sure?" Riggio nodded. "What's up top?"

Riggio looked grim. "The kid's up there," he said. "And DeGroot's got him wired up."

. . .

They came out of the trees at the top of the trail. There was a rock formation where a jumble of boulders had fallen against each other, then been worn down by the slow, patient sculpting of wind and water until they formed a hollowed area surrounded by sharply upthrust rocks at its back and on either side. Tourist guidebooks called it "the Devil's Throne." Ben sat in the hollow. He had some sort of vest on. When he got his first glimpse of Marie, he started to rise from the seat.

"KID!" Powell's voice cracked like a whip. "DON'T MOVE!" Ben sat down so quickly they could hear the sound of his rump hitting the rocks. "Mom?" he quavered.

"It's okay, baby," she said soothingly. "Just stay there. It's going to be okay." She turned to Powell. "What's wrong?" she hissed.

Powell's face was blank. "That belt he's wearing," he said. "It's loaded with C4. It's the same belt the Hajjis wear."

Marie's hand went to her mouth. "Oh my God," she whispered.

"Mom," Ben's voice was more insistent this time.

"Can you disarm it?" Marie said.

Powell took a deep breath. "I don't know," he said. "I don't know what kind of tricks our friend may have wired up."

"Demo's not really DeGroot's thing," Riggio offered. "It's probably pretty basic."

Powell shot him a dark look. "Thanks, buddy," he said.

"Come off it, bro," Riggio said. "You're going to try it. You know you are. You love that shit."

Powell sighed. "Yeah." He turned back to Ben. "Okay, kid," he said. "I'm coming over there. You need to sit there and stay absolutely still, okay?"

Ben began to cry. "I have to go to the bathroom," he whimpered.

"Oh, for Christ's sake," Powell muttered.

Marie began walking toward Ben. "It'll only be a few minutes, baby," she said. "I'll hold your hand." She glanced over in surprise. Keller had fallen in beside her. "Jack . . . ," she said.

Keller didn't answer her. "Ben," he said steadily. "You know how you always call me 'tough guy'?"

Ben quieted somewhat. "Yeah," he said uncertainly.

"Well, now it's your turn, kiddo," Keller said. "You've got to tough it out. Just for a few minutes. This guy here," he indicated Powell with a motion of his head, "is going to get that belt off of you. Then we're going to get the heck out of here. Sound good?"

"Yeah," Ben said. "I want to get out of here. I want to go home."

"I heard that," Keller said. He walked over and propped the shotgun against the rock. He knelt on one side of Ben and took his hand. Marie knelt on the other side and took his other hand. Powell came and knelt in front of him. They looked absurdly like some medieval tableau, supplicants kneeling before a prince. Powell studied Ben for a few moments, then gently reached out and opened the vest. To one side was a twist of multicolored wires, twined together like vines until a point where they separated and branched to the various pockets of the vest.

"What's wrong?" Ben said. "What is this thing? Why did that mean guy make me wear this?"

"Nothing's wrong," Powell said. From the suddenly professional tone in his voice, he might have been a pediatrician reassuring a patient that he only had a cold. "Mikey's right. It's simple. Basic stuff." He turned slightly. "Anyone bring a pair of wire cutters?"

There was a brief silence. "Shit," Riggio said.

Powell sighed. "Figures. How about a knife?" Keller reached into his back pocket and pulled out a small pocketknife. He handed it to Powell.

"Thanks," Powell said. He opened the knife and reached forward to pluck one wire out of the rest. Ben started to pull away.

Keller and Marie tightened their grip on his hands. "Shhh, baby," Marie soothed. "Just stay still."

"You sure about this?" Keller said. "What if your friend has learned to get tricky?"

"Then we'll never know," Powell murmured. "Well, Mikey might." He raised his voice. "Mikey?" he said. "You might want to get clear."

"Nah," Riggio said, as calmly as if he was turning down a last round of beers. "I'm good, bro. You've got it. Easy pickings, like you said."

"Okay," Powell breathed. "Here we go." He sliced through the wire.

Nothing happened for a moment. They all stood frozen, as if they couldn't believe they were alive. Ben spoke up. "Can I take this thing off now?"

Riggio laughed. "Yeah, kid," he said almost merrily. "You can take it off." Powell was reaching for the vest when there was a sudden sharp noise. Marie uttered a quick, cutoff scream. Keller jumped as if he'd been hit with an electrical shock. The noise came again, an abrupt bang from far away, down the slope.

The sound of gunshots.

DeGroot straightened up. He took the pistol he had just used on the wounded FBI agent and tucked it in the back of his waistband. He moved through the smoke, among the bodies, looking for more who might be alive. He found no one. He knew his time was running short. The FBI would be regrouping and coming back up after him, assuming there were any left in the vicinity. He glanced at his watch; only a few more hours of darkness. He began surveying the remaining vehicles. His own rental was a total loss, of course. The poor unsuspecting sod whose credit information and identity he had appropriated to make the rental was about to get a nasty surprise on his next Visa bill.

DeGroot's glance fell on the Jeep that Powell and Riggio had brought. Perfect. And there might be some useful information to be had. He walked toward it. As he did, he stumbled over an object lying in the gravel. He looked down. A child's toy frog. He kicked it out of his way and climbed into the Jeep. He took one last glance around the peaceful overlook he had so effectively turned into a killing zone and smiled as he started the engine.

"Sonofabitch," Riggio said. "He got past us. Slipped right through the line."

"You shouldn't use bad words," Ben said severely.

"Hush, baby," Marie said, scooping him up in her arms. Ben wrapped his arms around her, clinging to her like an infant.

"So he's down there, and we're up here," Powell said.

"He won't stick around," Riggio predicted. "Somebody down there hollered for help when the fireworks started. Guaranteed. He won't wait around to get caught again."

"Who the f—" Keller choked the curse back. "Who is that guy?"

"I'll explain later," Powell said. "We've gotta move."

"Move where?" Keller insisted. "I'm not going anywhere with anyone until you tell me what's going on. One minute I'm looking for a missing kid, and the next, some psycho has wired a five-year-old with explosives."

"Jack," Marie said, "He's right. We need to get out of here. I want to go home."

"Me, too," Ben said.

"Can we at least get off the top of this mountain?" Powell suggested. "I feel like I've got a set of crosshairs painted on my forehead standing out here."

"Okay," Keller relented. He walked over and picked up the shotgun.

"I got point this time," Riggio said. "Bobby, you trail. Keller, you stay in the middle and look after the woman and the boy." As they fell into line, Keller noticed Marie staggering slightly under Ben's weight. "Hey, big boy," she grunted with the effort, "You're getting too big for Mommy to carry. Can you walk?" Ben's answer was to draw his arms and legs tighter around Marie's torso and whimper.

"Here," Keller said, "Take the shotgun. I'll carry him."

Marie looked at him for a moment. Ben turned his head to look at Keller as well. Then Ben slowly relaxed his grip on his mother and slid to the ground. He and Marie walked over together. Keller handed the shotgun to Marie over Ben's head, then bent down to scoop the boy up in his arms.

"You won't drop me, will you?" Ben said softly.

Marie answered before Keller could respond. "No," she said. "No, he won't drop you." She looked back at Keller. "I was wrong to doubt you, Jack," she said. "I'm sorry."

"Uh . . . folks?" Powell spoke up. "We need to be going."

"Lead on," Marie said.

"You know how to use that shotgun, ma'am?" Riggio said pointedly.

Keller and Marie looked at one another for a moment before both of them started chuckling. This time it was Keller who answered. "Yeah," he said, "you could say that."

"I mean," Riggio insisted, "you ever shot anybody?"

The chuckling stopped. "Yeah," Marie said, her face expressionless. "I have."

"Marie used to be a cop," Keller said.

"Ah," Riggio said, looking embarrassed. "Sorry. I didn't . . ."

"We can debate unconscious sexism later," Marie said. "Let's move."

They worked their way back down the trail. As they reached the stream where the bodies of the FBI men still lay, Keller pulled Ben's head against his shoulder. "Don't look, Ben," he urged. The small fires were dying down, sputtering fitfully. The horrible miasma of burned flesh still hung in the air.

Burning oh God they're burning I've got to help them the whole goddamn world's on fire . . .

"Hey," Ben said, "you're shaking."

Keller's mind snapped back to the present. "It's okay," he said. "Just some bad memories."

"Are you scared?" Ben said.

Scared shitless, Keller thought, but he didn't say it.

"You can't be scared." Ben sounded alarmed.

"Shh," Keller said. "It's okay to be scared. Only really stupid or really crazy people don't get scared. But I'm not going to drop you. And I'm not going to let anybody hurt you, okay?"

Ben was silent for a moment. "That mean guy shot my dad," he said in a small voice. "I think he . . . I think he might have killed my dad." The boy's small body began to shake with sobs. Keller held him tighter, not knowing what to say. After a few minutes, Ben spoke again, into Keller's ear. "You get bad guys, right? It's what you do, right?"

Keller could see it coming. "Yeah," he said. "It's my job."

"I want you to get the bad guy that shot my dad, okay?" Ben said.

"We'll talk about it later, Ben," Keller said.

"You'll get him," Ben said, his voice suddenly drowsy. "You'll get him." By the time they reached the bottom of the trail, he was asleep.

eighteen

DeGroot drove with one hand and flipped the Jeep's glove box open with the other. He rummaged through the papers inside, his eyes flicking back and forth between the road and the dimly lighted glove box. The sudden turns and switchbacks in the road quickly made that idea unworkable. He had run into the opposite lane several times and almost crashed the guardrails at least twice before he gave up, fuming. He was going to need a place to go over the inside of the Jeep and gather what information there was to be gained. Then, he supposed, he needed to get rid of the Jeep. The FBI had probably sent in a description of the vehicle and a license plate number. He needed a quiet place, then a vehicle. In the cone of his headlights, he saw one of the wooden roadside signs that pointed the tourists toward the Parkway's facilities. This one had a simple carved relief of a tent and the legend "1 mi." A campsite, then. This had possibilities. He took the indicated exit off the paved road and immediately found himself crunching over a narrow gravel path. A few more turns and he began to see more wooden signs, directing campers to various spaces. The Jeep's headlights flashed off the chrome of vehicles in some of the spaces. A few dying campfires glowed dull orange in the dark. In the dim shadows at the edge of the light, he could barely make out the humped shapes of tents. There was no one up, no one stirring.

After passing a few of the tents, DeGroot found what he was looking for: an occupied site away from the others, with a Toyota 4×4 *bakkie* in the parking space. Perfect. He killed the lights, then the engine. He waited a few moments, letting his eyes get used to the darkness. He watched the tent closely, waiting for signs that someone had noticed his arrival and was coming out of the tent to investigate. Nothing. He picked up the pistol he had taken off the FBI man and looked around the inside of the Jeep. His eyes lighted on a bright yellow pillow in the back, where the little girl must have sat. He picked it up and noted with bemusement that the pillow was painted like a giant yellow sponge. A sponge with a face. A very imbecilic-looking face. DeGroot looked at it for a moment and shook his head. Then slowly, gently, he opened the Jeep door. It creaked slightly as he slid out of the vehicle. When he was completely out, he stopped and waited. Nothing.

Somewhere, far off, he heard the call of a whippoorwill. He took the pistol in one hand and tucked the yellow pillow under his arm. As silently as he had moved through the forest before, he advanced on the tent. It was a small tent, made for no more than two people. A couple of fishing rods were propped up on the picnic table by the fire pit. He'd be sure to take those with him. Tomorrow morning, he doubted that anyone would notice that the vehicle by the campsite wasn't the one that had been there before. And no one would notice that the campers weren't coming out of the tent. If anyone bothered to notice, they'd assume the campers had gone fishing, at least until the bodies started to get ripe. And by then, he'd be far away. He'd change vehicles again in a day or so, just to be safe.

He crouched down and fumbled for the zippered door on the tent. As his fingers located it, a horrible sound split the air. It sounded like the coughing roar of a chainsaw starting up, but there was a living quality to it, like the grunting respiration of some awful beast. It came from no more than two feet in front of DeGroot and he whipped the gun up to focus on the source of the awful din. Then he realized that it was and he almost laughed out loud with relief. DeGroot had spent enough nights in enough barracks and encampments to recognize the sound of snoring. This, he had to admit, was one of the more impressive examples he'd heard. He used the next great ripping inhalation to cover the sound of opening the zippered tent flap the rest of the way. There was a stirring on the right side of the tent and a vague mumble of complaint in the dark. DeGroot put the yellow pillow over the barrel of the pistol. He made out the shapes of two figures in sleeping bags. Another huge snore split the night, coming from the left-hand bag. DeGroot leaned over the figure in the other bag. It was a pretty dark-haired girl, about twenty. She stirred restlessly as her tentmate gave out with the biggest snore yet. Her eyes popped open just as DeGroot pulled the trigger and put a bullet through the pillow and between her eyes. The snorer stirred restlessly at the sound. He didn't wake up, though, and after DeGroot put a bullet in his temple, using the girl's blood-soaked pillow to muffle the shot, he never would.

Afterward, he carefully zipped the tent flap back up. He took a flashlight that he had found in the tent and walked back to the Jeep. He checked his watch and glanced up through the trees. Daylight was coming on and he had a feeling that campers woke early. Some of them, at least.

Back in the Jeep, he leaned back in the seat and closed his eyes. He suddenly realized how tired he was. He wanted this mess done. But in this condition, he'd be prone to stupid mistakes. He didn't know where his former partners would go. And he was still outnumbered. He couldn't forget that. DeGroot was not a man to play long odds. Powell and Riggio knew he was coming after them now. And there was the woman. DeGroot remembered the look in her eyes as she had demanded to know what he had done with her boy. A fighter. She'd be a handful. Like the lawyer. DeGroot had enjoyed the challenge of breaking that one. He found himself drifting, indulging himself in thoughts of how he'd go about breaking the woman, the sorts of pressure that could be brought to bear on a strong young body like that. Women were much stronger in many ways. They had to be able to bear the rigors of childbirth. They were naturally built to take more pain . . .

He sat up with a start. He realized, with a vague sense of unease, that he had become aroused. This was ridiculous. He was a professional. He didn't take pleasure in what he did, beyond the satisfaction of a job well done. He did it because he knew how. It was a usable skill and profitable. He thought back to his session with the lawyer. A shiver of disgust ran through him as he remembered. He had felt the same thing then. He had even had an erection.

"Gaah," he said out loud in disgust. "I've gone *bossies*, for sure. I need to get out of this fucking business." But to do that was going to require capital. And while he had saved prudently from his previous employments, he knew it wasn't enough to last him the rest of what he intended to be a long and peaceful and boring life. He might even go home and take up farming.

He reached inside his shirt and found the cord of a lanyard around his neck. He pulled on the cord and pulled out the object hanging on the lanyard. It was a slim plastic cylinder, about half the length of a ballpoint pen. It was colored a dull silver. DeGroot held it up before his face and looked at it. *There's the key,* he thought. *Or half of it, at least.* He studied it for a moment, then sighed and slid it inside his shirt. He returned to his contemplation of the odds. Powell. Riggio. The woman. He had heard the blond man call her Marie. The blond man was Keller. The one who had threatened to gouge his eye out. He felt a flash of anger at that. *I'll see you again,* boet, he promised. *And when I do, you'll learn that when you threaten to put a man's eye out, you do it, and worse after. Unless you want him to come back and do worse to you. Oh yeah, you'll learn that, and I'll take my time teaching you.* It was a different feeling than he had had thinking about the women, and it didn't raise in him any feeling of unease or disgust. In his profession, revenge was just good business. It kept other potential enemies respectful.

"*Kak,*" he said softly. These odds were impossible. There were too many of them, and they'd be ready. Slowly an idea came to him. He didn't like it at first. It would involve sharing some of the take. But he didn't see any other way around it. He needed information. He needed more people. More professionals, like him. He took out his cell phone. No service. No surprises there. He'd have to get down, out of these mountains, and make some calls.

"Shit," Riggio whispered. They stood in the parking lot, looking stupidly at the place where the Jeep had been.

"Dude," Powell cracked, "where's my car?"

"Funny," Riggio said. "Real funny."

"My car looks okay," Keller said. "We can take it."

"Check it, Dave," Riggio said. "We don't want any more surprises." Powell nodded and trotted over to the car. As he bent down to examine the undercarriage, Ben began to stir against Keller's shoulder. "Let me take him now," Marie said. She put the shotgun on the ground. Keller gently untangled Ben and handed him to Marie. The boy squirmed for a moment, then settled down as she stroked his hair and spoke soothingly to him.

Keller picked up the shotgun and dangled it by his side. "While your friend checks and makes sure that maniac hasn't booby-trapped my car, suppose you tell me what the fuck this is all about." Riggio hesitated for a moment, then held up his hands placatingly as he saw the look on Keller's face. "Easy, now," he said, "we're all on the same side here."

"I'll decide that," Keller snapped.

"I should talk this over with my partner . . ."

"Come on," Keller told Marie. "Let's go." He started walking toward the car. "You'd better get going," he said. "It's a long walk home."

"We need that car," Riggio said. His voice held a dangerous edge.

Keller raised the shotgun and pointed it at him one-handed. "You think you can take it?" Riggio started to raise the assault rifle. Keller's finger tightened on the trigger.

"Whoa, whoa, let's chill out a minute here." It was Powell, walking over from Keller's Crown Victoria. "Let's all get in the car and talk this over while we drive."

"You two aren't going anywhere until I find out what you've brought down on us."

"Jack," Marie began.

"I did just save the kid's life," Powell said. "That ought to earn us something."

"Thanks," Keller said. "Now tell me what's going on."

"Jesus," Riggio said, his voice tight with frustration.

"I want to know who's after us," Keller insisted.

"Fine," Powell said. "But while we stand here and argue, he could be in that tree line, laying a pair of crosshairs on your head. Or the kid's."

Keller was silent for a moment. Then he nodded. "Okay," he said. He jerked his chin at Powell. "You drive." He turned to Riggio. "Your rifle," he said. "It goes in the trunk."

"Now wait just a damn minute," Riggio sputtered.

"If I don't like your story," Keller said, "you're getting out. And I don't want any arguments. Either the gun goes in the trunk or you do."

"It's not all that uncomfortable," Marie said. "I've been there."

"Tell you what," Powell said to her, "Mikey'll put the weapon in the trunk if you promise to tell us *that* story."

Riggio glared for another brief moment, then his face split in a grin. "That's a deal I can live with."

"Done," Marie said. "But you go first."

"Deal," Powell said. He looked at Keller. "Deal?"

Keller hesitated, then lowered the shotgun. "Deal."

They walked over to the car, Keller bringing up the rear. Riggio turned to Marie and said in a whisper deliberately loud enough for Keller to hear, "He always this big of a hard-ass?"

"Yeah," Marie said. "Pretty much."

They loaded Riggio's rifle into the trunk. "Jesus," Powell said as he surveyed the trunk's contents. "At least it won't be lonely. You always drive around ready for a war?"

"Yeah," Keller said. "Pretty much. Your pistol, too."

"Yeah, yeah, right," Powell said. He laid his gun in the trunk. He climbed into the driver's seat. Keller got into the front passenger seat, the shotgun held on Powell.

"What happens if we hit a bump?" Powell said.

"Drive carefully," Keller said. Marie got into the back, holding

Ben on her lap. Riggio was last. He was holding something in his hands.

"This was lying in the parking lot," he said. "It must have been Alyssa's. You think your kid might like it?"

"Yeah," Marie said. "Thanks."

Riggio put the stuffed frog on the flat deck beneath the back window. "For when he wakes up."

nineteen

The valleys were still in shadow, but the sunlight was creeping slowly but perceptibly down the mountainsides as DeGroot steered the stolen Toyota truck down one of the steep off-ramps and exited the Parkway. He retraced the path he had taken to the meeting place, searching for one of the tiny villages he had passed through. Like most of the towns in the area, it made its living from providing the comforts of home and civilization to the tourists who told everyone they'd come to the mountains to get away from all that. After a short time, he located a place he had noticed and marked. The building had apparently started as a diner, but some subsequent owner had decided to try to dress the place up in a Swiss chalet motif with carved gingerbread trim around the edges of the roofline. A neon sign in the window advertised ESPRESSO. LATTE. SMOOTHIES in curlicued red letters, while another hand-lettered sign in the other side of the window promised INTERNET CAFÉ.

An electronic chime gave out with a grating electronic *bing-bong* as DeGroot entered. There was a plump teenage girl busy at the espresso machine. She and DeGroot were the only people in the café. She looked up and smiled at him through a mouthful of braces. "Be with you in a minute, hon," she said. DeGroot took a seat at the counter. After a moment, she finished whatever intricate operation the machine required and turned to DeGroot. "Welcome to Chez Espresso," she said in a cheerful mountain twang. "What kin I gitcha?"

"Coffee. Black," DeGroot said. "And I need to check my e-mail."

"Ain't even turned the computers on yet," the girl said. "But it'll be two shakes."

DeGroot was baffled. "What?"

"It'll be a just a couple minutes, hon," the girl said. She bustled off toward a back room.

"Dankie," he said absently.

In a moment, she was back. "Okay," she said. "They's bootin' up. Don't get much call for the Innernet this early in the mornin'. Most people just want the coffee. You want a granday or a molto granday?"

Degroot rubbed his hand over his face. What the devil was the bitch saying? "Just the coffee, *Dank* . . . ah, thanks."

"Yeah, but what size? Granday or molto granday?"

"Ahh . . . small."

"That'd be the granday. Just a sec." As she busied herself behind the counter, she chattered merrily. "I love your accent," she said. "Are you from Germany?"

"Ah, sure," DeGroot said. "Germany."

She nodded sagely. "I knew it. That's why you're up so early. You musta just got here. Jet lag, huh? I went to Los Angeles once to visit my cousin. I had jet lag somethin' awful." She handed a steaming Styrofoam cup across the counter. "That's three fifty," she said, "And five bucks for the Innernet." He handed the money to her across the counter. "Computer's in the back, hon," she said. "Enjoy your granday." She winked. "Hope you get good news."

"Thanks," DeGroot said. He shook his head as he walked to the back room. The computers were lined up on a counter that ran along three walls of the room. DeGroot glanced back over his shoulder. He hated sitting with his back to the door. He especially hated having the screen visible from the door. But the girl was busy setting up for the day. He would take the chance. He sat down and logged on. With another glance over his shoulder, he typed an address into the browser's location bar. The site had no name, just a series of numbers separated by periods. In a moment, he was looking at an online bulletin board only he and a very few men like him knew of. He scrolled through a few of the most-recent messages for a few moments and found nothing of interest. Then he began to type. The message was brief and cryptic, containing few particulars. He ended the message with a cell phone number. It wasn't his real number. Anyone reading the message who knew the code would know to subtract one from the first digit of the number, two from the next, and so on, to get the real number. It was a simple enough cipher and wouldn't stop a professional, but it would discourage anyone who had stumbled across the site by accident. He finished the message and logged off.

He took a long drink from the coffee cup. It was awful, but he'd had worse. He ran his hands roughly over his face again. He needed rest. There'd be a few hours before he began getting responses to his bulletin board message. Who knew how much time after that before he assembled his team? No, the smart thing to do was find a cheap and anonymous hotel and park off for a bit. No use staggering around in a *dwaal*. He swigged down the last of the coffee in one gulp and headed for the door.

"Good news?" the girl asked as he was walking out.

He flashed her grin. "Don't know yet," he said. "Fingers crossed, hey?"

"Where are we going?" Powell said. "And do you mind not pointing that thing at me while I'm trying to drive?"

"Just drive," Keller said. "I'll decide where we're going after we talk. I'll also decide whether to stop pointing the gun at you."

"All right, all right," Powell said. "Mikey, you tell him."

"What do you want to know?" Riggio said.

"First off," Keller said, "who the fuck is that guy?"

"His name's DeGroot," Riggio said. "He's South African."

"And how do you know him?" Keller persisted.

"We met in Afghanistan," Riggio answered. He didn't go on.

"Tell you what," Keller said, "I'm really not in the mood for Twenty Questions right now. So why don't you two get out of my car and walk home."

Riggio sighed. "First thing you need to know," he said. "He wasn't one of us."

"He wasn't Army," Keller said. "So who does he work for?"

"Now?" Riggio said. "He works for himself, looks like."

"And what about then?"

Riggio shrugged. "It was kind of a weird time," he said. "There were all sorts of people crawling all over those fucking mountains. Army. Agency. And a buttload of these contractor guys."

"Mercenaries," Keller said.

Riggio nodded. "Some of them . . . like DeGroot . . . were really in demand. They had, ah, special skills."

"I think I know what DeGroot's was."

Riggio made a face. "A couple of Agency guys told us he was a 'humint specialist'. Supposedly he was contracting for ISI— Pakistani Inter-Service Intelligence. But the Agency guys told us if we found someone we thought might have some intel we needed, we should bring him to DeGroot."

"And he'd start cutting pieces off until whoever you caught gave up what you wanted to know," Keller said.

"Hey," Powell spoke up. His voice was low and filled with venom. "You remember the World Trade Center, Keller? You re-member the Pentagon? Some of those cocksuckers were behind it. Or they knew where we could find the ones that were. You want apologies, you've come to the wrong fucking place."

"And before you get too goddamn high and mighty," Riggio added, "you were the one who was threatening to gouge a guy's eye out to get some intel."

There was a long silence. When Keller spoke again, his voice was quiet. "You said some," he said.

"What?"

"You said some of them were behind it."

"Yeah," Riggio said. "Well, there were all kinds of assholes roaming around. Warlords. Drug lords. Plain old everyday ban-dits. Sometimes it was hard to figure out who was on whose side. And sometimes it changed from day to day."

"We should have just nuked the whole fucking place and been done with it," Powell snarled.

"Roger that," Riggio said fervently. "If they give the world an enema, they'll stick in Afghanistan." He took a moment to gather his thoughts. "Anyway," he said, "we were out on patrol. Me, Dave, and Bobby. We had a couple of locals along as trans-lators. We caught this guy coming through one of the passes. He was dressed a little bit better than you'd expect for that part of the hills. The local guys swore up and down he was a bad guy.

'Osama, Osama,' they kept pointing at him. We knew he wasn't OBL, but they seemed to be telling us the guy knew where he was."

"But he didn't," Keller said.

Riggio shrugged. "Like I say," he went on, "there was more than one flavor of asshole roaming those hills. It was hard to tell who was who. For all we know, our guys may have owed the guy money and that was a good way to get rid of him."

"But you took him to DeGroot anyway."

Riggio looked glum, but nodded. "Yeah," he said. "We did. He was working out of this old house up in the hills. He'd set up with a couple of his merc buddies. They were running their own private prison camp up there."

"And DeGroot got something out of him."

Riggio looked haunted. "It took all night. We were outside the house. We could hear the guy screaming from inside. After the first hour, the locals bugged out. Even they couldn't take it anymore. And we're talking about some real mountain hard cases here."

Marie spoke up for the first time. "Did you even try to stop it?" she said softly.

"Yeah," Powell said. "Dave did. But it was too late."

twenty

The house was one of the type owned by relatively well-to-do Afghans in that part of the valley: a low, mud-brick compound with a main house consisting of several large rooms and several smaller outbuildings in a walled courtyard. An olive grove stretched up the gentle slope of a hill behind the main house. In front, the slope continued, down to the slow-moving river below.

The house had long been abandoned as its original occupants fled the region's endless conflicts. The roofs of some of the outbuildings had fallen in, and the untended olive trees drooped raggedly. But the main house was still in fairly good repair. DeGroot and the men he had working with him had turned some of the rooms into makeshift cells, stripping them of all furniture and placing heavy padlocked wooden doors in the doorways. Another room was where DeGroot and his cronies bunked. The remaining room, at the back of the house, had been set aside as the interrogation room. Only DeGroot and his "subjects" ever entered the room; even the other mercs avoided it as if it were a place of ill omen. Which, for the subjects who entered, it invariably was.

The three of them were camped out in the courtyard, huddled around a small fire they had built to ward off the evening chill. They were dressed in local garb. DeGroot had been the only one there when they delivered the prisoners. The other mercs were off on errands of their own.

Lundgren was poking the fire morosely with a stick. The screaming from inside the house had subsided for the moment.

"You think he's done?" Riggio said.

"I hope so," Lundgren replied. After a short pause, he said, almost reluctantly, "This shit isn't right, man."

"Don't pussy out on us now, Lundgren," Powell said belligerently. "This asshole's getting every fucking thing he deserves."

Lundgren and Riggio glanced at each other. They all believed in the mission. None of them had forgotten the sight of the towers falling or the Pentagon in flames. But Powell seemed to be the one most willing to push the envelope. He seemed to have taken it personally. Rumor was that he had known someone in either the Towers or the E-Ring of the Pentagon. No one asked, though. Personal questions were bad form.

It started again. The first sound was a high-pitched babbling with an edge of desperation, a frantic plea for mercy. Then it rose into an inhuman howling, a sound of agony, horror, and despair mixed into one awful shriek. It sounded like the gates of hell being pried open with a rusty crowbar.

Lundgren threw down the stick and picked up his assault rifle. "Fuck this," he said. He started for the house.

"You secure that shit, Sergeant," Powell began, but his voice lacked conviction.

Riggio picked up his weapon as well. "Come on, bro," he said. "Dave's right. This is fucked up."

"You know what this guy does," Powell said.

"Yeah," Riggio replied grimly. "But knowing about it and having to listen to it all night are different things, man. We've got to do something." Powell hesitated. Then he picked up his own rifle and followed them in.

The screaming had been bad enough from outside. Inside, in the narrow hallways, it rebounded and reverberated off the walls until they wanted to throw themselves on the ground and cover their ears. As they reached the door to the interrogation room, the noise weakened again. Only an indistinct murmuring penetrated the door. Lundgren pounded on the door. There was no response, just the blurred sound of voices pitched low.

"Open up, DeGroot," Lundgren said.

After a moment, the door swung wide. DeGroot stood there, stripped to the waist. His chest glistened with a thin film of sweat mixed here and there with stripes of blood.

"What is it, hey?" he said irritably. "I'm busy."

"No, sir," Lundgren said firmly, "you're done."

DeGroot looked at him for a moment, then burst into a laugh. "Right," he said. He started to close the door. Lundgren pushed forward. DeGroot, startled by the sudden aggressive move, stumbled backward before catching himself. They noticed something glistening in his right hand. A surgical scalpel. All three weapons came to bear on him at once. "Drop it, asshole," Powell snarled.

The scalpel clattered to the floor. *"Jislaaik,"* DeGroot said with an expression of wonder. "What the fuck is wrong with you three? You forgot your orders?"

"Our orders don't include letting you do . . . whatever it is you're doing in here," Lundgren said.

DeGroot's laugh was nasty. "That'll come as a surprise to my employer," he said. "Now if you don't mind . . ."

155

There was a sound behind DeGroot, a low bubbling groan.
"Step aside, sir," Lundgren said. DeGroot started to say something, then shrugged and stepped aside.

There was a man seated in a chair at the back of the room.
There was a table in front of the chair. Various objects glittered
on the table. The man's wrists and ankles were bound to the
arms and legs of the chair with heavy wire that cut cruelly into
the flesh. Then he raised his head to look at them.

"Oh my motherfucking God," Riggio said.

The skin on half of man's face had been flayed off. They could
see the white of teeth shining through the ruined flesh of his
cheek. More white bone glistened here and there where DeGroot
had cut through the soft tissue, digging to find and torment the
sensitive facial nerves before slicing through to the skull beneath.
It seemed impossible that anyone with that much damage done
to him should be alive. The figure in the chair tried to speak, but
the words came out as faint whimpers. Powell bent over and
retched. Lundgren swung his rifle back to bear on DeGroot.

"You're under arrest," he said flatly.

"You're making a mistake," DeGroot said.

"I don't think so. Mikey, get your medical kit. See what you
can do for this guy."

"Roger that," Riggio said. He ducked back out the door.

"My employer's not going to be happy," DeGroot said. "And
neither will your commanders."

"I'll take that chance, sir," Lundgren said.

DeGroot shook his head. "You don't understand, do you, *boet*?
You can't arrest me. There aren't any laws. Not up here." He gestured at the table. "Don't you want to know what that fellow was
carrying?"

Riggio came back in, clutching an olive-drab satchel. He

strode over to the man in the chair and began undoing the wires around his wrists.

"Why don't we discuss it outside," Lundgren said.

DeGroot shrugged. "Whatever. I was about done with him anyway." Lundgren stood aside to let him pass. He plucked his shirt off the nail where it was hanging by the door. They followed him into the courtyard.

DeGroot stood by the fire, warming his hands as nonchalantly as if they were on a campout. "That one was a good find, *brus*," he said. "You might even get a medal for it. "If "—he looked at them—"you decide to tell anyone. If you don't . . . well, let's say there might be a better reward than another pretty ribbon and a bit of tin."

Riggio came out of the house. He looked at them and shook his head. "He was too far gone," he said.

"*Ag* well," DeGroot shrugged. "He wouldn't have wanted to live like that anyway."

"You might consider shutting the fuck up," Powell snarled.

"In a minute," Riggio said. He held up a slender silver object. "First, I want to know what this is."

Right," DeGroot said. "Let's talk business, hey?"

157

twenty-one

There was a brief silence in the car. "Did you ever find out who the guy was?" Keller asked.

Riggio shook his head. "Not really. But no one up there, carrying what that guy was carrying, was any kind of innocent civilian."

"What was it?" Marie asked.

Another pause. "One thing all the bad guys up there have in common . . . the Al-Q's, the Talibs, the drug lords . . . is money. Lots of it. They need a way to move it from place to place. And it's not real bright to be carrying big satchels of cash over the hills and through airports. These days, most money doesn't move that way anyway. It's all just numbers on a computer screen. Why carry a bunch of green around when you can punch a few buttons and move it around the world?"

"What does that have to do with—"

"The guy was carrying a flash drive," Powell said. "You plug it into a computer. Into the USB port. They hold a lot of data."

"Including bank information."

"Right," Powell said. "Except that these gizmos took it one step further. You needed two of them. If you had them both, they acted like the keys to a safe-deposit box. Stick one into the computer, it loads a miniature Internet browser and takes you to a net address you won't find on Google. The second one unlocks the account and lets you send the money anywhere you want. All done electronically."

"How much money?" Keller said.

"DeGroot said it was between sixty and seventy million. The guy didn't know exactly. But it's a shitload. That's why it took two. Checks and balances. Whoever the money belonged to, it was probably more than one person. Or one group. No one can get to it with just one key."

"And DeGroot said he'd cut you in if you let him go."

Riggio shook his head glumly. "Yeah. Like I said, we may not have known exactly who the dead guy was or who he was working for, but we knew he was an asshole working for assholes. Stealing their money didn't seem like such a bad thing. Plus, Dave had something else working on him."

"His daughter," Marie said.

"Yeah. He'd been getting some e-mails from home. People telling him what was going on with his kid. What the Fedder woman was like. It was making him nuts."

"You said you needed two keys."

Powell spoke up. "The second key was held by a guy in Kabul. DeGroot got his guy to give up the address and the name. We went down to Kabul and got it."

"And killed the second guy," Keller said.

"Like I said," Riggio replied, "An asshole. Or working for assholes. He won't be missed."

"So what went wrong?" Keller asked.

Riggio sighed. "We were supposed to meet up after Kabul.

Put the keys together. Download the cash into numbered Swiss or Caymans accounts. But before any of that could happen, Dave called home to check on the kid. Carly Fedder answered the phone, drunk off her ass. That was the last straw. He went to the CO and got compassionate leave. He was gone the next day."

"He took the key with him?" Keller said.

"Yeah," Riggio said. He caught Keller's look and quickly added, "But we knew he wasn't selling us out. By then, we were starting to have second thoughts. We were thinking maybe this wasn't a good idea. Still, it was a shitload of money. DeGroot was still up in the hills, due to come down in two weeks. So we had a little time to think about it. We agreed we'd meet up when we got back to the States."

"Where?"

"A place we knew. Up here in the mountains. We trained a lot up here. There's a safe house we used sometimes."

"Did he make the meeting?"

"Yeah. And he had the kid. But he was AWOL. And by that time, so were we. Someone ratted us out. We're not sure who. Maybe one of the locals. We had Agency types crawling all over us, asking about DeGroot. And Dave. So we decided to disappear for a while and decide what to do."

"Not easy to disappear from the Agency."

"We always leave ourselves a backdoor, Keller. Especially with the spooks."

"Nice to know who you've got on your side."

"Comes with the territory. Sometimes we're in places we're not supposed to be. Someone gets burned, the Christians In Action want to be able to stand there in front of a congressional committee going 'Who, me?' You count on anybody but yourself and your people, you're a fucking idiot."

"So you made the meeting," Keller said. "What did you decide?"

"We decided, 'Fuck this,'" Riggio said. "The shit had just gotten way out of hand. We didn't want to spend the rest of our lives running from the army and the Agency both."

"And ourselves," Powell said quietly.

"Yeah," Riggio said. "We'd forgotten who we were. Dave reminded us of that. So decided to come back in. Dave was going to go back down, make contact with our command, and we were going to try to cut a deal."

"A deal?" Keller said disbelievingly.

Riggio shrugged. "What we do, there's a little more room for freelancing than most. I'm not saying they'd let us off the hook completely. But maybe we wouldn't end up in Leavenworth if we played our cards right." He sighed. "Except we didn't know DeGroot had made it to the States. He must have picked Dave up as soon as he surfaced."

"Did he have the key with him?"

"No," Powell said. "He wouldn't have died for that. And DeGroot wouldn't still be coming after us. He must have hidden it somewhere."

"Why wouldn't he have given it to you?" Marie asked.

"We told him not to," Powell said.

"You didn't trust yourselves," Keller said.

There was a long pause. "No," Riggio said finally.

"But you trusted him," Marie said.

"Yeah," Powell said. "He was always the best of us. He was . . ." He stopped, unable to go on.

"Okay," Keller said. "So we follow through with your original plan. We're headed back to Fayetteville. You can call your people at Bragg and make arrangements. We're going home."

"That may not be such a good idea," Powell said. "DeGroot's still out there. And I think he's a little pissed."

"He's right," Marie said after a moment of silence. "He's after anyone he thinks might know something."

"So we go back to the safe house," Riggio said.

"Okay," Keller spoke up. For the first time, he aimed the shotgun away from Powell. "We'll go there. Marie and Ben can stay there for a while. You guys can work things out with your people."

"What about you?" Marie said.

Keller chewed his lip, thinking. Finally, he said, "I'll decide what to do when you two are safe."

"Where are we going?" Ben spoke up sleepily.

"We're, ah, we're going to do some camping," Marie answered.

"I don't want to go camping," Ben complained. "I want to go home."

"We will, baby," Marie soothed. "In a little while."

"Is Grandpa coming?" Ben asked. No one answered him. After a moment, Marie spoke up. "Jack," she said.

"Yeah," Keller said. "I know." He pulled his cell phone off his belt and flipped it open. The NS light blinked at him.

"You got a signal?" he asked Marie.

"No," she replied.

Keller turned to Powell. "We need to get to somewhere where we can make some calls."

"What's up?" Powell asked.

"There are some people out there," Keller said grimly, "who your buddy might try to use to get at us. We need to warn them."

"You think he knows."

"We don't know how much he knows," Keller snapped. "We've got to try to cover all the bases."

"We're going to need some supplies, too," Marie said. "Ben can't wear these same clothes day after day."

Riggio sighed. "Jesus Christ."

"She's right, bro," Powell said. "It's a long drive. We need to top up on gas, anyway. We need to get off the Parkway."

"Pull over," Keller said. "I'll drive."

twenty-two

DeGroot's eyes snapped open. He didn't know where he was for a moment, and adrenaline jolted him to hyperalertness. He snatched the pistol from underneath the pillow and swung it toward the door, seeking whatever sound it was that had awakened him. There were voices outside the door. A man's voice called out. Another answered. DeGroot's finger tightened on the trigger. Then there was the sound of a car door opening and closing and an engine starting. He looked around the room at the rough wood paneling, the cheap prints on the wall, the simple furniture. It came back to him then. He was in a tourist motel. What he was hearing was probably nothing more than a family group coming back from a day's outing. He relaxed and let the gun drop to his side. He was feeling better than he had in days. In his years of warfare, he'd learned how to make even a brief rest count, and the sudden energy boost when he woke up had him feeling sharp and on top of his game. He checked the time. It was late afternoon. By now, he might have a few responses to his posting. He took the time to shower and shave before leaving the room.

The motel was tiny, only eleven rooms, with a cramped office at one end. It was clean enough, however, and perfect for his purposes, since it was the kind of small family-owned operation that wouldn't be fazed by someone paying cash for a night's lodging. Even better, it was within an easy few minutes' walk from the café where he had logged on to make his posting. He strolled down the narrow street, enjoying the coolness of the air and the view of the nearby mountains that loomed over the valley town.

The café was nearly as deserted as it had been in the morning. The only other customers were a pair of young men in hiking shorts and boots, sipping slowly at their lattes and conversing in weary voices. The girl behind the counter had been replaced by a dour man with a gray crew cut. From the look on the man's face and the sour way he looked over the nearly deserted establishment, DeGroot surmised he must be the owner. He paid over his money and took another "granday" coffee. He sipped it as he sat down at the computer and nearly gagged. It tasted as if it had been sitting in the pot since morning. Perhaps it had. He put the coffee aside and logged on. He arched his brow slightly in surprise at the number of responses. Times being what they were, he had expected a shortage of the type of skilled labor he sought. He sorted through the responses. No one, of course, used a real name or number, but he recognized a number of familiar noms de guerre. Some he didn't know quite well enough to propose this sort of operation; some, he knew, would have qualms about the nature of what he was proposing to do, fortune or no fortune. Some were too far away to meet with in the time frame he needed. He sat for a few moments, weighing the need for more hands against the desire to split the money among as few people as possible. Finally he had settled on four names. They

165

were men he knew, dependable men in their own way, especially where there was money to be made. And, more importantly, they were all either within the borders of the United States or close by. He could assemble them within a day or so, if . . . He opened another window on the Internet browser and did a quick search. He sighed. The nearest airport with the kind of access he needed was over two hours away. He'd just have to lose the time. This was the sort of business that could only be organized face-to-face.

He scratched the names and numbers down on a pad by the computer. Now all he needed was intel on his targets.

He glanced toward the front room. The hikers were gone. The proprietor was sitting on a stool, his arms folded across his chest, staring at a baseball game on a small television above the counter. The place was as good as deserted, and DeGroot didn't intend to give any truly incriminating details on an unsecure line. Still. He tossed the half-full coffee cup into the trash. The owner didn't acknowledge him as he left. He walked back to the hotel. Safe in the dim confines of his room he pulled out the sheet of paper and a cell phone. He had specially prepared the device with a "cloned" number stolen from someone else's account. No calls made on the phone would ever be traced to him. He began punching a set of numbers he knew by heart. A voice answered, reciting the last four digits of the phone number by way of greeting.

"Howzit, *bru*?" DeGroot said.

There was no response for a moment. Then: "Is this a secure line?"

"Secure enough," DeGroot said.

"You've been causing quite a stir," the voice said.

"It's not what I wanted," DeGroot admitted, "but here we are."

"What do you mean 'we'?"

"Playing innocent? That doesn't suit either of us, does it?"

"No," the voice said. "Neither one of us."

"The difference, *boet*," DeGroot snapped, "is that you've got a lot more to lose than I, hey? Farther to fall. Me, on the other hand, I've nowhere to go but up. And I might be tempted to trade certain information about certain, ah, incidents in exchange."

"Considering you just killed half a dozen federal agents, including an FBI SIAC, I don't think you'll find anyone in a bargaining mood."

"Maybe not. But maybe I'll just give them a few names, just as a gesture of good will. See what happens."

There was a pause. "What do you want then?" the voice said wearily.

"You remember the three fellows we worked with, about six months ago? The delivery team?"

The voice sharpened. "You know where they are?"

"Not exactly, no. But I have a general area. Maybe you can help narrow the search."

"How would I do that?"

"Please," DeGroot said. "Don't insult my intelligence. You have your fingers in everything."

There was a pause. "What area?"

"They're somewhere in the mountains in the state of North Carolina."

"Good place to disappear in. It took them five years to find that guy who bombed the Olympics."

"I can see that. But this group has a child with them. And a vehicle. They aren't likely living rough in a cave."

"Good point."

"They've got a safe house somewhere. Someplace not even their immediate command knew about. Help me find them."

"And what then?" the voice said.

"I'll put together a team," DeGroot replied. "I'll do the re-cruitment and the mission planning."

"With the mission being . . ."

DeGroot chuckled. "Best you not ask that question, hey?"

"It's like that then," the voice said.

"Yeah," DeGroot replied. "Just like that."

"It'll take some time."

"Time is something I don't have a lot of."

"You have a little more than you think. Your strike was very effective. You took out some of their key people in the area. The FBI's taking some time to regroup. But in a day or two, every agent on the East Coast is going to be arriving in those moun-tains."

"Kak," DeGroot swore softly.

"Why don't you let me find you a place."

DeGroot laughed out loud. "Right. *Dankie,* but I don't think I'll put myself in your hands right now. I'll call you tomorrow." He pushed the button that ended the call. He checked the names and numbers on his notepad and dialed again.

The heat draped itself around Danny Patrick like a wet blanket as he slid out of the front seat of the limo. He did his best to ig-nore it, his eyes sweeping the sidewalks and doorways on his side of the car. God damn, this suit was hot, though. For the amount of green it had set him back, the designer could proba-bly have afforded to put in an air-conditioning unit. But the clients demanded a certain level of class in the appearance of everyone around them, including the bodyguards, even if that meant wearing clothes that would slow him down if any real shit ever started. Not that anything serious would ever go down with this client. Nothing Danny would regard as serious, at least. The worst the spoiled little shit would ever face would be a love-struck fan or an overly aggressive paparazzo, and the little shit's management had been quite clear about a hands-off policy regarding those people. The last thing the little shit needed was another lawsuit. So Danny and his team had to intimidate, without actually getting physical. It worked on most fans, but the paparazzi knew that the team couldn't actually break cameras and heads anymore and acted accordingly, smirking as they snapped away, the flashbulbs going off like tracer fire. Sometimes the explosions of light transported him back to combat for a second. He felt the rush of adrenaline, the fear-rage combination that had once fueled him on the battlefield. He kept it under control, though. He didn't do to the photographers the awful things he knew he could, no matter how much he felt like it. But the intrusions always made the little shit furious, and he took it out on the security detail. Danny sometimes worried that he was going to start losing teeth soon, he spent so much time grinding them in frustration.

He finished his threat assessment. He'd found nothing and expected to find nothing. This was Coconut Grove, not Fallujah. He opened the limo door.

The little shit blinked up at him, his eyes red and squinting. Danny fought the urge to curl his lip in disdain. Not even six o'clock and the nation's newest teen pop idol was stewed to the gills. A few more expensive brandies at dinner, a few lines of blow in the restaurant crapper while the management looked the other way, and he'd be a raging monster. Danny sighed to himself. It was shaping up to be a long night. The little shit staggered out of the limo, followed by his current bimbo, the teenage star of a couple of slasher movies. The girl's eyes were as red and puffy as the client's, and one strap of her designer dress was askew, almost falling down in front. "Ma'am," Danny said politely, gesturing toward her dress. She recoiled from him as if she'd been struck, then glanced down and giggled. She looked up at Danny with a nasty smile and tugged the strap down further, revealing her breast to him for a second before pulling it back up. Her smile grew wider, smug and triumphant. Made you look, she was obviously thinking, Made you look at something you'll never have. She followed the little shit to the restaurant, where another member of the security team was already holding the door open. Danny felt a flush of rage rising to his cheeks. He briefly entertained the fantasy of stepping up behind her and snapping that skinny neck like a chicken's. He actually took a step toward her before he stopped himself. He thought about the message he had seen earlier on the bulletin board. Whatever the job was, he decided, he was going to take it. Fuck this shit. He was a soldier, not a goddamn babysitter. The phone buzzed in his jacket pocket. He pulled it out and flipped it open. "Go," he said.

"Long time, no see," a familiar voice said. "You got my message?"

"Yeah," Danny replied. "I'm in."

DeGroot sounded surprised. "You don't want to know what it is?"

"You said there was a possible big paycheck," Danny said. "That still true?"

"Yeah," DeGroot said. "But there's some risk."

Danny glanced up. The team leader was gesturing at him angrily from the restaurant door.

"Good," Danny said. "I'm bored off my ass."

DeGroot chuckled. *"Lekker,"* he said. He gave Danny a time and a place.

"North Carolina?" Danny said. "What the fuck's in North Carolina?" He shook his head. "Never mind. I'm still in." He snapped the phone shut. The team leader was walking toward him. He caught a flash of movement from the corner of his eye. A man with a large camera bag dangling from his shoulder was dismounting a small motor scooter a few feet away. Danny walked toward him, pushing past the team leader. The paparazzo came on, raising the camera, grinning from ear to ear. Danny could tell what he was thinking. A scuffle between two members of the security detail might not be as good as one of the little shit himself in some embarrassing situation, but it might be worth a few bucks. Danny grabbed the camera and jerked it away from the paparazzo. Then he whirled completely around in a 360-degree arc, generating the maximum momentum as he smashed the heavy camera into the side of the man's head. The paparazzo didn't have time to scream as he collapsed. Danny threw the camera down on the paparazzo's bleeding skull as hard as he could and turned to face the team leader. The man was standing there, his mouth open in shock. He shut it with an almost audible snap. His face contorted with rage. "You crazy bastard," he yelled, "What the fuck?"

Danny reached down to his belt. He wrapped his fingers around the plastic and metal object hanging there. It came free with one smooth motion and Danny pressed it to the team leader's stomach. He thumbed the button. The team leader stopped dead, then began to convulse as the stun gun slammed 80,000 volts of electricity through his body. Danny let go of the trigger and the team leader collapsed to the pavement.

"I quit," Danny said calmly. He turned and walked away. When he got to the corner, he raised his hand for a cab. He knew he didn't have long to get to his apartment and pack. By the time the cops got there, he'd be long gone. As the cab pulled to a stop and Danny got in, he started whistling.

twenty-three

"I can't tell you where I am right now, Dad," Marie was saying.
They were standing outside the car in the parking lot of a Wal-
Mart. Powell and Riggio were inside getting supplies. "Yes. Ben's
with me. I know. I know. No, Jack didn't have anything to do
with it, and neither did I. But, Dad, listen to me. If anyone
comes to the door that you don't know, don't let them in. Don't
even answer it. Anyone approaches you that you don't know,
don't talk to them. The man who killed Carson and took Ben . . .
he's loose somewhere. He's looking for us. He may try to find
out where we are by . . . by trying to get you. Yes, Dad, I know.
We're going to do that. But first we have to get somewhere safe.
And you need to be careful, okay? Okay? Dad?" She looked at
the cell phone in frustration. "Damn it!"

"He got the message, though," Keller said. He was sitting on
the hood of the car a few feet away from her. "That's the important thing."

"Yeah," Marie said. "He thinks this is your fault, by the way."

"Can't say I'm surprised," Keller said.

"Well, this time he's wrong," she replied. "I'm sorry, Jack. I never should have gotten you into this."

He shrugged. "I'm the one who offered," he said. "I volunteered."

"Kind of," she said, "but I could have turned you down." She hopped up onto the hood next to him. He put his arm around her shoulder and pulled her closer. "Are you all right?" she said. "Is all of this . . . you know . . ."

Keller examined his feelings. He felt fine. Better than fine, actually. He felt great. He sighed at the realization.

"You know me," he said. "I'm never happier than when I'm in the middle of a major shitstorm."

"I know," she said. "That's what worries me."

"I'll be okay," he said.

"I hope so." She kissed him. "Did you get hold of Angela?"

"Yeah. I filled her in. She's keeping a lookout. Oscar, too. She'll call Lucas."

"What about Scott?"

Keller flipped the phone open. "I need to call Scott myself." He hit a speed-dial button. After two rings, Scott McCaskill's confident baritone came on the line. "You've reached the law offices of Scott McCaskill," the recording began. At the beep, Keller said, "Scott, this is Jack Keller—" There was a click and McCaskill's voice came on. "Jack?" he said. "Where the hell are you, son?"

"Working late, aren't you, Scott?"

"I've been catching up," McCaskill responded. "Things have been a little busy around here, Jack, what with the local detectives, the FBI, Bragg CID, and about five different scary guys with credentials I never saw before wanting to know all about you. Mind telling your faithful attorney what the hell's going on?"

"What were they asking?" Keller said.

"Everything from where you lived to your shoe size. I told them nothing, of course."

"Of course," Keller said. "Were they asking about any, ah, incident in particular?"

"Yeah, son, they were," McCaskill said softly. "They were asking about Tammy Healy." There was a pause. "You didn't have anything to do with that, did you, Jack?" McCaskill said. His voice was bleak.

"No, Scott, I didn't. I swear it. But I think I know the guy who did."

"Good. I don't suppose I could persuade you to bring the cocksucker to me," McCaskill said. "Tammy Healy was a friend of mine. I'd surely like to have a little talk with the man who did that to her."

Keller was shocked at the savagery in his voice. "Actually, Scott," he said, "I'm trying to avoid him myself right now. And you may want to be careful about doing the same. He's not likely to be as nice about asking where I am as the cops were."

"Ah," McCaskill replied. "So that's how it is. He wants you bad, I take it."

"He wants information about some people I know," he said. "And I think I might have pissed him off a little."

"You do have a talent for that," McCaskill said. "This has anything to do with those missing guys from Bragg?"

"Have you checked this line lately?" Keller asked.

This time it was McCaskill who sounded shocked. "You think they'd tap my—" He paused. "Stupid question. Of course they would."

"Just be careful, Scott," Keller said.

"Jack," McCaskill said, "you think any of my staff people might be in danger?"

174

Keller looked into the car at Ben, who was playing with the stuffed frog they had picked up at the overlook. "Maybe. This guy's not really discriminating. If he thinks they might know something . . ."

"Got it," McCaskill said. "Looks like it's time for a little firm retreat. I can get Judge Waring to continue my cases for a few days. I hear Vermont's lovely this time of year."

"Impressive."

"These people have been with me for ten years or more, Jack," McCaskill said. "And I saw what that bastard did to Tammy. I . . ." He stopped. Keller heard his breathing on the other end of the line. When he spoke again, his voice was normal. "I was the one who ID'd the body."

"I didn't know you were that close," Keller said quietly. "I'm sorry."

"Thanks. You be careful. And Jack—"

"Yeah?"

"I was just kidding about bringing him to me."

"I figured."

"If you find him, kill the sonofabitch yourself. I'll defend you for free."

"Is that legal advice, Scott?"

McCaskill sighed. "No. So you should probably ignore it. Yeah, you should definitely ignore it."

"I probably will," Keller said. He hung up.

They drove for several hours. The terrain on either side of the road grew rougher, rocky bluffs rising abruptly to loom over them on one side of the road and dropping away precipitously on the other. Here and there, clumps of vegetation had forced their way between tiny chinks in the stone, patiently clawing

their own way into the mountain. These hills were already ancient, ground down to stumps of their former selves by the slow
abrasion of years. Man had added his own faster talent for de-
struction; the stone was gouged with long straight channels
where huge machines had ripped into the mountainside to cre-
ate the roadway. They looked like the marks of gargantuan
talons. Occasionally, the road widened enough for a small house
or tiny store to cling precariously to the roadside. They gradually
climbed higher into the hills, their ears popping as the air pressure decreased. After a while, they turned off the main road
onto a rougher and narrower two-lane byway. Now there were
trees on both sides of the road. There were no more houses.

"Turn here," Powell said. Keller stopped the car. A gravel road
led off to the right, heading upward. A wooden sign was nailed
to a tree at the entrance: COPPERHEAD ROAD. NO TRESPASSING.

"Friendly," Keller said. He wheeled the Crown Vic onto the
gravel track. The big car crunched and bounced over the ruts.

"Is this thing going to make it?" Riggio said.

"Don't worry," Keller said. "It used to be a cop car. And I
beefed the suspension up a little bit beyond cop specs."

"Not much further," Powell said.

They rounded a curve and came out of the trees. After the
bend, the road sloped sharply upward. Keller could see the steel
skeleton of a fire tower at the top of the rise. A small log cabin
crouched at its feet.

"Honey," Powell said. "I'm home."

twenty-four

The ringing of the phone jarred Holley's eyes open. He stared at the ceiling for a moment, trying to focus. His head throbbed and his eyes felt like the corneas had been rubbed with sandpaper. His right hand went automatically to the .357 revolver on the bedside table. He picked it up as he swung his legs to the floor. A nearly empty vodka bottle rolled beneath his foot. He kicked it away. He snapped the cylinder of the pistol open. One bullet, just like always. He spun the cylinder, then snapped it shut. He held the gun in his right hand and picked the phone up with his left.

"Yeah?" he said. His throat felt as rough and abraded as his eyes.

"So, Markey, *howzit?*" a familiar voice said.

Holley looked at the gun in his other hand. "Can't complain," he said.

"You're looking for work? Well-paying work?"

Holley continued to stare at the pistol. He brought the gun to his temple and closed his eyes.

"Hello?" DeGroot said. "You still there?"

"Yeah," Holley said. "Still here." His finger tightened on the trigger, just shy of the breaking point.

"So? Interested?"

The trigger broke. The hammer fell on an empty chamber. Holley opened his eyes.

"What was that?" DeGroot said.

"The alarm," Holley replied.

"Ah," DeGroot said. "Are you all right, *bru*? You sound like you got a bit of a *babalaas*," He used the Afrikaanas for hangover.

Holley looked at the vodka bottle. There was still some left. He felt the thirst pierce him like an ice pick. "Out late last night."

"That's fine," DeGroot said. "But I need you sharp for this one, Markey D. Can you manage that?"

"Yeah," he said. "I'm in."

"We're having a meeting tomorrow," DeGroot said. As before, he named a time and a meeting place.

"North Carolina?" Holley said. "Yeah. I'm only a few hours away."

"See you then," DeGroot said.

"Okay," Holley said. He hung up the phone. He picked up the bottle. A half inch of liquid remained. He sloshed it around and looked at it reflectively for a moment. Then he put it down. There was no need now. He had a mission. But his hands were still shaking. That wouldn't do. He opened the drawer of the bedside table and took out small plastic bag and a pack of rolling papers. Carefully, cursing his trembling hands, he rolled himself a conical joint of prime weed laced with a sprinkling of black Afghan hashish. He tucked the joint in his shirt pocket and rolled another. This one he lit. Ahhh. That was better. Once the shit started, he'd stay clean and sober. But for now, he needed a little lift. And if what DeGroot had told him about the mission was true, he'd have enough cash for all the drinks and weed a man could ask for.

"What is this place?" Keller said.

They were standing in the main room of the cabin. It was small but comfortably furnished. There was a main room with a wood stove in one corner. A tiny kitchen area was just off the main room to the right. Three bedrooms, two in the back and one to the left, opened on to the main room.

"Agency safe house," Powell said. "Back in the day, they used to bring Russian defectors up here to debrief. They don't use it much anymore."

"Mom!" Ben called from one of the bedrooms. "Bunk beds! I get a top one, okay?"

"Okay, honey," Marie called back. She turned to Powell. "How did you find it?"

"We were running an exercise five, six years ago," Powell answered. "The Agency lent it to us."

"And how long do you think it'll be," Keller said, "before somebody at the Army or the FBI puts two and two together once they realize that you're in these mountains?"

Powell sighed. "Not long," he admitted. "We may have to move again."

Riggio had entered the room from outside. "So where would we go?" he said.

Powell just looked at him. Comprehension dawned on Riggio's face. "Oh, no," he said. "Oh, *hell*, no!"

"You got any better ideas?" Powell demanded. "The place is a goddamn fortress. And no one would ever think of looking there. Hell, there probably aren't twenty people other than us who know the place even exists."

"If it still does," Riggio said glumly. He chewed at a fingernail. "Okay," he said. "We can check it out."

"What are you talking about?" Keller demanded.

"There's this guy . . . ," Powell began. "His name's Harland. He's got this camp up in the mountains, right on the edge of the national park. We sort of stumbled on him while we were out in the bush."

"What kind of camp?" Keller asked.

"A goddamn nuthouse is what it is," Riggio muttered.

"Harland was in Nam," Powell went on. "He was a Green Beret. He spent a lot of time raising hell up in the Highlands with the Montagnards. But it made him a little squirrelly. Or maybe it was coming back made him that way, I don't know. He started talking about the end of the world, the collapse of civilization, all sorts of shit like that. He'd racked up a lot of good operations in Nam, so they kept reassigning him, trying to keep him out of trouble. But he wouldn't shut up."

"That's for damn sure," Riggio said.

"Mike?" Powell said. "We get it, okay?" Riggio looked sullen, but quieted down. "Anyway," Powell said, "Harland got bounced out on a psycho discharge. So he came home."

Marie spoke up. "What happened to him?"

Riggio laughed. "He wrote a book. And the damn thing became a bestseller."

"Wait a minute," Keller said. "Are we talking about *Nathaniel Harland*?"

"Yep," Riggio said.

"I remember him," Marie said. "He was on a whole bunch of talk shows a few years ago. I remember he was really intense and spooky-looking."

"That's our boy," Riggio said sourly.

"What was the name of that book?" Marie wondered.

"*After the Storm*," Riggio and Powell said in unison.

"You read it?" Marie asked.

Riggio grimaced. "No. He read it to us."

"I thought he was dead," Keller said.

Powell shook his head. "Nope. He took the money and ran. Set up this camp way the hell back in the mountains. A whole bunch of other folks went with him. They were going to ride out 'the firestorm' they said was coming. Things really peaked right before Y2K. Must have been about a hundred people up there by then. After a while, though, civilization didn't collapse, and people got pretty tired of crapping outdoors. Folks started drifting away. But Harland's still up there." He glanced at Riggio. "And he's got food, and guns, and a position you'd need a battalion to take, and only then if you really didn't want to use the battalion for anything much afterward."

Riggio ran his hand through his hair. "I know, bro, I know. But, damn, I'm not looking forward to listening to that son of a bitch rattle on about the end of the world." He looked up. "And you know what? I'm tired of running. We never should have gotten ourselves in this mess in the first place."

"Roger that," Powell said sadly. "And now Dave's dead because of it. And a whole lot of other people."

"We should just turn ourselves in and take what's coming to us, bro," Riggio said.

"You may not get that far," Keller said. "DeGroot's still out there."

"He's not thinking about us," Riggio said, "He's running to save his own skin now."

Keller shook his head. "No," he said. "He's still after you. This guy isn't going to give up. He wants that money, and he wants us dead. And this guy isn't going to give up until he gets what he wants."

"How do you know that?" Powell demanded.

"Because, in some ways," Keller said, "he's a lot like me."

"Jack," Marie said, "You know that's not true."

Keller looked at her. "I wish you were right, Marie," he said. "God knows, I really do. But I've looked him in the eye. And I've seen that look. I've seen it in the mirror."

"Except," Marie said softly, "you're not a cold-blooded killer."

"Yet," Keller said. "And I've got you to thank for that." He shook his head. "But trust me on this. This guy's coming. He'll figure a way. And that's why I have to go after him."

"What!" Marie said.

"I'm not much good at waiting for people to come kill me, Marie," Keller said. "And remember how this guy works. He's willing to use the people you care about against you. And some of the people we both care about are out there. Angela. Oscar. Your dad."

"But we warned them," Marie said. "They'll be on the lookout. And the police, the FBI—"

"Couldn't protect us," Keller finished for her. "How are they going to cover everyone we know? Hell, they may be using them as bait just like they did us."

"They don't know anything," Marie said. "DeGroot has to know that."

"Maybe, maybe not. But then he'll just start killing them until we give up and come out."

"How do you think you're going to find him?" Riggio demanded.

Keller gave him a mirthless smile. "Finding people is what I do," Keller said. "And if I can't find him nearby, I know where he'll be going. While I'm out," he told Powell and Riggio, "I'll call the CID guy who was looking for you. The guy who was at the overlook. I'll tell him you want to come in. See what he says. Maybe he can run interference with the FBI for you. I don't know." He walked over and gently swung the door of the bedroom open. Ben was on the lower bunk, fast asleep. "Get him up," Keller told Marie. "This place may be blown. We need to head for this Harland guy. I'll go with you to make sure you get settled. Then I'll go after DeGroot."

"And when you find him," Marie demanded, "what are you going to do? Bring him in?"

Keller thought back to Ben's words. *Get the guy that shot my dad.* He thought of Scott McCaskill's last words to him. "I doubt he'll give me that chance," he replied. "But if he does . . ." He shrugged. "We'll see what happens."

twenty-five

Bernie Caldwell slid a burger off the grill with his spatula and onto a bun. He looked over at the picnic table. His twin girls were already chomping away eagerly. Normally he would have scolded them for not waiting for the grown-ups, but he was in too good a mood. It looked like the financial worries he'd been nursing the past few months—the twins' braces, his wife's back surgery—were about to come to an end. The fact that the job was being put together by DeGroot meant that it was probably illegal, which didn't bother Caldwell at all. Since Desert Storm, he'd worked on either side of the law so many times that the line had blurred for him until it vanished. The only thing that mattered was taking care of his family.

"Honey," his wife Gretchen called from the kitchen door. "Phone." She was a plump, cheerful woman in a flowered sundress.

"Coming, *Liebchen*," he said teasingly. They'd met while he was stationed in Germany, but he used her native tongue around the house more than she did. She swatted at him playfully as he pushed past her into the kitchen. "Get those last couple of burgers off the grill, okay?" he said as he picked up the phone. She nodded and headed outside. "Yeah," Caldwell said into the receiver.

"Sorry to interrupt your *braai*," DeGroot said, using the Afrikaans for "barbecue."

"No worries," Caldwell said. "Your message came at a good time."

"Glad to hear it," DeGroot said. "We need to move fast, though. Can you kit us out?"

"Depends on what you need," Caldwell said. "But most likely, yeah. Who else is in?"

"Mark Holley," DeGroot said. "And Danny Boy."

"Markey? You sure? He's been a little wobbly lately."

"Give him his toys to play with, and he'll unwobble," DeGroot said confidently, "and you're the toy man."

"Okay," Caldwell said. "Who else?"

A slight pause. "I'm going to try and get Mr. Phillips."

Caldwell whistled. "He won't work cheap," he said. "Besides, I thought he was back in England."

"I have different intel. And I need a good long-gunner."

"Well, Phillips is your guy, then. I won't need to get him anything. He always brings his own gear."

"Right, then," DeGroot said. He gave him the time and the meeting place. "This will be the last time we speak on the phone," DeGroot said. "Don't try to contact any of the others."

"Wait a minute," Caldwell said. "What's going on?"

"Things are going to get hot soon," DeGroot said. "Does that bother you?"

"Depends on how hot," Caldwell replied.

"Not so hot the payoff doesn't justify it," DeGroot said. "We'll talk more. Later. Just be there with the gear."

"Wait a minute," Caldwell said. But the line was dead. He looked at the receiver in frustration. He wanted to know more. He considered hitting star-69 to try and ring back, but he figured it would probably be fruitless. He had a vague sense of unease. He looked out through the open kitchen door into the yard. His wife was eating with the twins, but she stood by the table to eat, where they were sitting down. For time to time, when she thought the girls weren't looking, he saw her grimace in pain and put her hand to the small of her back. When the twins' attention was on her again, she was smiling.

Caldwell sighed. He couldn't afford to be picky. He went out and joined his family.

After dinner, as Gretchen was doing the dishes, he went out to the large storage shed that dominated the side yard. It was kept padlocked at all times, with Gretchen and the twins under strict instructions to never, ever go inside. Gretchen had been raised to believe a good wife never questioned her husband, so she complied without another word. He had caught the twins nosing around one time when they were six. It was the only time he had ever used his belt to spank them, and the experience so far had kept them terrified enough never to try it again.

Caldwell unlocked the shed and stepped inside. He carefully latched the door behind him before switching on the light.

The inside of the shed was an armory. Various rifles and shotguns hung on racks on the walls. Several automatic weapons were locked in cabinets with clear fronts. Caldwell was a federally licensed gun dealer, and he had permits for most of the weapons on display. Certain other more exotic items, however . . . Caldwell plucked a crowbar from a hook on the wall. He walked over to spot on the floor of the shed. There was a straight crack across the concrete floor of the shed. Caldwell shoved the sharp end of the bar into the crack and grunted as he lifted. He tried his best to spare his back; if he ended up like Gretchen, it would do none of them any good. He pried up the concrete slab, revealing a hole beneath. He put the crowbar down and slid into the hole. The area beneath the shed floor was cramped and smelled of Cosmoline. Caldwell worked quickly, selecting the items he needed and setting them carefully at the edge of the hole. When he had made his selections, he climbed out. With considerable effort, he fitted the slab back in place. He took the things he had chosen and set them by the door of the shed. He glanced at his watch. After the kids were in bed, he'd back his truck up quietly to the shed and load up. He'd have to leave early if he wanted to make the meeting, probably before the kids got up, but there'd still be time to say good-bye to Gretchen. Suddenly, he wanted very much to hold her in his arms.

I have a very bad feeling about this job, he thought.

"How do we get there?" Keller said. They were standing in front of the cabin, by Keller's car.

"There's an old logging road that starts out back of the cabin," Powell said. "We take it to the end, about six miles. Then we get out and walk," Powell said.

Marie glanced at Ben. He was oblivious to their conversation. He was holding some kind of conversation of his own with the stuffed frog he'd been carrying since they left the overlook. He had latched on to the toy as if it was a lifeline to a normal existence. Maybe it was. "How far do we walk?" she asked.

"Until Harland finds out we're there," Riggio said grimly.

"What happens then?" Keller said.

"Hope he doesn't shoot us," Powell replied.

"Whoa," Keller said, "You never said—"

"Relax," Powell said. "I'm kidding. I think." He glanced at the car. "I'm more worried this thing's going to bust an axle on the way. This road hasn't been maintained in a while. Harland only comes out of the woods about once or twice a year for supplies."

Keller opened the door. "Let's get moving."

The logging road was an old dirt trail, slowly being reclaimed by the forest. The car pushed over thick clumps of weeds like a tank. They weren't able to make more than a few miles an hour over the rough track. Keller steered as carefully as possible, but every now and then a hidden or unavoidable rut would rattle their teeth. The woods loomed around them on either side. The road began to slope sharply upward. The trees on their left side gave way to a weathered rock face. The trees on the right abruptly thinned, then the shoulder sloped away, revealing a broad vista. Unlike the others they'd seen, this view was not one of green and rolling forests. The forest down the slope was still standing, but the leaves were gone. There was some scrubby undergrowth beneath, but the taller trees stood bare and brown, stripped of all vegetation despite the fact that it was late summer.

"What the hell happened here?" Keller asked. He gritted his teeth as the car slammed into another rut.

"Acid rain," Riggio said. "Power plants and shit in Tennessee and the Ohio Valley. The wind blows the smoke right up here. When the clouds form, they're like battery acid. Any trees that don't die outright are so weak they're killed by bugs." As if to emphasize his words, a wisp of cloud blew by below them in the valley. It would normally have been a beautiful sight but for the army of dead trees beneath the cloud. Then the road took a hard left and the blasted hillside was out of view as they passed between upthrusting rocks on either side. Then the rocks were gone. The road suddenly widened out into a large circular clearing, like a parking lot. A battered and ancient Ford pickup sat to one side. There were pine needles covering the trunk and stuck on the windows. Keller pulled the car over next to the truck. They got out. Next to the truck, a gravel path led into the trees. Another NO TRESPASSING sign was nailed up by the path.

"Jesus," Keller said. "This guy really doesn't like company." He reached back into the car and pulled the shotgun from its rack.

"Hold it," Powell said. "You'd better leave that here."

"Like hell," Keller said.

"He's not going to like you coming onto his property armed," Riggio warned.

"He'll get used to it," Keller said. "You said you were on an exercise when you first met Harland. I don't suppose you were carrying bouquets of flowers."

Powell sighed. "Whatever. At least sling it on your back, okay?"

Keller thought for a moment.

"Look," Powell said impatiently, "We're here to talk, not fight. And if he does decide to fight, that thing won't do you a bit of good. You'll never see him coming."

"Okay," Keller said. He slung the weapon on his back. Powell and Riggio shouldered their packs. "Follow me," Powell said.

twenty-six

When the telephone rang, the man his colleagues knew only as Mr. Phillips was seated in his armchair, reading. He sighed and put the book aside. No one ever seemed to call until he was sitting down engrossed in a book. And the book was one of his favorites, too. He picked the phone up. "Hello?" The voice was soft but steady, with a distinctively British accent.

"How's retirement treating you, *rooinek?*"

Phillips grimaced. DeGroot never tired of calling him by the Afrikaans term for an English speaker. It literally meant "redneck," but any of the ironic humor of the term being applied to the soft-spoken and reticent Phillips had long since been bled away by repetition.

"I'm well," Phillips said politely. "And you?"

"Fine. I scheme that retirement's gotten a bit boring for you, else you wouldn't have answered my little message."

"It was the bit about a potential large payoff that caught my eye."

"Need some money, hey?"

"Who doesn't, really?"

"Willing to take a few risks for it?"

"If the payoff is sufficient."

"Don't worry. As always, no one will ever know you're there. Not until it's too late. Still got your skills, have you? Still in practice?"

In fact, Phillips had taken his rifle out to the range the day before and fired over two hundred rounds through it. He didn't stop until he could consistently put six consecutive bullets into a one-inch circle at a hundred yards. "Not bad for an old guy," another shooter had remarked. Phillips had ignored him.

"Yes" was all he said.

"*Lekker,*" DeGroot said. "So you're in, hey?"

"Yes," Phillips said again.

"Got a pencil?" DeGroot asked.

"I don't require one," Phillips said. "Just tell me the meeting place."

DeGroot chuckled. "Still showing off, I see." Phillips didn't answer. DeGroot gave him the directions. Phillips said good-bye and hung up. He looked at the phone for a moment, then dialed again. The voice on the other end answered by repeating the last four digits of the phone number.

"He called," Phillips said.

"You told him yes?" the voice said.

"That's what you asked me to do."

"Good. I've booked a flight for you. It leaves at six thirty."

Phillips grimaced. "Commercial?"

"Anything else would be too conspicuous. When you reach your destination, I've rented you a car."

This was the second time the man on the other end had said "I" and not "we." This operation must truly be off the books. It wouldn't be the first time, but, Phillips thought, it was going to be the last if he could help it. The comments of rude Americans aside, he was getting old for this sort of thing. He hung up the phone and glanced at his watch. He sighed. If he was going to make his flight, he'd have to leave immediately. Properly cased and unloaded, his rifle could be checked as baggage, as could his specially hand-loaded ammunition when properly stowed. Eventually, the airline security people could be convinced that he was harmless, just a rich hunter traveling to find big game. But that took time. The one thing he dreaded, especially where he was going, was when some security guard wanted to talk deer or dove or some other kind of actual game hunting with him. He had no interest in killing defenseless animals.

Phillips stood up and stretched. He picked up his book again. He would finish it on the plane, but he didn't think he'd bring this copy. It was a rare first edition and he didn't want to risk damaging it. He ran his finger over the raised letters of the title. *Red Harvest.*

"Whoa," Keller said.

The path ended abruptly at the edge of a deep ravine. A hundred or more feet below, the stream that had cleaved the cleft of the mountain foamed over rocks. A narrow wooden trestle spanned the gap to the other side, a distance of forty to fifty feet. Rusted railway tracks ran down the center, ending where the trestle joined the trail.

"What is this place?" Marie asked.

Powell gestured to the other side. "There's an old played-out mine on the other side. It dates back to before the Civil War. This is what's left of the tracks for the train that brought the ore down the mountain. The trail we just came up is the old railroad bed."

"You were right," Keller said. "You could hold off an army from here."

"Told you," Powell said. "This is the only way in from the road, across here. Down the other side is just woods. It's where the national park begins."

"So where's your friend?" Keller said.

Riggio cupped his hands around his mouth. "*Hey!*" he yelled. "*Hey!*" The sound bounced and echoed off the walls of the gorge. There was no response.

"He had to have heard that," Powell said. "Let's go on."

"I don't want to go on there," Ben said. "It's scary."

Marie bent down and picked him up. "Just put your head on my shoulder, baby," she said. "I'll carry you." Ben looked dubious, but he put his head against Marie's shoulder and closed his eyes.

They picked their way carefully across the bridge in single file. Halfway across, Keller looked down. He saw several familiar objects fastened to the supports of the bridge. He pointed. "Are those what I think they are?" he whispered to Riggio, who was right behind him.

Riggio nodded. "Yep," he said, "he's got the trestle wired."

He gave a tight humorless grin. "Don't worry, though," he said. "He wouldn't blow it just to kill us. He could have just picked us off if he wanted to do that."

When they reached the other side, they could see the mouth of the old mine, recessed slightly into the cliff ahead. The opening was sealed shut with heavy timbers nailed close together, the whole construction overgrown with a snarl of vines and creepers. A well-worn path led past the mine, into another stand of trees.

"The camp's through there," Powell said. "When we get to the edge, we'll stop and call again until somebody answers."

"How do you know anyone's still here?" Keller asked. "Maybe Harland gave up, too."

Powell shook his head. "No," he said. He gestured at the path. "That's been kept clear."

"Okay," Keller said. "Let's go." The woods were thick here, arching over the path like the roof of a tunnel. They fell naturally back into single file, Powell in the lead, Keller behind him, then Marie with Ben in her arms, then Riggio bringing up the rear. After a few hundred yards, they began descending. They had to pick their way carefully; even though the way was clear of brush and vine, rocks jutted up through the clay soil. Finally, the trail and the trees ended together at a low stone wall with a wooden gate. Beyond the wall was a large rectangle of flat ground, about the size of a football field, where the slope of the mountain leveled off before beginning its descent again. The long sides of the rectangle were lined with small log houses, a half dozen on either side. The area between them was grass, as flat and well trimmed as a parade ground. On the opposite end of the rectangle was a larger building, two stories tall, also made of hewn native timber. An American flag hung limp on a pole in front of the broad wooden doors.

Powell cupped to his hands to his mouth and called out. "*Hey! Hello!*" There was no answer. He called again. Still nothing.

"Maybe he's out hunting," Powell said. He turned to them. "I think we should . . ." He stopped, his eyes widening. "Where's Mikey?"

Keller looked around. Riggio was gone. He reached for the shotgun slung on his back.

"I wouldn't," a voice said.

Keller froze.

194

"Put your hands down," the voice said. "Where I can see them."

The speaker was standing a few feet away. She seemed to have materialized out of the trees. She was a short woman, barely over five feet, dressed in green camo. She looked to be barely out of her teens. Her features were clearly Asian, but she spoke with no trace of accent. Her dark eyes were hard and appraising. She held a shotgun of her own trained on Keller's chest.

"Lisa?" Powell said.

Her eyes flicked toward him briefly, then took in Marie and Ben before returning to Keller. "Hi, Bobby," she said. "Long time no see. Who're your friends?"

"Lisa," Powell said, "we need a place to stay for a few days."

"Plenty of hotels around," she said.

"We've, ah, run into some trouble," Powell said.

"And this is our problem? Why, exactly?"

"Ma'am," Marie interrupted softly, "could you please stop pointing that gun at us? You're scaring my son."

The woman looked at Marie and Ben expressionlessly for a few moments. Ben stared back, wide-eyed and trembling. She looked back at Keller. "Reach back," she told him. "Slowly. Grab the shotgun by the barrel. Put it on the ground." Something in Keller's eyes made her hands tighten around her own weapon. She raised it slightly. "No stranger comes armed into camp," she said, as if reciting from a rule book.

"Please, Jack," Marie said. Gritting his teeth, Keller complied. As he straightened up, Lisa lowered her own weapon, then slung it on her back. She walked over to where Ben huddled against Marie's leg and went to one knee. "I'm sorry if I scared you," she said gently, "but we have to be careful of strangers." She held out a slender hand. "My name's Lisa," she said. "I live here with my dad."

Ben looked dubious for a moment, then reached out and shook her hand. "I'm Ben," he said in a small voice. "My dad got shot."

A look of shock crossed her face for a moment, then she re-formed her features into the impassive mask. "I'm sorry to hear that, Ben," she said. She looked up at Marie. "You'd better come in," she said. She straightened up, walked to the gate and swung it open. "Welcome to Camp Phoenix," she said formally.

They looked at each other, then preceded her through the gate. "Lisa," Powell said, "Mike was with us . . ."

"I know," she said shortly. "He's fine. I sent him to the mess hall." Then, unexpectedly, she grinned. The smile made her look almost impish. "Boy," she said, "was he surprised when I took him down!"

"Wait a minute," Powell said. "You took him down?"

Lisa looked smug. "You betcha," she said. "Things have changed a lot around here since you guys were here last."

"Looks like it," Powell said. His face split into a grin. "Man," he said, "am I going to give Mikey some shit about this." He began to laugh. Lisa laughed along with him. Then so quickly that her figure seemed to blur, she dropped to the ground in a curious twisting motion. One leg came around viciously and swept Powell's feet from beneath him. He gave a startled yelp as he crashed heavily to the ground. He looked up dumbfounded at Lisa, who had sprung back to her feet and was smiling wickedly down at him.

"Now you've both got something to laugh about," she said brightly.

Keller bent down and helped Powell to his feet. Powell looked furious for a moment, then he chuckled. "Pretty good, Lise," he said ruefully. "I underestimated you." His face hardened. "But you won't get a chance like that again."

"I only need one," she said. She turned and began walking again.

As they walked across the commons, Keller noticed that the log houses on either side were boarded up. Padlocks fastened every door. They drew even with the flagpole. Keller glanced up. The American flag was hanging upside down in the symbol of distress. The sight stopped him in his tracks. "What's the emergency?" he asked.

She followed his gaze, then looked at him stonily. "You must not have been paying attention the last thirty years or so." She swung open the door of the large building. "Come on in," she said. "Dad'll want to talk to you."

They stepped inside, into a large room. The only illumination was provided by the sunlight coming in through the high windows down either side of the room. At the far end of the room, interior serving windows opened into a kitchen.

A long wooden table ran down the center of the room, with wooden chairs on either side. The table was long enough to seat twenty people, but only two of the chairs were occupied. Riggio sat at one of them, eating from a wooden bowl. The smell of meat and broth reached Keller, and his stomach growled.

The man sitting across the table from Riggio stood up. He was tall and slender, almost gaunt, with a face lined and seamed from years of wind and weather. Beneath that, however, his chiseled features and high cheekbones spoke strongly of Native American ancestry. His eyes, however, were a piercing blue. His jet-black hair was streaked with silver, hanging halfway down his back in a long ponytail. He stood before them for a moment, looking them up and down. His face was as impassive as Lisa's. Keller felt as uncomfortable under that sharp gaze as a recruit on his first inspection. Finally, the man held out his hand to Powell. "Good to see you back, Bobby," he said. His voice was deep and soft, but there was the promise of steel beneath it. This was a man to whom command of other men was as natural as breathing.

"Thank you, sir," Powell said as he took the man's hand. "I'm sorry to impose on you like this, but . . ."

"I'll decide later whether you're imposing," the man said. "For now," he gestured toward the serving windows at the back of the room, "there's stew in the kitchen. Venison. It's fresh."

"Colonel," Powell said, "we need to tell you . . ."

The man waved him off. "Eat first. Then we talk." Powell nodded and headed for the back of the room. The man turned his gaze back to Keller. Keller had to fight the impulse to salute. Instead, he held out his hand. "I'm Jackson Keller, sir," he said.

The man took it. "Nate Harland." He looked at Marie, who stepped forward. "Marie Jones, sir," Harland gently took her hand in his and bowed slightly. It was an archaic gesture, almost medieval in its formality. He released Marie's hand, then bent down and took a knee so he could look Ben in the eye.

"Are you an Indian?" Ben blurted out. Marie put her hand warningly on his shoulder, but Harland only smiled.

"My father's mother was Tsalagi," he said, "what white men called the Cherokee. My mother's grandfather was, too. My father's father was Irish, though, and my mother's grandmother was a lady from Scotland. What do you suppose that makes me?"

The boy looked confused. "I don't know," he said uncertainly.

"American," Harland said.

Ben gestured to where Lisa was standing. "That girl there says you're her dad."

Harland looked at her and smiled again. "I am. In a way."

"What way?" Ben insisted.

"Ben!" Marie said. "Stop being nosy."

Harland laughed and stood up. "I'll tell you the story later, Ben," he said. "Now, I bet a fellow like you, who's been doing some hard traveling, has got to be hungry. Am I right?" Ben nodded. "You ever eaten deer meat?" Harland asked him.

"Oh yeah," Ben said, "Lots of times. My grandpa hunts deer. My mom used to."

Harland looked at Marie appraisingly. "That so?" he said. He smiled and gestured back toward the kitchen. "Help yourselves. More where that came from." He went to the door. "We'll be back in bit," he told them. He looked at Lisa and gestured slightly with his chin. She followed him, casting a worried look over her shoulder at them.

"I hope we haven't gotten her in trouble," Marie said.

"Nah," Riggio said. "Believe me, we'd be hearing it now if he was going to dress her down. He's probably just getting her report."

"Report?" Marie said, "She's his daughter!"

"She's also a soldier, at least as far as he's concerned," Riggio said. He laughed. "In fact, from the looks of things, she's his whole damn army."

"Where are all the people?" Keller wondered. "It looks like this place was built for at least a hundred."

"It was," Riggio replied. "Harland had a regular little village going up here at one point, waiting for the end of the world. But," he shrugged, "civilization didn't collapse."

"Oh, didn't it?" Lisa said as she reentered the room. "So why exactly are you people up here? What are you running from?"

"And, more important," Harland said as he followed her in, "what are the chances that you're going to bring it here to us?"

They looked at each other. Marie looked at Ben. Harland followed her gaze.

"Lisa," he said. "Take the boy outside. Show him around the camp."

"Sir," she began to protest.

"You'll be briefed on all the information I get," he said. The words were reassuring but the command in the voice was unmistakable. She stood up, her face stony. "Yes, sir," she said. She extended a hand to Ben and smiled. "C'mon, Ben," she said, "You want to see a waterfall?"

Ben looked dubiously at his mother, who nodded at him. "Go with Lisa, Ben," she said. "I'll be out to get you in a little bit." Ben left with her, still clutching the stuffed frog to his chest.

"Now," Harland said as they walked out, "Since no one's volunteered to lead this briefing, looks like I'll need to pick a volunteer." He looked at Keller. "Mister Keller," he said. "What's going on here?"

twenty-seven

DeGroot punched the numbers into his cell phone. On the second ring, he got the usual numerical response. He engaged in no pleasantries. "What do you have for me?" he said.

"It wasn't easy," the voice said.

"If it was easy," DeGroot replied, "I could have gotten anyone to do it."

"The fact that I was nosing around those files . . . There may be questions."

"Give me what you've found, or there won't be any questions. Or any doubts in anyone's mind."

A sigh on the other end. "All right. The Agency has an asset in the area you described. An old cabin. They bought it from the Parks Service in the eighties when the service decommissioned one of the old fire watchtowers."

"And what," DeGroot asked, "did the Agency want with an old cabin in the mountains?"

"It was a place to take defectors for questioning. Isolated. Quiet."

"Easily defensible."

"Probably."

"So what does this have to do with our friends?"

"Their unit used it for an exercise a few years ago. They ran a simulated attack and hostage rescue there."

"How'd they do?"

"According to the after-action report, brilliantly."

"So they might have gone back there," DeGroot mused.

"They'll be ready for you," the voice warned.

DeGroot heard a car pull up outside the motel room. He moved the curtain aside as a red Corvette pulled into the parking lot. Danny Patrick was behind the wheel. DeGroot waved. "They won't be ready for what I'm bringing them," he said. He snapped the phone shut.

When Keller was finished, Harland looked around the table. "Anyone have anything to add?" he said. No one said anything for a moment. Then Marie spoke up.

"Sir," she said, "I know you don't know us. You don't have any reason to trust either Mister Keller or myself." She took a deep breath. "But believe me when I tell you, the man following us is a monster."

"I believe you," Harland said gently. "Trust me, Miss Jones, I know better than most men what monsters there are in this world. But you may have brought this one to my doorstep."

Riggio spoke up. "He's only one man, Colonel. And I don't think he knows anything about this place."

Harland smiled tightly. "One man?" he said. "Never underestimate what one man, properly motivated, can do. You and

Sergeant Powell should know that. It's an article of your faith."

"Please, Colonel," Marie said, her voice nearly breaking "That man tried to kill my son. I'm afraid if he catches us . . ." Her voice did break then. She looked down at the table and ran the back of her hand over her eyes.

Harland stood up. "I'm not making a decision this second," he said. "It'll be dark soon. Even if I decide you can't stay, I won't send you out on that road in the dark." He walked over to a cabinet against one wall and opened it. Inside the cabinet was a board studded with hooks. A variety of keys hung from the hooks. "You can bunk in the empty cabins," Harland said. "They may take a bit of airing out." He tossed a key to Riggio. "Riggio, you and Powell have number five." He looked at Keller, then Marie. "You two are together, I take it?"

They looked at each other. They realized that each was waiting for the other to answer, and they laughed.

"Yeah," said Keller, "we're together."

"And the boy?"

"He's with us," Keller said. Marie reached across the table and squeezed his hand. Harland tossed her a key. "Number seven," he said, "it was built for a married couple."

Ben came crashing back into the mess hall, followed by Lisa. He was breathless with excitement. She was bright-eyed and laughing.

"Mom," Ben said. "There's the coolest waterfall. It must be a hundred feet high! You gotta come see!"

"In a little while, Ben," Marie said.

"Now," Ben insisted. He grabbed at Marie's hand.

Harland laughed softly. "I think you've been given an order, Miss Jones," he said. "You might as well go. The waterfall's very pretty in the sunset."

"Lisa," Ben said, turning to the girl, "tell them how cool it is."

"It's very, very cool," Lisa said with mock gravity.

"Come on, Mom," Ben insisted.

"I'll take you back if you want to go," Lisa said.

Marie looked down at Ben's impatient face. He was so serious and determined she had to laugh. "Okay," she said. She turned to Keller. "Jack?"

"Sure," he said. "You guys go on. I'll be along in a minute."

Marie allowed herself to be pulled to her feet and out the door. Lisa followed, still laughing.

Harland's voice was almost a whisper. "She misses the children most of all," he said as if to himself.

"Sir," Keller said, "whatever you decide about me, or these two," he gestured at Powell and Riggio, "let Marie and the boy stay."

"That's one of the options I'm considering," Harland said.

"Consider it real carefully," Keller said, "Because I'll do whatever I have to do to keep them safe. Sir."

Harland looked at him. "Is that a threat, Mr. Keller?"

"No, sir, Colonel," Keller said. "I just wanted you to have all the information you needed to make a good command decision."

They stared at each other for a moment. Outside, the shadows were lengthening as the sun eased toward the peaks of the mountains. Powell and Riggio looked uncomfortably at each other. Finally, Harland broke the silence. "I'll let you know my decision in the morning."

"Yes, sir," Keller said, "Thank you, sir." He stood up and walked out.

"Ben!" Marie called out. "Come back!"

Lisa was walking side by side with Marie, her shotgun slung across her back. She walked with an easy, confident stride over the uneven rocky ground. Now she cupped her hands around her mouth. "Hey, hold up!" she called. Only then did Ben stop pounding down the path into the trees behind the mess hall. He stood waiting, practically vibrating with impatience.

"Oh, *you* he listens to," Marie said wryly.

Lisa grinned. "He's a lot of fun," she said. "I've missed having kids around."

"Where did everyone go?" Marie asked.

The smile vanished. "Back into the world," she said with a trace of bitterness. "Back into the shit."

"You didn't go with them," Marie said.

"I still believe in my father," she said. "I still believe in his work."

"Your father," Marie said tentatively. "I couldn't help but notice—"

Lisa chuckled. "Yeah. I'm adopted."

"I didn't mean to pry."

"It's not a problem." They had entered the woods now. Ben was a few feet ahead of them on the trail, zigzagging back and forth. "My birth father and Colonel Harland fought together in Vietnam. After the war, things got pretty nasty for my folks. The government treated everyone who'd fought on the American side . . . Well, it got pretty bad. Colonel Harland and some of the other men who'd fought with them worked hard to get them out of Vietnam and over here. My birth father was the only one of the family who made it."

"I'm sorry," Marie said.

Lisa shrugged. "It all happened before I was born. Anyway, my birth father came to America, got married again, and opened a convenience store. Two weeks after I was born, he and my mother were shot to death by an armed robber."

"I'm sorry," Marie said again. She couldn't think of anything else to say.

"Like I said," Lisa replied, "I don't remember any of it. Dad . . . Colonel Harland . . . had promised my birth father he'd take care of his family if anything happened. He adopted me. I've lived up here all my life."

"What was it like?"

"It was a great place to grow up," Lisa said. "There were lots of people around, woods to play in . . . Sure better than living down in the shit." She shook her head. "I don't understand why anybody would want to live like that," she said.

"Don't you ever get lonely?" Marie asked.

"Here we are" was Lisa's only answer.

Marie looked. They had come out of the trees to a broad ledge of rock. A massive stone overhang, the size of a small building, loomed to their right. A fast-running stream had a groove into the rock, through which it shot out like a horizontal geyser, tumbling down the sheer rock face below. Ben stood at the lip of the ledge, looking over to where the rushing water disappeared from view. Marie's heart leapt into her throat. "Best step back a bit, buddy," Lisa said calmly. "Long way down."

Ben complied with obvious reluctance. "Come see, Mom," he said. Marie stepped to him and looked cautiously over. The water roared and hissed and tumbled through the air until it smashed against the stone a hundred feet below, exploding into a cloud of mist before continuing its journey down to the valley below.

"Isn't it cool?!" Ben said.

"It's gorgeous," Marie said truthfully.

"Can we stay, Mom?" Ben said.

"I hope so," Marie said. "But you've got to promise never to come here without a grown-up. You might fall."

"I won't fall," Ben said.

"Promise," Marie insisted.

"Okay, okay," Ben said. He brightened. "I can get Lisa to bring me. Right, Lisa? Right?"

Lisa laughed. "Sure, kiddo," she said. "Any time."

Holley squinted into the late-afternoon sun. The day's hangover had subsided somewhat, but the sun's rays still made his head hurt. He reached over and fumbled the glove compartment open. The road climbing into the mountains had grown more winding, so it was an exercise in divided concentration to locate the last hashish-laced joint. Finally, his fingers encountered the softness of the stuffed rolling paper. He smiled. He put the joint between his lips and popped the cigarette lighter. *Last one,* he told himself. *Then it's showtime.*

The miles passed more quickly in the haze of the black Afghan hash. It began to get dark. He almost missed the turn to the town where DeGroot had told them to meet. He found that hilarious. He was laughing as he got back on the right road. Finally, after a timeless interval, he saw the lighted sign of the small motel where DeGroot had said to meet. He pulled into the parking lot. A Toyota 4×4 and a red Corvette were the only vehicles parked in front of the units. Holley crushed out the joint and got out of his car. The crunch of his combat boots on gravel sounded unnaturally loud in his ears as he walked into the office, blinking against the bright fluorescent lights. "Room for the night, dude," he told the elderly man behind the desk. He was dark-skinned, with a full beard. A dark-red turban was wrapped around his head. The man's lips pursed in disapproval as Holley filled out the register.

"Markey D?" the man said. "What kind of a name is that?"

"It's my stage name, dude," Holley said. "Like Ice-T. 50 Cent. You know the drill."

"I need your full name," the man said irritably.

207

Holley briefly toyed with the idea of fetching his pistol from the car and teaching the Indian fuck some manners, but put the pleasant idea aside for another time. The old man slapped a key down on the counter. Holley picked it up and squinted at it. The number made no sense to him. *Jesus,* he thought, *I am ripped straight to the tits.*

"Can't you read?" the old man said. "Number thirteen."

"Lucky number thirteen," Holley grinned. "Thanks, dude."

As he walked down the row of units, a door opened. Danny Patrick stepped out. "Danny Boy!" Holley said happily. He began to sing. "Danny Boyyy . . ." he crooned in an unmelodious voice, "the fuck-ing pipes are callllling . . ."

"Jesus," Patrick said. "Are you fucked up or something?"

"Good to see you, too, brudda," Holley said. "Where's our friend?"

"He's in his room," Patrick said. "Come on." He led Holley down the row of units. He knocked at a door. Holley could see a thin sliver of light across Patrick's face as the door was opened a crack. Then the door swung wide. Holley followed Patrick into the room. DeGroot was seating himself on the bed. He held a 9-mm automatic in his right hand.

"Howzit, *bru?*" DeGroot asked.

"Aiight," Holley replied. "What's with the iron?" He gestured toward the gun.

"Can't be too careful, hey?" DeGroot said easily.

"Can you drive?" Patrick asked him.

"I drove here, didn't I?"

"Good," Patrick said. "Come on." He tossed Holley a set of keys. He turned to DeGroot. "We'll be back," he said.

"Where are we going?" Holley said as he deftly plucked the keys out of the air. He followed Patrick out the door.

Patrick pointed at the Toyota. "We've got to ditch this

somewhere," he said. "It's gonna be reported stolen pretty soon. DeGroot'll be happy he doesn't have to drive. He doesn't want to get out any more than he has to."

"What's going on?" Holley said. "Is our old buddy bringing down the heat?"

"Yeah," Patrick said. "But if we do this right, it'll be okay. And the payoff . . ." He stopped.

"The payoff?" Holley said helpfully.

"Millions, Markey," Patrick said. "Fuckin' millions."

The cabin was small, two bedrooms and a tiny front room that served as a parlor and work space. There was no kitchen; apparently all meals were supposed to be prepared communally. Ben's nose wrinkled at the musty smell of a building left unoccupied for too long.

"It smells weird in here," he said.

"It just needs airing out," Keller said. He put down the propane lamp he'd been carrying. Its intense white light burned like a tiny star, almost too bright to look at directly. It made Keller's shadow seem enormous as he walked over and opened a window. The old wood of the window frame screamed in protest at the unaccustomed movement. Marie put down her own lamp and opened another. The cool night air rushed in, fragrant with the smell of the surrounding forest. "See?" Keller said. "Better already." They checked the bedrooms. The bedsteads were wooden and appeared handmade. Worn mattresses were rolled up against the headboards. Dust puffed up from them as Keller unrolled them.

"No linens," Marie said.

Keller opened a cabinet. He pulled out a pair of rough Army blankets. "We've got these," he said.

"Just like basic, huh?" Marie said.

"Yeah."

"You think he'll let us stay?" Marie said.

Keller tossed a blanket to Ben. "Go get set up in the other room, buddy," he told Ben. "Take one of the lamps." Ben struggled for a moment, trying to arrange the blanket, the lamps and the ever-present stuffed frog. As he walked out, Keller told Marie, "He'll let you stay. I'll make sure of it."

"What if he says no?" Marie said.

Keller shook his head. "He won't say no," he said. "I'll talk to him."

"Jack," Marie said, "I don't want you to do anything . . . I don't want you to hurt them. Either of them. Or threaten them. These are good people."

He looked at her. "So are you and Ben. And you two are my responsibility."

She shook her head. "No, Jack. I'm my own responsibility. And Ben is my responsibility. I'm a grown-up. I get some say in this. And I'm telling you, I don't want any violence against these people. I don't want that on my conscience. And I don't think you do, either."

Keller tensed for a moment, but the reply he was getting ready to make died in his throat. He took her in his arms. "Sometimes," he said, "you're the only thing that keeps me from going completely off the rails."

"I know," she said. "It worries me."

"Yeah," he said, "Me, too." He kissed her.

"Eeuuuw," Ben said as he came back in. "Get a room."

Keller broke the kiss and laughed. "We've got a room, smart guy," he said. "And you've got yours, and it's time for bed."

Ben ignored him. "Mom," he said, "there's something wrong with this frog." He turned the creature over. There was a tear in the plush green fabric, along one of the bottom seams.

Marie took the frog from him and sat on the bed. "Hmmm," she said. "Looks like it should be easy to fix. I'll check in the morning and see if they have a needle and thread." She poked lightly at the rent in the fabric. Her brow furrowed. There was something buried in the stuffing, something hard. She dug inside with her fingers.

"Mom," Ben said with alarm.

Marie drew out a small silver cylinder. She looked up at Keller. "Jack," she said.

"Is that . . ." he began.

She grasped one end of the cylinder and pulled. It came apart easily. There was a flat plug in one end, clearly designed to slide into some sort of socket.

Keller reached out and took it from her. "He hid it in his kid's stuffed frog."

"What do we do now?" she said.

He walked to the door. "We talk to Powell and Riggio."

twenty-eight

"Bad craziness," Holley said.

The Toyota was still crashing and bouncing through the undergrowth, down the cliff face he and Patrick had just pushed it over. As they watched, enough of the thick brush pushed aside by the truck's passage sprang back to cover all but the most obvious gouges made by the truck as it fell. It was like throwing the vehicle into a green sea.

"Come on, man," Patrick said. "We need to haul ass."

"What if somebody finds it?"

"They'll have a hell of a time getting it back up here," Patrick said. "Come on, Markey, before any more cars come."

"What the fuck is going on here, anyway?" Holley asked as they got back into Patrick's Vette.

"Well," Patrick said, "some old partners of DeGroot's took something from him. Something worth a boatload of money. And he wants it back. So he got some new partners, namely us. That's all I know right now. He'll tell us more when the others get here."

"Who else is coming?"

"Caldwell. And Phillips."

"Be good to see old Bern again," Holley said. "He always has some cool shit to play with. But Phillips—" He gave an involuntary shiver. "Man, that dude gives me the creeps sometimes."

"Right," said Patrick, "and DeGroot doesn't?"

"Oh, I know DeGroot's a bastard," Holley said cheerfully. "But he, like, admits it. Phillips, though. I can never figure out what he's thinking."

"You don't need to know," Patrick told him. "All you need to know is, he's on our side."

"You sure about that?" Holley said. Patrick didn't answer. Holley looked out the window into the darkness. "Bad craziness," he muttered again.

"Well, I'll be damned," Powell said.

The cabin assigned to Powell and Riggio was bigger than Keller and Marie's, but the inside was even starker. It had clearly been designed as quarters for the unmarried men or women. Rows of bunk beds with rolled-up mattresses lined the walls. A long table, a smaller version of the one in the mess hall, ran down the center of the room. The computer flash drive lay in the center of the table.

"So what do we do now?" Riggio asked.

"Now that you know where the key is," Keller said, "maybe we have something to bargain with."

"Bargain?" Powell snorted, "with who? DeGroot? You can't bargain with that sonofabitch, Keller. He'll catch you and then he'll take you apart."

"All he wants is the drive," Keller argued. "Give him that—"

"And he kills us anyway, to keep us from telling anyone else," Powell snapped. "No. No way."

Keller thought for a moment, then sighed. "Yeah," he said. "You're right."

"Only thing to do," Riggio said, "is hole up. Hope the FBI finds DeGroot. Then maybe we can make a deal with our people to come in."

Keller stood up. "That means," he said, "that I need to talk to Harland."

Keller found Lisa outside the mess hall. She carried her shotgun unslung. Before he could ask, she gestured with the barrel of the weapon, toward the door of the hall. "He's in his office," she said. "Go to the back, then up the stairs. He's waiting."

Keller moved carefully through the darkened mess hall, waiting for his eyes to become accustomed to the darkness. He could sense rather than see Lisa's slim form blocking the entrance door. He could barely make out the reflected flicker of a lamp at the other end of the building. He found the stairs and began to climb. They were noisy, he suspected deliberately so. It would be nearly impossible to come up those stairs undetected.

The stairs came up directly into the office. The room was large; it seemed to take up nearly a quarter of the top floor. Bookshelves lined the walls. Harland had chosen the older-style kerosene lamps rather than the brighter propane ones for this room; the light was dimmer and redder. It flickered, making the shadows seem to move even when the person behind them was still. The only other light in the room was the soft electronic glow of what looked like a bank of radios that crowded a table on one side of the room, next to Harland's desk.

Harland sat behind the desk. It, like all the other furniture in the camp, was handmade and rough-hewn. A pistol lay on the desk in front of Harland. It was within easy reach of his hand.

"You won't need that," Keller said. "Besides, I'm not armed."

Harland didn't speak for a moment. He regarded Keller with grave eyes that seemed to have sunk slightly into his craggy face. Finally, he spoke.

"What weapon has the lion," he said, "but himself?"

"What?" Keller said. Then, "Uh . . . thanks. I guess."

Harland didn't move. "Don't thank me, Mr. Keller," he said. "You're a violent man. You can mask it in front of others, but I know. I spent much of my life in the company of violent men. I know the signs. I see it. It comes off you like steam." He picked up the gun, but gently. He looked at it and turned it over and over in his hands. "What we call civilization," he said, "is a thin veneer. It's like a beautiful, delicate vase. It sits on the mantel and everyone admires it, saying how fine it is. Oh, there are flaws in the finish, but we can fix them. No need to do it right now, because isn't the vase pretty? The flaws, we tell ourselves, even add to the beauty. But the vase is full of corruption, Keller. It's brimming up to its lid with pus and blood and maggots. And the flaws in the finish are turning into cracks. Soon it will shatter completely, and the world will drown. Drown in its own corruption." He put the gun down and looked at Keller.

Crazy as a goddamn loon, Keller thought. "Seems to me you've been saying that for a while," he said.

Harland turned to him. "My only mistake," he said, "was that I hadn't any sense of the timescale involved. I'm an American, after all. We think in terms of years. Maybe decades, if we're particularly visionary. I didn't realize how long it would take. But it's an accelerating process. I was only off by a few years."

"I need to talk to you," Keller said, "about—"

"You know, Keller," Harland interrupted. "You know what I'm talking about. You've been there. You've seen what men can do to each other. You've seen the fire from the sky."

Keller shook his head. Suddenly, in his mind's eye, he saw the white flash out of the desert night, felt the heat of the impact wash over him.

Burning, they're burning . . .

Keller shook his head savagely, to clear it. He looked up and saw Harland looking at him. "Yes," he said. "The fire. You've seen men pull fire down from the sky. On other men. On women. On children."

"Yeah," Keller said. "What about it?"

Harland picked up the gun again. "I've seen it, too. I've seen the fire come down. I called it with my own voice." His eyes went far away. "The planes screamed like enraged angels as the fire fell. Afterward, I walked on the blackened earth. Everything was black. The ground, the trees, the children . . ." He stopped and shook his head. "We should never have been given that power, Keller. We're killer apes that can bring the heat of the sun to touch the earth. In the end, we'll bring the fire down. We can't help ourselves." He paused and stood up. "Do you read Yeats, Keller?"

Keller shrugged. "I remember the name from high school."

Harland walked over to the bookshelf, ran a finger over the spines of the books 'Mere anarchy is loosed upon the world,' he quoted. 'The blood-dimmed tide is loosed, and everywhere, the ceremony of innocence is drowned; the best lack all conviction, while the worst are full of passionate intensity." He turned back to Keller. "Are you paying attention at all? Can you deny that's what's happening now?"

Keller stood up and dusted off his hands on his pants. "Look," he said, "are you going to let us stay or not?"

Harlan's smile was a spear of ice. "It's that simple to you?"

"Right now, yeah," Keller said. "There was a time I might have eaten this stuff up, Colonel. The world's a shithole. Fine. I know it. You know it. Maybe soon it'll finally implode and take us all with it. But right now, I've got people I care about. People who depend on me."

Harland's cold smile didn't change. "It won't change the final outcome. Nothing will."

Keller shrugged. "Maybe. But I'm just fighting each battle as it comes."

"And that's the problem for me, Keller. Your battle isn't mine. And I don't want my home turned into a battlefield."

"You won't have to. I'm going after DeGroot. You just look after the woman and the boy. That's all I ask."

Harland sat back down. "I'll give you my decision in the morning." The dismissal was obvious. Keller stood watching him for a moment. Finally, he walked out.

As he exited the building, he stopped and took a deep breath of the cool, moist night air. He shook his head to clear it. Harland's words had shaken him more than he had thought originally. Or maybe it was Harland himself.

Like Harland, Keller had seen horrible things. He had taken other men's lives. It had changed him in ways he sometimes hated to think about. He wondered if after a few more years of this, he'd be as batshit crazy as Harland. He looked across the parade ground at the cabin he shared with Marie and Ben. He saw the light of the lantern flickering in the window. He walked toward it.

twenty-nine

Dawn was breaking over the mountains as Caldwell reached the first roadblock. He saw the stopped traffic first, the brake lights of cars glowing in the early morning light as the sparse traffic piled up. Then the strobes of the highway patrol and county sheriff's cars. He felt a brief rush of adrenaline. A few deep breaths brought that under control. His disguise was perfect. The brown truck he drove was practically an icon. So was his brown uniform. People saw those and instinctively relaxed. No one would suspect that they were both bogus. After all, who suspects the UPS man of carrying an illegal arsenal?

As he reached the roadblock, the young sheriff's deputy on his side of the road started to just wave him past, then thought better of it. Caldwell came to a full stop and levered the door open. The young deputy came around to the exit side of the truck. He leaned in and put one foot on the bottom step of the truck entrance.

"Gettin' an early start, ain't ya?" the deputy said. Caldwell relaxed slightly. There was no explicit challenge in the voice. The man was just being friendly.

"Gonna be a long day," Caldwell said.

"I heard 'at," the deputy said.

"So what's up?" Caldwell asked.

"Some guy shot it out with some FBI agents up on the Parkway," the deputy said.

"And he got away?" Caldwell said. His voice was calm, but his mind was working furiously.

The deputy nodded. "Yep," he said. "Kilt half a dozen of 'em. Must be one mean sumbitch."

"Must be," Caldwell replied. He had half-heard reports of the incident on the radio, but he had been too preoccupied with his preparations to make any connection. "I'll, uh, I'll keep a lookout for him."

"Oh, hell," the deputy said. "That ol' boy's long gone from here by now. But you caint tell the FBI that. Dumb sonsabitches. I ain't complainin', mind you. I can use the overtime." He stepped back out of the truck. "You have a good day, now," he said.

"You, too," Caldwell said. He closed the door. *What the hell is DeGroot getting me into,* he thought as he pulled away.

They were seated at the table in the mess hall: Keller, Marie, Powell, and Riggio. Lisa bustled back and forth from the kitchen, bringing bowls of homemade muesli. Ben followed in her wake, ostensibly helping, but mostly getting in the way. Lisa didn't seem to mind. She was laughing and joking with him. It made Marie smile despite the obvious tension in the room.

Harland entered the mess hall. He came to stand at the foot of the table. "You can't stay," he said without preamble.

Lisa stopped dead in her tracks, the laugh dying on her lips. "Sir," she began.

Harland cut her off. "I've made my decision," he said to her curtly. He turned too address the group. "You're a threat to the security of this camp. I want you gone after you finish eating. Lisa will escort you off the premises." He turned on his heel and walked out. Lisa slammed the bowl she was carrying down on the table and ran out after him. They looked at each other for a moment without speaking.

Ben broke the silence. "What's going on? What's wrong?" he said. There was an edge of panic in his voice. Marie opened her arms and he ran into them.

"Nothing's wrong, baby," she murmured. "We have to get ready to go, though."

His voice was muffled against her. "I don't want to go," he whined. "I want us to stay here with Lisa."

From outside they heard voices raised in argument. Keller stood up. "Where you going, Keller?" Powell said.

"To change his mind," Keller replied tightly.

Riggio shook his head sadly. "No, man," he said. "That won't work."

"And the other thing you're thinking about," Powell added. "That won't work, either." He gestured toward the door. "You try to take him on, you've got Lisa to deal with. She's good, but you could probably take her. But are you ready to go that far?"

Keller had to think about that for a minute. "Yeah," he said finally. "I am."

"Well, we're not," Powell said. "There's been enough good people hurt."

"What are you talking about?" Ben piped up. "You're not going to hurt Lisa, are you?" he looked at Jack. "Jack," he said. His voice was near hysteria. "Lisa's my friend. Don't hurt her. Jack?"

Keller gritted his teeth. His head felt like it was about to explode. It took an enormous effort of will for him to keep his voice low and steady. "Okay, buddy," he said. "Don't worry. I'm not going to hurt anyone. Not here."

"Promise?" Ben said.

Keller looked at Ben. Ben drew closer to his mother. *He's afraid of me,* Keller realized. *Afraid of what I'll do. And he's right.* The revelation broke his heart. "I promise," he said. He had trouble getting the words out. Something seemed to be caught in his throat.

Lisa came back in, slamming the door behind her. Her face was a mask of barely contained fury. Her shotgun was slung over her shoulder again. "I'm to escort you back to the parking area," he said, her voice expressionless. "You've got ten minutes to get your things together. Meet me on the parade ground." She turned and walked out. "Hey," Ben said weakly. She didn't appear to hear him. "Is Lisa mad at us?" Ben asked his mother plaintively.

"No, honey," Marie said. "She's just sad because we have to leave."

Ten minutes later, they were assembled on the parade ground. Lisa stalked up. She had lost the look of fury. It had been replaced with a blank look, as if she was an automaton. Keller's gun was slung across her shoulder. She held her own shotgun loose in her hands. It wasn't pointed at anyone, but the threat was there. "Mike, you know the way," she said curtly. "You lead. I'll be behind."

"Lise," Riggio said. "We don't blame you . . ."

She cut him off. "Good. Get moving."

They walked out of the camp, back up the trail to the old mine entrance. At the edge of the trestle, they paused. Lisa unslung Keller's gun and handed it back to him. "Here," she said. "Good luck." She turned as if to go.

"Lisa," Ben said. "Aren't you coming with us?"

She stopped, still facing away from them. Her shoulders slumped. After a long moment, she turned around. She looked at Ben and smiled. "You know what, kiddo?" she said brightly. "I think I am."

"Are you sure about this, Lise?" Riggio said.

"Yeah, Mike," Lisa said. "I am." She shook her head. "Twenty years, I idolized my father. He was like God to me. I've never seen him do anything cowardly. Until today."

"He's just trying to keep you safe," Marie said softly. "That's not cowardly."

"When he throws innocent people to the wolves, it is," Lisa said.

"Wolves?" Ben said. "What wolves?"

Lisa grinned. She reached out and tweaked Ben on the nose. "Figure of speech, kiddo," she said. She looked up at Marie. "Dad told me your story. Told me about what you did for that little girl. I admire that." She turned to the others. "Let's go."

Phillips was tired and irritable. The screeners at the airport had given him more than the usual amount of red tape and aggravation over checking the rifle through, even though it was locked up and the ammo stored in compliance with all federal regulations and the rules of the airline, rules which he had apparently researched more carefully than the people charged with enforcing them. He had tried to sleep on the plane, but the man in the seat next to him had been a nervous flyer, jacked up on adrenaline and bad airport coffee. He had jabbered incessantly throughout the flight, seemingly oblivious to the fact that he had received only monosyllables in reply. The Charlotte airport had been nearly deserted when he arrived in the early morning hours, yet it seemed to take an eternity to get his checked luggage back. And when he had, the hard-sided flight case in which his rifle and ammo were locked had been badly scuffed on one side and corner, as if an angry baggage handler had taken out his frustration by flinging the case repeatedly against the concrete. Phillips sighed. The case was supposedly shockproof and the rifle inside was designed for field use, but he'd have to check the weapon carefully to feel confident that none of the optics in the scope had been damaged. As a final indignity, the car-rental agency had botched his reservation. The unobtrusive midsize car he had reserved under his bogus identity was unavailable. He ended up with a monstrosity of an SUV. The rental agent was nonplussed that Phillips didn't seem more grateful for the upgrade. "Usually, you know," the woman said, "these are fifty dollars more a day. We're going to give you the upgrade for free. And look," he said, "it even has GPS." Phillips almost told her what a ridiculous waste is was to have one person driving such an enormous vehicle, but he held his tongue. He tried to leave few memories of himself behind as he moved toward an assignment. He took the keys and thanked the rental agent. As she walked him out to the vehicle, she gestured at the rifle case. "Doing some hunting?" she said.

"Thought I might, yes," he said.

Her brow wrinkled. "But wait a sec. Deer season doesn't start till September. That's a month off."

"Oh dear," he said, "I must have been misinformed."

When they reached the parking area, Lisa brushed the pine needles and leaves off the window of the old pickup. She fished a set of keys out from beneath the front seat. "Hey, buddy," she said to Ben, tossing the keys in the air and catching them deftly. "You want to ride with me?"

Ben looked at Marie. "Can I, Mom?"

She looked reluctant for a minute, the glanced at Keller. "Yeah," she said. "Sure."

They headed back out on the old logging road. Keller drove the Crown Vic, with Lisa and Ben following behind. They were silent most of the way. Marie looked out the window, chewing at her lip.

As they approached the area of the cabin, Riggio called them to a halt. "We'd better go check it out," he said. "Make sure we don't have any unwanted company."

Keller nodded. Powell and Riggio fetched their weapons from the trunk and slipped off into the woods. Keller got out and sat on the hood. He lit a cigarette.

Marie came up and sat beside him. "Jack," she began, then stopped.

He looked at her. "What?"

"I'm scared."

"Yeah," Keller said. He slipped an arm around her shoulders. "So am I."

"When we get to the cabin," she said, "are you still going after him? After DeGroot?"

"Yeah."

She reached up and took his chin in her hand. Slowly she turned his face toward her until she was looking into his eyes.

"Jack," she said, her voice shaking a little, "I want you to find him. And I want you to do anything you have to do to stop him. *Anything.*"

Keller looked back at her steadily. Her eyes were fierce and unyielding. "You know what that could mean," he said.

"Yeah, Jack," she said. "I do. I wouldn't ask you to do it for me. But that bastard tried to kill my son."

"I know," Keller said. "Don't worry. I'll find him."

She kissed him. "I know," she said.

Riggio was back. "All clear," he said. "Come on ahead."

thirty

Keller pulled out of the long gravel driveway onto the hardtop road. The shotgun rode upright in its rack beside him. He snapped on the radio and began seeking through stations, looking for a news-talk station. He finally found one, even though the reception was shaky and faded in and out. Next he flipped on the police scanner slung beneath the dashboard. He adjusted the volume of each of the radios until they were roughly equal and just below the threshold of his immediate conscious attention. If something relevant came over the airwaves, he knew from experience, his subconscious would pick it up and alert him. He drove as if on autopilot, paying barely enough attention to keep the car from plunging into the chasms on one side or scraping the rock faces that loomed above. Most of his mind was concentrated on the hunt.

Most men on the run seek safety in the familiar—old haunts, old girlfriends, old acquaintances. That made them easy to find. DeGroot offered none of these. He was a stranger in a strange land. But that gave Keller another angle to work. DeGroot would stand out. His accent would mark him. So would the fact that he was traveling alone in an area where most strangers traveled in groups of families or friends. The only difficult question would be where to start.

Something on the radio caught the edge of his hearing. He turned the news station up. Authorities were seeking the arrest of a man who had escaped after attacking and killing several FBI agents in a gun battle at a Blue Ridge Parkway overlook.

Gun battle, Keller thought. There was no mention of explosives. *Interesting.*

The announcer went on to state that the FBI was seeking the arrest of a South African national for involvement in the murders. However, the announcer stressed, the FBI was not considering this an act of terrorism.

Trying to keep the panic down, Keller thought. *Or maybe,* he thought more cynically, *they just won't call it terrorism if white guys do it.* He turned the radio back down and returned to his thoughts.

A man on the run needed things. Gasoline. Food. Rest. Keller decided to head back to the Parkway exit near where he had last encountered DeGroot. If the man had decided to wait until he reached one of the bigger towns like the college town of Boone, he knew the trail would probably turn cold. But if DeGroot's need had been sufficient to risk the smaller towns, there might be some hope. He'd check along the highways and in some of the smaller communities.

The fear in him was gone. The uncertainly and worry was gone. All Keller felt was the eerie combination of adrenaline and mental calm that accompanied the hunt.

· · ·

"This," DeGroot said as he laid a silver cylinder on the table, "is what we're looking for."

They were crowded into the tiny hotel room. DeGroot was seated at the table, with Caldwell seated at the only other chair. Holley was reclined on the bed, his legs crossed at the ankles. Patrick and Phillips leaned against the walls.

"What the hell is it?" Patrick asked.

Caldwell answered for him. "USB flash drive," he said. "You stick it in a computer. Holds a lot of data."

"So where's the money?" Holley said.

"In a bank in Indonesia," DeGroot said. "At least that's what my source told me."

"And this source was reliable, I trust," Phillips said in his quiet, precise voice.

DeGroot nodded. "He wasn't going to lie to me. Not then."

"Wait a minute," Patrick spoke up. "No one said anything about going to fucking Indonesia."

DeGroot sighed. He reminded himself that Patrick had been selected for his capacity for violence, not his intelligence. Before he could explain, Holley spoke up.

"We don't need to go to Indonesia," he said. "At least not in person. All we need's a computer and a Net connection. And that little gizmo right there." He looked at DeGroot. "Unless I'm mistaken, that there is the key to the vault, right?"

"One of them," DeGroot confirmed. "My former associates have the other one."

Patrick clearly still didn't understand, and it was making him angry. His jaw clenched and he began opening and closing his fists. Holley grinned at him.

"That money's everywhere, dude," he drawled, "and nowhere. All at once."

"Stop baiting him, Holley," DeGroot snapped. He turned to

Patrick. "With both keys," he explained patiently, "we can go on-line. With the crypto . . . with the codes on these keys, we can get into the computers of the bank where the money is."

"And get them to send the money anywhere in the world," Caldwell said.

Holley nodded. "Slick."

Comprehension dawned on Patrick's face. "So where are these guys?" Patrick asked.

"First," said Caldwell, "I want to know *who* they are."

DeGroot had considered not telling them, but had finally decided they needed to know the truth. "A pair of Special Forces soldiers. Deltas."

Holley sat up. "Whoa. Whoa. We're going up against *those* guys?"

"So fucking what?" Patrick sneered. "Those cocksuckers aren't as tough as they think they are. They got their asses kicked in Somalia. By a bunch of fucking savages."

"Took a few thousand fucking savages to do it," Caldwell said glumly.

"There are only two, yes?" Phillips said.

"They may have another pair with them," DeGroot said. "A man and a woman. But they're amateurs." He glanced at Caldwell and decided not to mention the child. Caldwell was a family man, DeGroot knew, and he already looked dubious. "I don't believe they have any heavy weapons," he said. "Which is where Mr. Caldwell comes in. You brought the items I requested?"

Caldwell nodded.

"Awright," Holley said. "I get to blow shit up!"

"Thought you'd like that, *bru*," DeGroot said.

"So where's this party at?" Patrick asked.

DeGroot unrolled a map on the table. "There's a cabin on the edge of the national park boundary," he began.

thirty-one

"Naw," the old man behind the counter said. "Ain't seen nobody like 'at."

The roadside store was tiny, with a pair of rusting gas pumps out front. Fishing lures and other small items hung from a pegboard behind the battered sales counter. A drinks cooler with a cracked front glass rattled and wheezed at Keller's elbow.

"Thanks anyway," Keller said. He took out one of his business cards and laid it on the counter. "If he turns up," Keller said, "I'd appreciate it you'd call and let me know. My cell phone number's on there."

The old man looked at the card on the table distastefully, as if Keller had laid a fresh turd there. "You a bail bondsman?" he said. "What's this feller s'posed to've done?"

Keller read the suspicion and the skepticism in the man's voice. This was not a place, he realized, where law enforcement, even unofficial law enforcement like himself, had ever been much welcomed.

"It's not a bail matter," Keller said. "This guy tried to kill a friend of mine."

The old man's eyes brightened a little at that. Personal vengeance was something closer to his heart. He picked up the card and stuffed it in a pocket in his creased overalls.

"Awright," he said. "I'll keep an eye peeled."

"Thanks," Keller said. "And let me have a pack of Marlboros." The old man reached up and pulled a pack down from the plastic rack that hung over the counter. "You catch this fella," he asked casually, "you aim to bring him in to the law?"

"Guess that depends on him," Keller said as he handed the money across.

The man grinned, revealing several missing teeth. "I heard that," he said. "Good luck, now. And have a nice day."

"You, too." Keller walked out and got in the car. He punched the lighter and tapped a cigarette out of the pack. He sighed. This was getting him nowhere. He had ruled out the tourist traps peddling gimcracks like flimsy Taiwan-made "Indian" dolls. Even so, there were dozens of places DeGroot could have stopped for gas or food, assuming he needed to stop at all. It was easy to disappear into these mountains, even for a man traveling the roads. He needed some way to narrow his search.

The police scanner crackled on the edge of his hearing. He leaned forward and turned it up. The dispatcher spoke in the harsh mountain twang that made a jarring contrast to the familiar cop talk.

"All units, be on th' lookout," the voice said, "fer a 2004 Tiyota four bah four, Tenn'see license MJH 4490, ref'rince stolen vee-hicle, in conjunction with homicide at Folger's Gap campground on the Parkway. Approach subject with caution."

Keller reached up above the visor and pulled out the Parkway map he had bought at one of his roadside stops. The Folger's

Gap campground was only a few miles from the overlook where DeGroot had escaped.

The radio crackled again. "Dispatch," a laconic voice said. "10-21 Highway Patrol reference that Toyota. I think they got a 10-78 on 'at one near Banner Elk."

Keller started the car.

They stood silently looking down at the map. The plan seemed simple enough. "Any questions?" DeGroot asked. There were none. "Tell it back to me, then." He looked at Patrick. "You."

"Markey and I take the front," Patrick said promptly. "If we can get close enough without being seen, we force entry. If not, we suppress."

Caldwell spoke up. "DeGroot and I take the thumper out back," he said, using the slang term for his weapon of choice, the grenade launcher. "If there's a back door and we can get to it undetected, we force entry. If not, we use the thumper or the LAW."

"I ingress first," Phillips said. "I start by taking out anything in this tower. Then I move to provide overwatch from this tree line." He ran his finger along the edge of the forested area on the left side of the clearing. "I aid in suppressing fire coming from inside the house, and mop up any strays outside." He looked at DeGroot. "I'd feel better if there was a bit of higher ground. The way the terrain slopes away from the house, I'm always firing uphill."

"I'll be sure to ring you up a nice hillside," DeGroot said. "Any other questions?" He looked around. Again there was no answer. "Fixed up, then. Everyone grab a quick graze. There's a café down the road. We leave right after."

•   •   •

231

Keller hit pay dirt in a tiny café in one of the valley towns.

"Sure," the plump girl behind the counter said. "Big feller. Short hair, talked foreign. I think he was from Germany or someplace."

Keller sipped at the wretched coffee and tried not to show his excitement. "He say where he was going?"

"I don't think he was goin' nowhere," the girl said. "He's stayin' around here, I think. Came in two or three times to check his e-mail." She gestured toward the computer room in back.

"Where's he staying?" Keller asked. "Do you know?"

The girl was suddenly suspicious. "Wait a minute," she asked. "What business you got with this feller? You a policeman or somethin'?"

Keller pulled a business card from his pocket and handed it to her. She looked at it, then back up at him with a shocked expression. "This guy some sorta criminal?"

"Yeah," Keller said. "I need to catch up with him."

She shook her head in disbelief. "Wow," she said. "That's wild."

"So where'd he be staying around here?"

She popped her gum. "The Mountain View's closest," she said. "Right up the street." She nodded decisively, her mind made up. "Yep, that's gotta be it. He din't park out front, so he musta walked."

Keller stood up. "Thanks," he said. "You've been a big help." A thought occurred to him. "You remember which computer he used?"

She shook her head. "Ain't but three, though. Why?"

"You mind if I have a look? It might give me some information."

She looked dubious. "It's five bucks for . . ." Keller already had his wallet out. She took the bill and gestured toward the back room. "Knock yourself out, hon."

Keller walked to the back. All three computers were on. The name of the café scrolled slowly across the screen. He sat down at the first one and moved the mouse. The screen saver disappeared, to be replaced by the computer desktop. He clicked the icon for the Web browser. When the home page came up, he checked the browser history. EPSN.com. CNN.com. Stocks.com. He moved to the next one and repeated the procedure. The history was blank. Someone had cleared it.

He heard someone come in the front of the café. He got up and looked out into the front room. Three men where standing there, scanning the menu. The first thing Keller noticed was the similarity in their haircuts: all short, all cut above the ears. He had worn his hair like that for years, even after the military. He glanced down. The boots all looked the same. All military or military surplus. An alarm began to sound, quiet but insistent, in the back of Keller's mind. He walked toward the front door, not looking at the three men. They moved slightly to let him pass, their eyes glancing over him, then away with the dismissive disinterest of the professional who's assessed a situation and sees no threat.

"Bye, hon," the girl called out to him. He didn't look back or answer as he headed out the door.

On the sidewalk, he looked around. He saw the sign for the Mountain View Motel up the street. He got into his car and started it. He glanced back inside the café. The three were still ordering. They didn't look outside. Keller reached into the back seat and pulled the shotgun out from beneath the blanket he had used to cover it. He propped the shotgun in the rack beside the seat and pulled out of the parking area.

In a few moments, he was pulling into the parking lot of the motel. He parked next to a large brown truck with the UPS logo. Keller surveyed the line of doors. Which one would DeGroot be behind? He glanced over at the office. They'd know. As he got out of the car, a door opened about halfway between Keller and the office. A familiar figure stepped out. Keller reached into the car and yanked the shotgun from the rack. *"DeGroot!"* he yelled. *"Freeze, motherfucker!"*

DeGroot stopped dead in his tracks, looking stunned. *"On the ground!"* Keller bellowed. *"Now!"* DeGroot hesitated. Keller racked the slide on the shotgun. Slowly, DeGroot sank to his knees. Keller advanced on him, the shotgun held at the ready. "Give me a fucking excuse," he snarled. "Any excuse at all."

"Easy now, *boet*," DeGroot said soothingly. "We can do business, you and me."

"On your belly," Keller said. "Hands behind you." He stopped just out of DeGroot's reach. *"Now!"* As DeGroot began to comply, Keller heard a door open, just to his left. He began to turn, prepared to order whoever it was back into the room. He felt an object pressed against his side. He felt a burning sensation, then he couldn't breathe. His muscles wouldn't answer him. His arms and legs began to jerk uncontrollably. Then the pain came as he collapsed to the pavement.

"Good work, Danny," DeGroot said. They stood over Keller's twitching body. Patrick still held the stun gun loosely by his side. He leaned over and gave the helpless man another jolt. He was grinning as Keller went into a fresh set of convulsions.

DeGroot looked over at the office. The manager was standing there, his mouth opening and closing like a fish's. "Danny," DeGroot said in a low voice. "Go see if you can dissuade that *kaffir* from calling the police." Patrick moved off toward the office. The panicked manager tried to run back inside, but Patrick was on him before he could get the door shut. DeGroot bent down and frisked Keller quickly and professionally. He pulled a set of nylon flex cuffs from Keller's back pocket. "Handy," he observed. By the time Keller was regaining some control, Keller's hands were securely fastened behind his back.

Caldwell and Holley came jogging up, Phillips trailing behind. "Whoa, dude," Holley said. "What the fuck?"

"Old friend," DeGroot said, gesturing at the bound man on the ground. Keller looked up at him with pure hatred in his eyes. He started to turn to get his legs beneath him. With casual cruelty, DeGroot kicked him in the solar plexus, doubling him over with pain.

"Shit," Caldwell said. "This is bad. If he trailed us, who else might have?"

"He's not a problem," DeGroot said. "In fact," he said, looking at Keller's car, "he might just give us certain advantages."

"I'm not telling you shit," Keller growled up at him.

DeGroot laughed and bent down. "You don't have to," he whispered. "I know where they are." He straightened up. "Change in plans," he announced. He gestured down at Keller. "Get him in the trunk of his car," he ordered. "The targets will recognize it. It'll help us get closer."

After a couple of hours on the hardtop road, Keller felt the vehicle slow, then stop. The doors thunked open, then Keller was blinking in the light as the trunk lid was wrenched up. DeGroot stood looking down at him. He was holding a scalpel in his right hand.

"A word of advice," he said. "You tell a man you're going to put his eye out, you *bladdie* well do it, hey? Then you kill him. Because if you leave him alive, this is what could happen. He could come back and take both of yours." He bent down, placed the scalpel at the corner of Keller's right eye. "I'll leave you one," he said, "For the moment. Because I want you to watch me with the boy. Then the woman. But you won't need both your eyes for that." He moved the tip of the blade slightly. Keller could feel a coldness, then a burning sensation, then a trickle of moisture as the blade drew blood. "You pick," he said softly. "The one that winks first is the one you lose first."

Keller tried to control his breathing, fought down the urge to buck and squirm and try to get away. It would be useless. The blade would find him anyway. He glared up at DeGroot. He tried to keep his eye from blinking, held them open by force of will until they burned. Then he realized that was part of DeGroot's game, to force him to try something useless to avoid the agony, then laugh at his pitiful efforts as he hurt him anyway. Slowly, deliberately, he winked his right eye. Do it, the gesture said, Get it over with.

DeGroot laughed in delighted surprise. "Very good," he breathed. "You've got balls, I'll grant you that. Maybe I'll take those last." Then the blade moved in a quick slashing movement. Keller screamed against the gag as he tried not to flinch away and failed.

thirty-two

Holley and Patrick exchanged worried glances as DeGroot slammed the trunk on the still-screaming man and walked to the front of the car. Caldwell strode up to where they stood. "What the fuck?" he asked.

"Yeah, man," Holley said to DeGroot, "what the fuck?"

"Shut up," DeGroot said. He opened the passenger side door and got in.

As the door slammed, Caldwell turned to the other two. "Guys," he said, "I don't think we're being told everything we need to know."

"Are we ever?" Holley said.

Patrick walked to the driver's side, opened the door. "Let's go."

Keller was curled in the darkness, shaking and sweating. He felt the blood trickling down into his right eye from where DeGroot had opened a gash just below the line of the eyebrow. He wondered for a moment why the man hadn't taken his eye as promised. Then it dawned on him. Keller had called his bluff. He had dared DeGroot to take the eye. But DeGroot wanted to show he was still in control. Keller had no doubt that when the time came, it would be the other eye that he took, before he started working on Ben and Marie. He would undoubtedly play the same games with them. The thought choked him with despair. *No,* he thought, his teeth clenched. *This is not over. This is not. Fucking. Over.* He began feeling as best he could with his fingers looking for any sharp edge, anything he could use to try to get these cuffs off. He shifted and squirmed, searching with his fingers, which were rapidly becoming numb. He felt the coldness of a piece of metal. It was the jack. He ran his fingers over the serrated edge of the upright. Better than nothing. He pressed the nylon cuffs against the jack and began sawing back and forth.

They stopped at the turnoff and got out of the vehicles. DeGroot gathered them at the rear of the UPS van. "Time to kit up," he said. Caldwell opened the latch on the van and pulled. The cargo door rattled as it slid up in its tracks. "Help me get this stuff out." In a few minutes, they had removed the boxes and laid them out on the ground. A few moments of knife work and the boxes gaped open, revealing the deadly cargo within. A few more moments and all four men were dressed in heavy armored vests and black "Fritz" helmets. Each sported a commo headset with a microphone poised before his lips. Holley gripped an AK-47 in his hands. "AK-47," he quoted, "when you absolutely, positively got to kill every motherfucker in the *room!*" He cackled. "Accept no substitutes."

"Spare us," DeGroot snapped. He looked the men over, then nodded his satisfaction. "Right," he said. "We'll approach in the car. Patrick, you drive. Caldwell, you and Phillips follow behind in the truck. When we get close, we'll dismount and approach on foot. He put his foot on the bumper of the Crown Victoria and rocked it. "We'll march this bastard out ahead of us." The men nodded. "If need be," DeGroot went on, "We'll unload some of the other surprises Caldwell brought us. Now let's go."

Riggio heard the sound of an engine, coming toward him up the road. He picked up the sniper rifle and stood, resting the heavy weapon on the metal wall of the tower. He saw the nose of the Crown Victoria coming around the bend. His brow furrowed. *What's Keller doing back here?* he thought. *And without calling first?* He settled the butt against his shoulder and peered through the scope. He waited for the car to stop and signal.

As the car came around the bend, Patrick saw the tower looming ahead, with the cabin beneath. He slowed down. "Shit," he muttered. "I think I made one turn too many."

"Back up," DeGroot hissed. "This is too far!"

"DeGroot," Patrick said, "you see anybody in that . . ." He saw a metallic glint flash from the top of the tower, sunlight reflecting off something metal, something like . . .

Patrick rammed the car into reverse and stomped on the gas. *"Gun!"* he hollered. *"Everybody down!"*

Riggio saw the car slow down, then stop. He waited for Keller to flash the headlights as they'd instructed him. Suddenly, the car's big engine roared. The tires spun in the gravel as it tried to back up. Reflex took over as he squeezed gently, felt the trigger give, heard the roar as the huge rifle fired.

The sudden movement of the car had put the vehicle at a slight angle to the tower. Had it hit them straight on, the high-powered round would have blown a hole in Patrick, then gone straight through to kill Holley in the backseat and, most likely, Keller in the trunk. As it was, the enormous projectile blasted Danny Patrick's head into bloody mist before blowing out the back passenger window. Blood spouted from the stump of Patrick's neck and sprayed all over the inside of the car. His body bowed backward, then slumped forward onto the wheel. The horn began to blow. Patrick's body slumped to the side, carrying the wheel with it part of the way. The car continued to roll backward, swerving hard, until it ran off the road and slammed trunk first into a large oak by the roadside.

"Fuck!" Holley screamed as he was suddenly covered in blood and pellets of safety glass. He yanked the door open and bailed out just before the car hit the tree. He hit and rolled, then he scrambled to his feet. The car had ended up at a ninety-degree angle to the road, between Holley and the tower. He dropped to his belly and looked beneath. He could see DeGroot's feet pumping as he bolted for the trees. A geyser of dirt erupted beside him as the sniper in the tower fired and missed. "Fuck, fuck, fuck," Holley muttered. In his panic he'd left his AK propped in the backseat. But he was damned if he was going to expose himself to whatever terrible weapon had just turned Danny Patrick into bloody meat. He heard a sharp, familiar report as the weapon fired again. The car rocked and the blowing horn was silenced. *Barrett sniper rifle,* his brain registered. *Fifty cal. Jesus H. Tap-Dancing Christ, we are fuuuuuucked.*

"DeGroot, you shithead!" he yelled over to the invisible figure in the tree line. "You didn't tell us they'd have anything heavy!"

"Calm down, *boet*," DeGroot called back. "And use your damned headset."

Holley flicked the device on. "Fall back to the truck," DeGroot said in his ear. "We'll get something that'll take care of this problem. On my count of three. One . . ."

Holley slumped back against the car. He closed his eyes and gathered his courage.

"Two . . ."

He came to a crouch, still sheltered by the vehicle.

"Three!" There was a sudden *pop pop pop* of small-arms fire as DeGroot opened up from cover on the man in the tower.

Holley sprang to his feet and ran like hell for the truck.

The people in the truck had their own problems. At the first sound of gunfire from in front, Caldwell had thrown the truck into reverse and begun backing down the gravel road. He misjudged the width of the road and the right rear tire went into a shallow ditch. Caldwell yanked the wheel back the other way. The truck slewed across the road, overbalanced, and tipped over. It came crashing down on its left side with a sound of rending metal. Caldwell heard Phillips shout from the cargo compartment as some of the boxes came unsecured and tumbled about in the back. Then there was silence, broken only by the ticking of the hot engine, now dead and cooling. In that silence, Caldwell heard another rifle shot, then shouting from up ahead. A third shot. He began crawling backward into the cargo compartment. It would be easier to get out the back than to try the driver's door which was now pointing skyward.

Phillips sat among the jumble of boxes. There was blood on

the side of his face, yet he appeared calm. He had his rifle out of its case and was checking it over. He looked up at Caldwell. "Nice driving," he said.

"Fucking Patrick," Caldwell fumed. "He went too goddamn far."

"Hm," Phillips agreed. "Well, he is known for that." He set the rifle aside, apparently satisfied that it was undamaged. He took the fighting knife from his belt and used it to slice open one of boxes. He pulled out something that looked like a large bundle of netting, with leaves and branches woven into it. He gestured toward the back door. "I assume that's the best way out?" he said. Caldwell nodded. Phillips reached out and groped around till he found the latch. Then he yanked hard sideways. The door rattled as he pulled it along its track. Daylight filled the interior of the truck. Phillips climbed out and slung the netting over his shoulder. Caldwell followed, wincing at the aches and pains as he straightened up. He saw Holley running down the road toward them. He pulled up at the sight of the upended truck. "Whoa," he said.

"What happened up there?" Caldwell asked.

"Sniper," Holley said. "In the fire tower. Danny didn't see him until it was too late."

Phillips just nodded. His face showed only minor irritation, as if this was of no more import than a flat tire. "I'll have to deal with him, then."

"Wait," Caldwell said. He reached into the back of the truck and began overturning boxes. As he searched, DeGroot jogged up. "*Bladdie* idiot!" he spat. He looked at Holley and laughed nastily. "Caught a bit of a *skrik* there, hey? Didja piss yourself?"

"Hey, fuck you," Holley snapped back. "You didn't fucking tell us they'd have a fucking Barrett. What else do they have that you forgot to fucking tell us about?"

"Hah!" Caldwell said. He pulled a box about a yard long from the back of the truck. He laid it on the ground and slit the package with his knife. The box was filled with plastic packing peanuts. He reached into the mass of white and pulled out an olive-drab tube slightly under a yard long. There was a web sling attached to the tube like that of a rifle.

Holley, his irritation forgotten, grinned like a child at Christmas. "That what I think it is?"

"Yep," Caldwell said.

Holley held out his hands. "Gimme," he said. Caldwell handed it to him and he slung it on his back.

DeGroot turned to Phillips. "Find a place to give us some overwatch."

"Yeah," Holley said. "See if you can keep that bastard's head down in the tower. I'm gonna get a little payback for Danny Boy." Phillips nodded and slipped off into the woods.

"Let's try this again," DeGroot said.

Keller felt the crunch of the gravel under the car's tires. They had reached the long driveway up to the cabin. He redoubled his efforts, raking the zip cuffs as hard as he could against the rough metal. It wasn't working. He wasn't going to have time. He felt the car lurch to a stop. Then the tires were spinning in gravel. There was the sound of a gunshot and the car came to a stop. Someone was screaming. The car was rolling. There was a bone-jarring impact and Keller's head banged against the inside of the trunk. He heard more shouting, the horn blowing, then the car rocked again with an impact like a hammer blow. The horn stopped. Keller looked up, gasping for breath, his mind fogged with pain. He didn't realize at first what he was seeing as he looked at the trunk lid. A thin sliver of daylight.

thirty-three

Inside the house, Marie had been dozing on the couch when she heard the sound of the rifle. She leaped to her feet. Powell came piling out of the back bedroom. "We've got company," he said grimly. He picked up the assault rifle propped by the door. Marie opened the door of the bedroom where Ben had been napping. He was sitting up on the lower bunk, blinking in confusion. "What's going on?" he said. The rifle fired again. Ben flinched at the sound.

"Get under the bed, baby," Marie whispered frantically.

"Don't come out till I say so, okay?" Ben nodded. She could see the whites of his eyes in the dimness of the room. He swung his legs off the bed and dropped to the floor before scooting his body underneath the lower bunk. Marie ran back into the front room. Powell was at the window, his rifle at his shoulder. "Where's Lisa?" Marie said as she picked up her own weapon.

"Outside somewhere," Powell said. His voice was detached, as if they were discussing a trip to the store. "Said she was going to reconnoiter."

"Well," Marie said, "she left her rifle." She gestured to where the weapon sat propped by the front door. Marie went to the other front window. She saw the familiar shape of Keller's vehicle. It was resting at a slight angle, off the road, the trunk jammed against the trunk of a tree. She raised her rifle to her shoulder and peered through the scope. There was nothing moving. "It's Jack's car," Marie said. "Did you see him?"

"No," Powell said. "I saw some guys tear-assing back toward the woods. None of them was Keller." Powell hesitated. "If he'd been driving," he said, "He would have stopped and given the signal like we told him."

Marie felt her heart die in her. "Oh God," she whispered. "DeGroot . . . he must have . . ."

"I'm figuring that's how he found us," Powell said. "He must have gotten it out of Keller."

"No," Marie said, shaking her head. "Jack wouldn't give us up." Powell was silent. She knew what he was thinking. That everyone could be broken if you put them through enough pain. And there was no denying someone had found them. A tear rolled down Marie's face. She brushed it away with the back of her hand. She could see DeGroot's calm, mocking face in her mind's eye. The emptiness in her was changing, turning to a savage re-solve. *All right then, you bastard,* she said silently. *You've fucked with me and mine long enough. Today you die for it. Come on then. Come on and die.*

Riggio scanned back and forth with the scope, searching for tar-gets. He wasn't worried about warning the people in the cabin.

The report of the huge sniper rifle would have been more than enough to send everybody to battle stations. He trusted Powell. He always had. A flash of movement to his left caused him to swing his sights to bear on a rapidly moving figure below. He saw a quick glimpse of old-fashioned green camo before the figure disappeared into the trees. *Lisa,* he thought. *What the hell does that girl think she's doing?* He turned his attention back to the area of the wrecked car. He saw the slightest flicker of movement behind a large boulder at the edge of the treeline. Riggio had only a second to register the flash and hiss of a rocket launch, less than that to see the quick plume of smoke from the back blast. Then Holley's antitank rocket blew him and the top of the fire tower to flaming pieces.

"Mike!" Powell screamed. Marie could see burning debris raining down into the yard in front of them. Powell screamed again wordlessly and cut loose with the assault rifle.

"What was that?" she yelled over at Powell.

He stopped firing. "Fucking LAW, man," he said, his voice choked. "They just killed Mike with a fucking rocket."

"Where did they get that kind of firepower?" Marie said.

"I don't know," Powell said more calmly, "but we are in some deep shit." He looked around. "Get to the back bedroom," he said. "Make sure no one gets in that way." Marie nodded and headed back. On the way she stopped and poked her head into Ben's room. "Mom?" she heard his voice from beneath the bunk. "Is that you?"

"Yeah, baby," she said, trying to keep the tremors from her voice. "Stay down."

"Is Jack coming to save us?" Ben asked. She didn't answer.

Ben spoke up again. "He'll be here," he said almost cheerfully. "Jack won't let us down."

Marie tried to say something in response, but she couldn't trust her voice. She headed for the back room.

Keller was curled on his back, his wrists going numb beneath him from his weight. He had been repeatedly smashing at the nearly sprung trunk lid with his boots. As the abused latch finally gave way and the trunk popped open, he heard the hiss of the rocket, followed by the shattering blast of impact. It was a sound he had heard in a thousand nightmares. In his mind, he saw the arc-light glare of rockets, heard the screams of dying men as he lay helpless in the sand . . .

He snarled and turned his body, struggling to a kneeling position in the trunk. He got his legs under him and stood up. The huge tree blocked his most direct route out of the trunk. He tried to go over the side, stumbled, and came crashing to the rocky ground with an impact that knocked the wind out of him. He lay there in agony, struggling for breath. As his lungs finally drew air, he became aware of a heavy sweet smell and the sound of something liquid trickling onto the ground. He looked over at the car. The violence of the rear impact had crumpled the Crown Vic's rear end and cracked the gas tank. A thin stream of clear fuel was pooling between the rear wheels.

"Dude," a voice said, "looks like you're having some serious aggravation."

Keller looked up. A stocky man dressed in camouflage stood a few feet away, grinning at him. He had on a Kevlar vest that barely fit across his massive chest. The olive-drab tube of a LAW rocket lay at his feet. An AK-47 was strapped across his back. As

Keller watched, the man unslung the assault rifle and raised it
to his shoulder. "Look at it this way, man," he said conversation-
ally. "This'll be a damn sight easier than what my old buddy
DeGroot had planned."

Keller gritted his teeth and struggled back to a kneeling position. The mercenary laughed with delight. "Yo, respect," he said.
"Never say fuckin' die, man. I like that." He lowered the gun.
There was a manic grin on his face as he propped it against the
tree. "Tell you what, dude," he said as he drew the fighting knife
that was hanging from his belt. "I'll make it a little more fair."

Phillips gritted his teeth, trying to control his irritation. The
whole operation offended his sensibilities. Everything was being
rushed. He hated being rushed. Sniping, to him, was a matter of
deliberation, of planning, of picking just the right position and
calculating the shot. Sniping was like surgery. This, on the other
hand, felt sloppy and improvised. This was just butchery.

"Any time today, *bru*," DeGroot's sardonic voice sounded in
his earphone.

Phillips grimaced in disgust. He flopped down and pulled the
camouflaged ghillie suit over him. He raised the rifle and scanned
the killing zone. He could see the wrecked car to his right across
the broad clearing. The house was to his left, the tower looming
above it. Suddenly, the top of the tower exploded in a gout of red
flame and black smoke.

"Boo-yah," he heard Holley's whisper in the phones. That was
another thing that rankled Philips. The total lack of radio disci-
pline. At least the threat from the tower was neutralized. Phillips
saw the trunk of the car pop open. He swiveled the rifle to bear
on the movement. He was amazed to see Keller rise halfway out
of the trunk. He lined up the shot. As his finger tightened on the

trigger, Keller disappeared from his view as he fell over. Phillips bit back the curse that rose to his lips. His shot was obscured by the bulk of the car and the tree it was resting against. He scanned a bit to his left. There might be a shot through the windows. One was blown out, leaving only the one on the far side to obscure his vision. Still, it would be tricky. He saw Holley. He was moving in from the right, his AK at the ready. Phillips could see the grin on his face. Then Holley propped the gun against a tree and drew his knife.

You idiot, Phillips thought.

He keyed his microphone. "Holley," he whispered furiously, "what in the bloody hell are you doing?"

There was no answer.

"I'll be damned," Powell said. He saw the trunk lid pop up, saw Keller stumble and fall from the car. He took a breath to yell the news back to Marie, then stopped as he saw another figure step out into his sight. The other figure dropped a familiar-looking cylinder on the ground in front of him. *That's the bastard that killed Mike,* Powell thought. His finger tightened on the trigger. But Keller had moved. He was between Powell and his target. "Come on," Powell muttered. "Move, damn it."

The man with the knife moved toward Keller with an easy assurance, like a cat stalking on wounded prey. He feinted with the knife, laughed again as Keller staggered to his feet. "Just wish I had more time to play," he said, "but you know how it is. So many engagements, so little time." His face became taut with concentration. There was a sudden blur of movement in the leaves behind him. As the man started to turn, a hand snaked

249

across his throat. There was a brief glint of steel and the hand was suddenly gone. The man had a stunned expression on his face. His hand went to his throat. The hand turned suddenly crimson as the severed arteries sprayed bright red blood across them. He tried to cry out, but all that came out was a bubbling wheeze as the air from his slashed windpipe mixed with the spurting blood. He turned as he fell, trying to see who it was that had killed him.

Lisa stood behind him, her own crimsoned blade clutched tight in one hand. She looked at Keller, a stunned expression on her face. "I never actually killed anyone before," she whispered.

The man had fallen to his knees, blood coating the front of the vest. He seemed to hear Lisa's words and looked up. An expression of disgust crossed his face as he toppled over. Lisa looked at him lying in front of her and took a step back. She laughed, a little hysterically.

"Come on," Keller said. "Cut these damn things off me."

Lisa looked up, confusion in her eyes. She shook her head as if to clear it and stepped forward. Keller turned around to give her access to his bound wrists. He felt the knife sawing at the plastic of the cuffs.

"How many of them are there?" Lisa asked.

"Three now," Keller said. "They started with five. Whoever was in the tower got one of them. You took out another one. Thanks, by the way."

"Don't mention it," she replied in a subdued voice.

The damned car was still in the way. Phillips's vision was partially obstructed by the remaining car window, but he could still see the two figures, Holley and Keller. Abruptly there was a third figure, a commotion, then blood everywhere

"Idiot," he muttered out loud for the first time as he saw Holley's body fall out of his sight.

"What was that?" DeGroot asked in the earphone.

"Keller's out of the trunk," Phillips whispered. "Holley tried to play silly buggers and take him with his knife. Someone else got Holley from behind. He's down. Permanently, judging from the amount of blood."

"Who took him?" DeGroot demanded. "Powell or Riggio?" DeGroot asked.

"Can't tell."

"Whichever it is," DeGroot said, "take him out. And Keller as well." Phillips merely clicked his mike on and off one time to signal the affirmative. He could dimly make out two figures still standing. They were slightly downslope from the car; he could just make out the top of Keller's head. It was a shot he knew he could make, but there was a higher percentage shot available. Phillips always took the higher percentage shot when possible. He lowered his sight and prepared to fire through the remaining window.

The cuffs fell away from Keller's wrists. He grimaced at the pain as blood began to flow freely again. He turned around. Lisa was standing there, between him and the car. She stared at the bloody knife in her hand. She looked up at him with an uncertain smile. "I did the right thing," she said, "right? I didn't have any choice."

"Yeah," Keller said, "you did the right thing. We need to get away from the car. The gas tank's ruptured." She nodded.

The air was suddenly filled of flying glass.

Lisa made an abrupt sound, midway between a grunt and a sigh, as if she'd been kicked from behind. She sagged forward into Keller's arms. Instinctively, he dropped to the ground, pulling her on top of him to cushion her fall. He rolled her off of him. She cried out in pain as she landed on her back. There was a stunned look on her face. "I . . . I . . . ," she whispered. He gently turned her onto her side.

The entry wound was in the center of her back, slightly below the shoulder blades. Bright red blood pumped rhythmically onto the leaves. The sharp coppery smell of it mingled with the gas fumes, nearly choking him. As he watched, the rhythm slowed, stopped. He turned her back. Her eyes stared sightlessly into the sky. Keller reached out and gently closed them. He dropped down and looked underneath the car, toward the other side of the clearing. He couldn't see the shooter, but he could feel him there, feel the watching presence, waiting for him to make the wrong move. He was pinned down. He crept up to the open front passenger door and hoisted himself prone onto the seat.

Patrick's body lolled against the driver's side door. Everything above the lower jaw was gone, the muscle and veins stretched across the back of the seat like severed cables.

Keller reached over and pushed the cigarette lighter in. He popped the glove box open and rummaged through it. As the lighter popped back out, he pulled out a sheet of flimsy paper marked "Vehicle Inspection Report." He rolled it into a loose cylinder. It caught easily when he touched it to the glowing lighter. Keller slid back out of the car and crawled to the rear of the vehicle. He took a deep breath. The paper was burning quickly, almost scorching his fingers. He tossed it into the puddle of gasoline. There was a soft *whump* as the gas caught. Keller sprang up and bolted for where Holley's AK was leaning against the tree. He was halfway there when the tank exploded.

• • •

Phillips lay still, poised in a state of total alertness, waiting. Waiting was the sniper's gift. The shot would come. The target would move. He had to. Phillips didn't, and that unbalanced equation was why Phillips knew he'd win.

There. A sudden flurry of movement, toward the back of the car. He was going for Holley's weapon. Phillips's brain swiftly calculated range, elevation, target speed. His muscles, in perfect synchronization, made the minute adjustments needed to bring the bullet to its target. His finger tightened on the trigger . . .

A huge ball of black and red flame erupted from the wrecked vehicle. The sound of the explosion rolled like summer thunder across the clearing. Phillips's attention was yanked toward the car just enough to jerk his hands ever so slightly to the side. But it was enough. He knew the shot would go wide even as the silenced rifle gave a soft cough. Phillips tore his eyes away from the scope. The car was an inferno. The smoke billowed and rolled around it. Phillips could see nothing. "Clever boy," he muttered.

"What was that?" DeGroot demanded.

Phillips keyed his mike. "I got one target," he said. "But Keller torched the car. I can't get a clear shot for all the smoke."

There was a moment of silence. Then, "Okay. Concentrate on the house. Keep anyone from getting out the front. We're in position around back." Phillips keyed his mike once in acknowledgement.

"What was that?!" Marie yelled from the back bedroom.

"It was Keller," Powell called back. "He set the car on fire. For a diversion, I guess."

"Jack!" Marie said. "He's here? He's alive?"

"Yeah," Powell answered. "I saw him."

"I knew it!" Ben called from the bedroom. "I knew he'd be here!"

"Ben!" Marie yelled. "Get back where I told you!"

"It's okay, Mom," Ben said. "Jack's here."

"Ben!"

"*Okay*, Mom." Ben sounded exasperated.

"Any sign of Lisa?" Marie asked.

Powell didn't know what to say. He had seen Lisa fall. But he didn't want the boy to know. "Yeah," he said finally.

"And?" Marie insisted. Powell hesitated. "There's a sniper somewhere in the front," he said finally.

"Okay," Marie said. "I get it." After a moment, she said, "I've got movement around back." Powell heard the bark of her rifle.

There was a brief rattle of answering gunfire and the sound of breaking glass. "Jones?" Powell called back.

"Mom?" Ben cried with an edge of panic in his voice. "*Mom?*"

"Okay," Caldwell said. "We've got them bottled up. Now what?"

DeGroot fired a three-round burst at the window where the shot had come from. "Now," he said, "while I keep their heads down, I need you to take your grenade launcher and put a WP round on the roof of that cabin."

Caldwell stared at him. "Why? Just order them to come out with the key. They know by now they're surrounded. We let them walk if they give up the key."

DeGroot's grin was like a death's head. "I think we'll be in a stronger negotiating position if the house is on fire, hey?"

Caldwell shrugged. He reached into his bandolier and pulled out a fat, stubby grenade. It looked like an exaggerated cartoon version of a bullet. Caldwell cracked the grenade launcher open at the breech and slid the round in. He snapped it closed and nodded to DeGroot. DeGroot began firing short, precise bursts, first at one window, then another. Caldwell sat the butt of the launcher on the ground and pointed the barrel toward the house at a steep angle. He squinted at the house and adjusted the barrel. He pressed down on the trigger.

The round arced up in a long parabola. It came down on the roof of the house and burst in a ball of brilliant white smoke. The smoke arced up in long spider-leg trails. At the end of each leg, a flame burned like a tiny sun. In a moment, the roof was aflame.

"I'm okay," Marie said. She picked herself up off the floor of the back bedroom where she had thrown herself to avoid the hail of bullets. She heard a hollow *thunk* from outside. She dared to peek up over the windowsill. One of the men was picking a familiar-looking weapon off the ground. Marie heard something land on the roof, then the flash of the explosion drove her back down to the floor. *"Grenade!"* she yelled. The room was filling with white, choking smoke. She had to get to Ben. She began to crawl toward the front of the house.

Keller hadn't heard the sound since the desert, but he recognized it immediately. *Thumper.* He looked toward the house. Through the pall of black smoke that surrounded him, he saw the bright star of the white phosphorus round arcing high above. He bent back to his task with grim determination. Sweat poured down his face from the heat of the blaze only a few yards away. He pulled harder. Holley was a big man, and hard to move. Keller grunted with the effort as he pulled the Kevlar vest free. A stray breeze blew a gust of smoke into his face and eyes. The smoke was thick with the stench of burning meat from the body in the car. Keller coughed and gagged as he slipped the vest on over his head, trying to ignore the bloodstains on the front. He picked up the AK and thumbed the selector level to full auto. He glanced up at the opposite tree line. He tried to keep the pall of smoke between him and whoever was up there as he faded back into the trees. The brush was thick, with clinging vines that clutched and dragged at his ankles as he moved from tree to tree. He caught a glimpse of the house through the trunks of the trees. The roof was burning, the smoke white in contrast to the black oily smoke of the car. He could hear shouting from inside the house.

Smoke and fire and screaming . . .

White fire from the sky, out of the night . . .

Burning, they're burning . . .

Darkness rose in him like a tide. He had fought it for so long, the black rage that had pulled at him like an undertow. He had spent so much of the last fifteen years fighting it, trying to keep the rage at bay. Now he opened himself to it, letting it take him. He had always thought of it as an ocean trying to drown him, to drag him away from himself. But this was like a homecoming. And home was a yawning abyss of dark fire. He knew the fire would consume him, leaving nothing behind. But that was all right.

The noise of voices was closer now. He could make out DeGroot's voice, shouting what sounded like orders. And he could hear the sound of a child crying.

They could hear the crackling of the cedar shingles from inside the house. In one corner of the main room, the ceiling was beginning to crack and char from the flames working their way down. The inside began to fill with smoke. Marie had Ben clutched to her. Powell was soaking towels in the sink. He brought one over to them and wrapped it around Ben's nose and mouth. "Breathe through this," he said. "It'll help with the smoke." He handed another soaked towel to Marie. She wrapped it over her own face.

"What now?" she asked, her voice muffled by the towel.

"Inside the house!" DeGroot's voice came from outside. "Come out. Hands up. Throw the key out first." There was a pause. "Or stay in there and burn."

Powell picked up his rifle. He stood beside the window, his back to the wall. "You can have the key!" he shouted back. "I'll bring it out! But you let the woman and the boy go."

"You're not in much a position to deal, *bru*," DeGroot called. He sounded amused.

"Oh yeah?" Powell said. "How about I run into one of the rooms and hide the key? Think you can find it after the house burns down around it? Or it'll be any good to you then?"

There was a pause. "All right," DeGroot said. "Throw the weapons out. Yours and the woman's. Then they come out, hands up."

"You let them go," Powell yelled. "When I see they're leaving, I come out. Anything happens to them, I toss the key into the fire."

"Agreed. Now the weapons."

Powell picked up his rifle by the barrel and shoved it, stock first, out the window. Marie hesitated, then followed suit.

"I don't want to go out there," Ben whimpered. "That mean guy is out there. That's the guy that shot Dad. The guy that hurt me up on that mountain." He started to cry. "Mommy, please. I don't want to. Please. Please."

Tears were running down Marie's face. "We don't have a choice, Ben. The house is on fire. We have to get out." As if to confirm her words, there was a crash as a section of ceiling fell in the main room. She bent down and gave Ben a short, fierce hug. "It'll be all right, baby," she whispered. "I promise." She took a deep breath, then turned to stand in the window. Nothing happened. She crawled out, dropping to the rocky ground behind the cabin, before turning and holding out her arms. Ben was already on the windowsill. Powell helped hand him into her arms.

"Hands up," DeGroot ordered. "Above your heads. Now."

They turned slowly. DeGroot and a man Marie didn't recognize were lying prone in the grass, about forty feet away. She could see the barrels of their weapons. They looked as big as the mouths of caves.

"March," DeGroot said. "Toward me."

"You said you'd let us go," Marie said.

"And I will," DeGroot said. "In good time. Now walk to me, or I cut you both down where you stand."

"Mom?" Ben said, his voice quivering.

"Do what he says, baby," Marie whispered.

They began to walk together.

"You son of a bitch," Caldwell hissed viciously.

"What are you on about?" DeGroot whispered back. He had laid his rifle down beside him. He reached down and drew his sidearm.

"You didn't say anything about any kids," Caldwell said.

"What's the difference?"

"I don't kill children," Caldwell said.

"Is that so?" DeGroot said. "You've been lucky up to now, then."

"I mean it," Caldwell insisted. "I don't kill children, DeGroot."

The woman and the boy were only few feet away. "That's no

problem," DeGroot said. "Because I don't mind it." He leaped to his feet. He took one quick step to where Marie and Ben had come to a surprised halt. He grabbed Ben and pulled the boy to him. Ben cried out. DeGroot held the barrel of the gun against Ben's head. "No," Marie cried out.

"I think I like this deal better," DeGroot called out. "With that Keller fellow running around the woods somewhere, I think I'll need a little more insurance." Holding Ben so tightly by the shoulder that he cried out in pain, he lowered the gun so it was pressed against the middle of the boy's back. "Now," he called. "Come on out, Bobby. And bring the key with you. Any more tricks and I blow the boy's spine in two." There was no answer. "You want that, Bobby?" DeGroot asked. "You want him to be a cripple, if he lives at all? You know I'll do it, Bobby. You know what I'll do. He'll live in a chair and shit in a bag for the rest of his life."

"Okay," Caldwell said as he stood up. "That is fucking enough." He dropped the grenade launcher and reached for his own sidearm. Before he could draw it, DeGroot raised his own gun and shot Caldwell in the face. Caldwell was knocked off his feet by the impact of the bullet. Marie and Ben screamed at once. Caldwell made no sound. His body twitched and spasmed. DeGroot returned his weapon to Ben.

He raised his voice again. "I'm counting to three, Bobby. One . . ."

"I'll kill you," Marie said, her voice choked with tears. "So help me God, I'll kill you if it's the last thing I do."

"No," DeGroot said. "No, you won't. Two . . ."

Powell appeared at the window. He slowly climbed out.

"The key, Bobby," DeGroot said. "Let me see the key."

Powell raised one hand. The silver cylinder gleamed briefly in the sunlight.

"Good," DeGroot said. "Now walk to the point halfway

between me and the house. Slowly." Moving like a sleepwalker, Powell complied.

"Put the key on the ground." Powell bent over slowly. As he straightened up, his face lost its blank expression and twisted in a snarl of rage. He sprang at DeGroot, his arms in front of him. DeGroot raised the gun and fired. The bullet took Powell in the throat. A fine pink mist blew out of the back of his neck. His charge became a stumble, then a limp collapse, facedown.

"Good," DeGroot said with satisfaction. "I was beginning to think he wasn't going to try. I would have been disappointed if he hadn't tried."

Marie was beyond screaming. Ben, likewise, was catatonic with fear and shock.

"Please," Marie said, "Don't hurt my son. I'll . . . I'll do anything you want."

"Here's the thing, cherry," DeGroot said. "When I get done with you, you'll do anything I want whether I hurt him or not. But I want your friend Keller to join the party. He's tuned me a bit of grief, and I owe him." He reached up and switched on his headset microphone. "Mr. Keller," he said into the mike. "I'm sure you've got poor Markey's headset. You know what's happening. And what's going to happen. So if you'd like to . . ."

"You don't need that," Keller spoke. "I'm right here."

DeGroot turned, Ben still clutched in front of him. Keller was standing a few feet away, the AK-47 at his shoulder pointed at DeGroot.

DeGroot used his grip on Ben's shoulder to shake him like a dog with a toy. "I'll shoot," he said. "I'll kill the boy." To emphasize the point, he pressed the gun into Ben's back until the boy cried out.

"And then I'll kill you," Keller said. "I know you don't want to die. You value your own skin, I know that."

"True enough," DeGroot said genially. "It's a matter of who values what the most, hey?"

"We don't have to play chicken to figure that out," Keller said. "I know what you really want. Marie," he said, "go get the key."

She walked on shaky legs to where the silver computer device lay gleaming in the grass. Her path took her between the bodies of Caldwell and Powell. She didn't look at either body as she bent down to pick it up.

"Your choice, DeGroot," Keller said. "The boy for the key. Everybody walks away. No one else has to die."

"You've forgotten one thing," DeGroot said. He smiled. "The remaining player on the board. Are you in firing position?" he said.

Keller realized he was speaking into his headset mike. The whispered voice that replied in Keller's own headset had a trace of British accent. "Roger that."

"Take the shot, then."

Phillips had begun to move his firing position as soon as he saw the flames engulfing the front of the house. Nothing was coming out that way, and it sounded like the action was moving to the rear anyway. He was in the vee of a huge oak, sighted in on the group below. A tree wasn't the ideal firing position, but he had elevation and a clear line of sight. Keller had his back to Phillips, with DeGroot slightly to his left, holding the boy. Phillips adjusted his aim slightly for the range, the slight drop of the bullet, and the light wind and prepared to shoot.

Thunder split the sky open.

All four of the people on the ground reflexively looked up at the blast of noise that filled the air, drowning out even the crackle of

the flames. An enormous double-rotored helicopter roared overhead. A huge bag hung from cables suspended beneath the
chopper. The aircraft made a slow turn directly above the burning building. They saw a logo printed on the side, a stylized fir
tree inside a badge-shaped outline.

A cable moved, the bag seemed to tip slightly, and an ava-
lanche of water poured down like an airborne Niagara. The del-
uge hit the burning building dead center. Some flashed into
steam that leapt toward the sky. The falling water blew out the
remaining windows and rolled out of the house in all directions
like a tsunami. It rolled over them, knocking all three of them
from their feet like tenpins. When the flood passed, Keller was
the first one on his feet. He had lost the AK-47, so he launched
himself at DeGroot bare-handed. DeGroot had lost his grip on
Ben, but he had managed to hold on to the pistol. He tried to
bring it to bear on Keller, but Keller was inside his reach in an instant. He locked DeGroot's elbow with his left arm and brought
the heel of his right hand up under the man's chin as hard as he
could. The force of the blow snapped DeGroot's head back. He
sagged. Keller's armlock kept him from falling. Keller drove his
fist up under DeGroot's sternum as hard as he could. DeGroot
grunted and his body tried to double over, tried to curl around
the pain. Keller prevented that by slamming his hand up under
the chin again. Only when he heard the thud of the pistol landing on the ground did he release his hold. DeGroot sagged to his
knees, retching. Keller stood over him, guarding against any further attempt the man might make to stand. He was dimly aware
of the sound of the helicopter receding.

"He'll be back," Keller said. "This late in summer, dry
weather . . ." He jerked a thumb back over his shoulder at the
house, which was now a smoldering wreck. "That much smoke's
going to bring every firefighter and smoke jumper in three states.

That tanker was just the beginning. This place'll be crawling with them any minute. It's over."

"Not yet," he heard Marie say.

Keller turned. Marie stood there, holding a pistol. It was pointed at DeGroot. "Step away, Jack."

"What are you doing?" Keller asked.

She glanced at him, then back at DeGroot. "Do you remember something he said back at the overlook, Jack? He said he wanted the FBI guy to talk to someone. He had this . . . this smug look on his face when he said it." She raised the gun a little higher. "This fucker's got some kind of connection. Some kind of get-out-of-jail-free card. And I'm not going to let that happen."

DeGroot wiped his mouth with the back of his hand. "I'm not armed," he said.

"Bad luck for you," Marie said.

"You're a police officer," he said. "You won't shoot a man in cold blood."

"You fucking *bastard*," she said, her voice rising. "You tried to kill my *son*." Keller could see her knuckles whiten around the grip.

"Mom?" Ben's voice said. He was standing behind her, his eyes wide with fear.

"Get back, baby," she said. Her eyes were hard as flint. "Mommy has some business to take care of."

DeGroot's eyes went to Ben. He smiled nastily. "So you think you can kill a helpless man in cold blood? In front of your son? I don't think you'll do it."

"No," Keller said. "But I will." He held out his hand. "Give me the gun, Marie."

She didn't move. "No way, Jack," she said. "He doesn't walk out of here. Not when there's a chance he'll ever get free. Not when there's a chance he'll ever threaten Ben or my family again."

"He won't walk, Marie," Keller said. "I promise. He dies to-day. But he's right. You can't kill him. Not in front of Ben." She still didn't move. She stood there, as pitiless as a Fury. Keller tried one last gambit.

"You've saved me twice," he said. "Now it's my turn."

She looked at him. She glanced back at Ben who was still star-ing at her as if she'd grown horns. Slowly, she walked over to Keller, the gun still held on DeGroot. Keller took it from her and took aim. "Go to Ben," he said. "Don't let him look."

DeGroot looked up at him, a sickly smile on his face. "*Blad-die* idiot," he spat. He looked off toward the tree line. "Shoot him," he called.

There was no response.

DeGroot's face went blank with shock. "*Shoot!*" he screamed.

"I don't think he can hear you," Keller said. He looked over. Marie had knelt on the ground and was clutching Ben to her. He turned back to DeGroot.

"A word of advice," he said. "You tell a man you're going to put his eye out, you do it. Then you kill him. Because if you leave him alive, this is what could happen."

He fired. DeGroot went over backward. Keller stepped over to him and straddled his twitching body. He fired again. And again. The killing rage was on him. He let go of it, gave it free reign. It flared through him like a forest fire. His lips drew back from his teeth in a feral grin. He fired again.

"That should be sufficient," a voice said.

Keller looked up. A man in camouflage uniform was standing a few feet away. He held a long rifle pointed at Keller. His face was obscured by a mask in the same camouflage design as his cloth-ing. "Drop the gun, please," he said in a clipped British accent.

The rage was still howling through Keller, screaming at him to fire again, to draw blood again, to kill again. But with the rifle pointed at him, it would have been suicide. Keller dropped the pistol by DeGroot's body. He was shaking like a man in the throes of a fever.

"Miss," the man said over his shoulder, "I'll have to ask you and the boy to come over here. I'll need you all together."

Marie stood up. Ben had his face buried in her hip, as if he couldn't bear to see any more. It made movement awkward, but they eventually ended up by Keller.

"Now," the masked man told Keller. He gestured with the barrel of the rifle "Search him. Find the computer drive."

Keller bent down. He rifled through DeGroot's pockets. He found the drive in the shirt pocket and held it up. "Toss it here," the man said. Keller did. It landed at the man's feet. He stooped carefully to pick it up. "Miss," he said to Marie, "do you still have the other one?"

She shook her head. "I dropped it when the water hit."

The man nodded. "Then the three of you will go over there and look for it, please."

It took them fifteen minutes, while the man watched. He had lowered the rifle, but it never left his hands. Finally Marie saw the drive glittering in the wet grass. She held it up silently.

"Right," the man said. "Toss it to me." She tossed it. He bent and retrieved it. The four of them stood watching each other for a long moment. Finally Marie spoke.

"Are you going to kill us now?"

"No," the man said. "You are not my mission. And since you have no idea who I am, nor any real evidence of who employed me, there's no need." He gestured at DeGroot's body lying in the grass. "Unlike our late friend over there," he said. "I try to maintain a certain professionalism." He sighed. "Mr. DeGroot had become what I believe one of your detective novelists called 'blood-simple.'"

"What?" Keller said.

"It's a quote from one of your detective writers. Mr. Dashiell Hammett. Something of a passion of mine, really. Detective fiction, I mean. Anyway"—he gestured at DeGroot again—"Mr. DeGroot had gotten to like killing a shade too much. My employers were finding him a bit of an embarrassment."

"So if I hadn't killed him . . ."

The man nodded. "I suppose I should thank you. Sorry, but I won't be sharing the retainer with you. I'm sure you understand." The rotor blades sounded again in the distance. "Ah," the man said, "time for me to be leaving. I've quite a hike to make." He raised one hand in an ironic salute. "Cheers." He backed away slowly, never turning his back on them. Then he was in the trees and gone.

Marie sank to the grass. She drew Ben to her lap. He threw his arms around her, sobbing. Keller walked over to them. He knelt down on the grass next to them. He put out his hand to touch Ben on the shoulder. Ben turned to look at him.

And screamed.

Keller reeled backward. He almost fell, but recovered his balance and stood up quickly. "Ben," he said in a choked voice.

"Go away!" Ben cried, his voice muffled by his mother's shoulder. *"Go away! Make him go away, Mommy!"*

"Ben," Marie soothed, stroking his hair. "It's okay, baby, it's okay."

Ben was nearly hysterical. *"I don't want him here! Make him go away!"*

"Did he see?" Keller whispered.

"No," Marie said. "But he must have heard. You . . . you were laughing, Jack. You were laughing when you killed him."

Keller didn't answer. He turned away and walked toward the house. A few hot spots were smoking here and there, but the fire was mostly drowned. He stood there watching for a moment, then walked around to the front. The burning car had set the big oak tree on fire. The pillar of smoke reached upward like a dark prayer. He shaded his eyes and looked into the empty sky for a moment. He looked back down. He saw Lisa's body lying at the edge of the woods. The grass and leaves nearby were beginning to catch. Keller strode rapidly over to where she lay. He knelt down and got his arms under her. Grunting with the effort, he stood up, cradling the girl's body. He walked back behind the house. The pickup truck was parked there at the edge of the woods, at the entrance to the logging road. Keller walked past Marie and Ben. "Jack," Marie said. Keller didn't speak as he passed.

When he got to the truck, he hesitated. It seemed wrong somehow to pile Lisa's body into the truck bed like a load of firewood, but to put her in the front seat seemed even more grotesque. As Keller stood there, a figure came striding out of the woods. It was Harland. His face was grim and determined. When he saw Keller standing there, however, he stopped. He looked like a man who'd been punched in the stomach. "No," he said. "No." He strode rapidly over to where Keller stood. "Put her down," he said in a tight, furious voice. "Put her down, you bastard." Keller knelt and gently laid Lisa's body on the ground. Harland knelt on the other side of her. He ran a hand gently over her still face. A single tear ran down his dark, craggy face.

Marie had come over. "Colonel," she said quietly. "How did you get here?"

Harland looked up. "You think I can't walk through these mountains?" he said.

Marie looked down at Lisa's body. "I'm sorry," she said. "She was very brave."

"I don't want to hear it," he snarled. He looked at Keller. "You," he said. "You did this."

"No," Marie said.

Harland didn't answer her. He continued looking at Keller. "You may not have pulled the trigger. But you brought this on her. You brought it on us all. You bring the fire with you. You bring death, and hell follows with you." He got his arms under Lisa and picked her up. As they watched, he loaded her into the truck bed. He started the truck and backed up. He made a quick, savage, three-point turn and rattled off down the logging road.

Keller was still kneeling. Marie put her hand on his shoulder. "Jack," she said. He didn't answer. "Jack?" she said, more alarmed now. She got down on her knees in front of him. His eyes were blank and unseeing. *"Jack!"* she yelled. No answer. He didn't even look up as the helicopters began to land.

thirty-four

"There's nothing physically wrong with him," Lucas Berry said. He sat at his desk in the drug rehabilitation center that he directed. Angela and Marie sat across from him.

"He's a little banged up, of course," Berry went on. He rubbed his face with his hands. "But that's not unusual for Jack Keller."

"What about his mental state?" Angela asked. "Aren't you worried about that?"

Berry grimaced. "Of course I am. Considering his prior PTSD and everything he's gone through recently, I suppose it's a miracle he hasn't gone either screaming insane or completely catatonic. As it is, he can care for himself. He's just not speaking."

Angela's voice was calm. "What can you do, Lucas?"

"Not much at this point," Berry sighed. There are a number of medications . . ."

"He hates drugs," Angela said.

"I know. And he's still refusing to take them. And we can't

keep him in the hospital if he doesn't want to stay. Just refusing to speak isn't reason to involuntarily commit him."

Angela stood up and picked up her cane. "Do whatever you can for him, Lucas. And send the bills to me," she said. She looked at Marie and walked out.

Berry looked across the table at Marie. Marie sighed. "She blames me. She didn't even really want me here."

"What about you?" Berry asked gently. "Do you blame yourself?"

Marie shook her head. "I don't know, Lucas," she said wearily. "Sometimes I do. I let him take the gun from me. But he did what he did of his own free will."

Berry nodded. "True enough," he said neutrally.

"But I knew what it would probably do to him," she went on. "And I put the gun in his hand anyway."

"Also true," Berry said.

She looked at him. "You're no help at all."

"It's going to take a while for you to work this out, Marie," Berry said. "I suggest you find a therapist for yourself as well as for Ben when you get back to Oregon."

She stood up. "Yeah," she said. She extended a hand across the desk. "It's been nice knowing you, Lucas."

He stood up and took the extended hand. "You, too," he said. His voice softened. "You take care of yourself, girl."

"Thanks," she said. "You, too."

She walked out into the parking lot of the restored Victorian home that housed Berry's drug rehab center. Angela stood between her car and Marie's. Marie squared her shoulders and walked over.

"Are you coming to the hospital?" Angela said.

Marie shook her head. "I went earlier this morning," she said. "I have to get back and finish packing."

270

"Did you at least tell him good-bye?" Angela asked.

Marie sighed. "I'm not going to fight about this anymore, Angela," she said. "Ben's doctor says he needs to get away from places and things that remind him of what happened."

"And people."

"And people, yes," Marie snapped. "You think this is easy for me? He's my *son*, Angela. I'll do whatever it takes to keep him safe and healthy. Even if "—her voice caught in her throat—"even if I have to do something that breaks my own heart." She began to sob. Angela stood and watched her for a moment. Then her face softened. She took a handkerchief out of her pocket and handed it to Marie. Marie took it and wiped her eyes. "Thanks," she choked out.

"It's okay," Angela said. Marie started to hand the handkerchief back, but Angela waved it off. "Keep it." She opened the door of her own car. "Have a good life, Marie," she said.

"Thanks," Marie said. "You, too."

Angela drove to the hospital. She walked past the desk and took the elevator to Keller's room.

It was empty. The bed was neatly made. It was as if Keller had never been there.

Angela turned and walked back to the nurse's station. The young blond nurse behind the counter looked up as Angela approached. She stood up and picked up a chart that rested on the counter.

Angela tried to keep her voice steady. "Where's . . ."

The nurse shook her head. Her lips pursed in a look of disapproval that belonged on a much older face.

"Mr. Keller checked himself out."

Angela's mouth snapped shut. After a moment, she said, "Checked . . . himself out?"

The girl nodded. "AMA." She held out the chart. Angela

could see the letters at the bottom of the page, scrawled in an angry hand. Apparently, the doctor had been irritated that Keller had left against medical advice.

She pulled out her cell phone and flipped it open. Keller's number was first on her speed dial. The phone rang twice, then the recorded message came on telling her that the subscriber was not available.

"If you're trying to call him," the nurse said, "you should know he left this here." She held out Keller's cell phone.

Angela took it from her. She stared at it for a moment. Then she raised her own phone again and hit the number for H & H. Oscar picked up the phone on the first ring.

"Oscar," she said, "has Jack called?"

"No," Oscar said, surprise evident in his voice. "Is he not at the hospital?"

"He just walked out," Angela said. "If he calls or comes in, let me know."

"Of course," Oscar said. Angela looked again at Keller's phone in her hand. She hit Keller's home number on her own phone. After fifteen rings, she gently closed the phone.

Harland used the shovel to pat the last of the earth onto the grave. He had performed the old Hmong ceremonies as best as he could remember from his time in Vietnam. He had to hope his old friend would understand any of the lapses. He stood looking at the grave for a long time. Finally he turned and walked away. There was one last thing to do.

He reached the old mine entrance near the trestle. It was sealed up by a heavy wooden wall built across the entranceway. There was a door cut into the wall, with narrow firing ports on either side. Harland took a ring of keys from his belt and opened the padlock on the door. He stepped inside. Just inside the door, a pair of wires stuck up from the earth. A molded plastic detonator box lay next to them. Harland picked up the detonator and connected the wire to it with a practiced hand. When the wires were connected, he didn't hesitate. He turned the crank on the detonator.

There was a quick series of bangs from outside that echoed back and forth off the walls of the gorge. Then a deep rumble that gained in volume as the trestle began to collapse. Harland stepped outside and watched the old wooden bridge sag, then topple sideways into the gorge. It seemed to take a long time, and when it was done, the echoes resounded for almost a full minute. Harland looked across the chasm that separated him from the world. Then he walked back to camp.

Phillips sat in his study, in front of his computer screen. The two flash drives lay on the desk next to the monitor, side by side. He didn't know which one went first, so he took a guess. He picked up the one on the right and slotted it into the small rectangular port on the front of the machine. There was a brief pause, then the soft chime that signaled a device being plugged in. A small balloon popped up in a corner of the screen to indicate "new hardware found." A screen popped up asking him what he wanted to do with it. He clicked the icon that opened the flash drive. Another brief pause. Phillips held his breath. Suddenly a Web browser page flashed up on his screen. It was in Arabic. He had expected as much. It was, fortunately, a language which he had learned in the course of his travels. He followed the instructions on the screen. When prompted, he inserted the second flash drive into the slot. There was a pause and a whirr as the program read the encrypted passwords on the second drive. Then another screen popped up. Phillips felt his heart rate accelerating.

He had been paid well for the job, but his employer was a fool if he thought Phillips was going to simply turn this much money over to some bureaucrat. They'd be angry, of course. They would, most likely, come after him. No matter. This much money could buy a great deal of protection.

Finally, the screen was done loading. Phillips scanned it for a few moments. His eyes widened. Then he sat back in his chair and started to laugh. It began as a small quiet chuckle, then expanded into a great roaring belly laugh. Every time Phillips looked back at the screen, he began laughing again.

The account was empty. Someone else had had access and had cleared it. Or his employers had hacked it. No matter. It was a fine joke on everyone.

Still chuckling, Phillips stood up and walked over to his bookshelves. He had finished *Red Harvest* on the plane ride back. Often, what to read next was a difficult decision for him. Something new? An old favorite? But this circumstance allowed for only one choice. He pulled the book down, took his position in his easy chair, and began to read:

Samuel Spade's jaw was long and bony, his chin a jutting V under the more flexible V of his mouth . . .

"Hey, *amigo*," a voice said. "Wake up, *amigo*."

Keller opened his eyes and straightened up. He had fallen asleep leaning against the doorpost of the car. He looked over. The driver was a burly Mexican in his late twenties. He had told Keller his name, but sleep had chased the information from his head.

"The ranch where I work is up ahead, man," the driver said.

"I better let you off here. Maybe you can get a ride to"—he hesitated—"wherever you're going."

Keller looked out the window. It was early morning. The sun was coming up over a distant range of barren hills. They were parked in the gravel lot of a small diner. There was a small gas station across the road. There were no other buildings. The road stretched out before and behind, totally flat and straight until it narrowed to a point in the distance.

Keller looked back at the driver. "Thanks for the ride," he said. He noted the man's look of relief as he opened the door. The driver had been friendly and chatty early on, but he had grown noticeably more uneasy at Keller's monosyllabic replies and long silences in the long hours since he'd picked Keller up by the side of the road in Louisiana.

Keller got out and fetched his backpack from behind the seat.

"Take care, man," the driver said.

"Thanks," Keller said. "You, too." He shut the door. The car kicked up dust and a spray of gravel as it pulled away fast. Keller watched it until it dwindled in the distance. He glanced at the diner. There were a few people inside. He could see a table of older men in trucker caps, joking and laughing with a middle-aged waitress. Keller turned away and looked into the rising sun. Heat waves were already beginning to shimmer up from the hard-packed brown earth that stretched to the hills on the horizon, broken here and there by outcroppings of rock. Keller gave the people in the diner one last look. Then he started walking along the side of the road toward the hills.

He was back in the desert. In many ways, he'd never left.